Edgewater Angels

doubleday

new york london toronto sydney auckland

Edgewater Angels

Sandro Meallet

PUBLISHED BY DOUBLEDAY
a division of Random House, Inc.
1540 Broadway, New York, New York 10036

DOUBLEDAY and the portrayal of an anchor with a dolphin
are trademarks of Doubleday, a division of
Random House, Inc.

The first chapter of *Edgewater Angels* first appeared as the short story
"Fish Heads" in the July 2000 issue of *Atlantic Monthly*.

Library of Congress Cataloging-in-Publication Data
Meallet, Sandro, 1965–
Edgewater angels / by Sandro Meallet. —1st ed.
p.   cm.
1. San Pedro (Los Angeles, Calif.)—Fiction. 2. Boys—Fiction.
I. Title.
PS3563.E1933 E34 2001
813'.6—dc21
00-065882

Book design by Terry Karydes
Title illustration by Christian Engel

To Melissa,
my absolute everything

Edgewater Angels

Sometimes we fished and crabbed behind the Maritime Museum or from the concrete pier next to the Catalina Terminal underneath the San Pedro side of the Vincent Thomas Bridge. Sometimes we silently borrowed a rowboat from the tugboat docks and paddled to Terminal Island across the harbor just in front of us and hid the rowboat under an unbusy wharf, then strolled over to Berth 300 with droplines, bait knives, and gotta-have donuts all in one to two buckets. Sometimes as an extra we got to watch the big gray pelicans just off the edge of Berth 300 headfirst themselves into the wavy seawater with the small trailer birds hot on their tails hoping to snatch and scoop away any overflow from the huge bills. And sometimes as we fished and watched the pelicans dive we tripped that Berth 300 was next to the federal penitentiary where rich businessmen spent their caught days. It was also where the gangster Al Capone from Chicago was prisoned many many years ago.

But mostly we headed to the Pink Building over by Deadman's Slip and back on the San Pedro side because the fish there bit hungry and came in spread-out schools. Often the fishschools jumped greedy from the water for the baited ends of our lowering droplines as if they couldn't wait for the frying pan. And always at each spot Tom-Su sat himself down alone with his dropline and stared into the water as he rocked back and forth.

Besides Tom-Su tagging along, the summer was a typical one for us. We fished and crabbed for most of each day and then headed to the San Pedro fishmarket. We sold our catch to locals before they got into the market—mostly Slavs and Italians who usually bought up everything—and split up the money between us. Whenever we couldn't sell the catch, it went to the one whose family needed it the most.

Tom-Su spoke very little English and understood even less. He was new from Korea and had a special way of treating caught fish that wiggled at the end of his dropline. We'd never seen anything like it.

"Tom-Su," one of us once said, "tell us the truth. Why do you bite the heads off of fish—while they're still alive!"

"Dead already." And that's all he said with a grin.

Tom-Su had bucked teeth and often drooled as if his mouth and jaw had been forever dentistnumbed. He always wore suspenders with his jeans, which were too high and tight around his waist. But we didn't know how to explain to him that it was goofy not only to have his pants flooding so hard, but to also be putting the visegrip on one's nuts. Me and the fellas wondered on and off just how we could make Tom-Su understand that down the line he wasn't gonna be a daddy, disrespecting his jewels the way he did. To top it off, Tom-Su sported a rope instead of a belt, definitely nailing down the supersorry look.

"Tom-Su," one of us once said, "pull your pants down a little so you don't hurt yourself!"

"You welcome." And that's all he said with a grin.

He was goofy in other ways, too. His baseball cap didn't fit his misshapen head; he moved as if he had rubber for bones; his skin was like a vanilla lampshade; and he would unexpectedly look at you with these cannibal-hungry eyes, complete with underbags and socketsinkage.

"Tom-Su," one of us once said to him, "what are you looking at?"

"That's good." And that's all he said with a grin.

The drool and cannibal eyes made some of us think of his food intake. And if Tom-Su was hungry we couldn't blame him. His diet was out there like Pluto. In his house once with his father not at home, we opened the fridge to see it packed wall-to-wall with seaweed. Green ocean plant in jars, in plastic bags, in boxes and open on the shelves, as if it were growing on vines. It gave the fridge a smell of musty freon. Hell, my teeth might've bucked on me too with nothing but seaweed for breakfast, lunch, and dinner.

"Tom-Su," one of us said to him in his kitchen, "is this all you eat?"

"Pretty good." And that's all he said with a grin as he opened up a cupboard to show us a year's supply of the stuff.

A seaweed breakfast? Know what I'm saying? Out there.

So when Tom-Su got around the live-and-kicking-for-life fish—and I mean meat and not some ocean plants—well, he got very involved with the catch the way none of us would, or could, or maybe even should. Early on, though, I guess we mainly thought his fish head biting a hobby within a hobby or maybe a creepy-gross natural ability—one you wouldn't want to be born with yourself.

But Tom-Su was cool with us because he carried our buckets wherever we headed along the waterfront and because he eventually depended on us—though none of us knew how much at the time. Wherever we went, he went, tagging along in his own speechless way, yessing his head, drifting off elsewhere, but always ready to bust out that buckedtooth grin.

In the beginning it had bugged us that Tom-Su went straight to his lonely area, sat down, and rocked rocked rocked. But eventually we got used to it or forgot about him altogether. After all, we had our fishing to do. Bait, for example, and not Tom-Su's state of mind, was something we had to give serious thinking to. If the fish weren't biting we had to get experimental on them. Sometimes we'd bring anchovies for bait. They were salty and tough and held fast to the hook. The fish loved to nibble then chomp at them. Sometimes, when we were interested in the bigger mackerel or bonita that brought us more than chumpchange at the fishmarket, we'd bring squid. Sometimes, when no other bait could be found, we'd bring lures and would be lucky to catch a couple of perch or buttermouth that were probably the dumbest and hungriest fish in the harbor. And sometimes we'd put small pear or apple wedges onto our hooks to catch some smelt and mackerel and even an occasional halibut. Bananas, grapes, peaches, plums, mangoes, oranges—none of them worked, though we'd once snagged a moray eel with a mediumsized strawberry and fought him for over an hour. After the moray snapped the dropline we talked about how good that strawberry must've tasted for him to want it so bad. A few times a tightlywadded piece of paper worked to catch a flounder; as did a button, a cube of stanky cheese, a corner of plywood, and an eyeball from a dead harbor cat to catch other things. The last several baits had been good only when the fishschools jumped like mad and our regular bait had run out and the buckets were near full. Oh, and once we accidentally caught a seagull using a chunk of plain bagel that the bird snatched right out of midair. We pulled the seagull in like a wild-and-desperate-winged kite and removing the hook from its beak dropped enough feathers for a well-stuffed baby's pillow.

———

One afternoon as we fought a recordsized bonita and yelled at each other to pull it up, Tom-Su sat to the side and didn't notice or care about the happenings at all; he didn't even budge—just stared straight down at the water. At the time we thought that he was maybe trying to spot the fish moving around beneath the surface or that maybe his brain shut down on him whenever he took his seat. But not until Tom-Su had fished with us for a good month did we realize that the rocking and numbheaded gaze were about something altogether different. Like that fish-head business. Only every so often, when he got a nibble, did Tom-Su come out of his trance, spring to his feet, and haul his dropline high over his head, fist by fist, until he yanked a fish from the water. Tom-Su then grabbed the fish from its jerking rise, brought it to his mouth in one fast motion, and clamped his teeth down right over the fish's head.

The previous May, Tom-Su and his mother had come to the Barton Hill Elementary principal's office. I'd been caught fighting Lowrider Louie again, this time because I'd looked at him a second too long, and was ordered to the office. Principal Dickerson sent Louie home on his reputation alone. Tom-Su sat in the chair next to me while his mother spoke to Dickerson at a nearby desk.

"He twelve year old," she said.

"Yes, I know, Mrs. Kim," said Dickerson. "He can't start here this summer or next fall. He's too old. Take him to the junior high—Dana Junior High, okay?"

"Tom-Su have small problem, Mr. Dick'son," she said and pointed to her temple. "No big problem; only small problem—very very small. And no speak English too good."

"Then take him to Harlem Shoemaker, Mrs. Kim," said Dickerson. Harlem Shoemaker was the school for retarded children. "I'm sure they'll have room for him there."

Tom-Su's mother gave a confused face as Dickerson wrote on a piece of paper. I looked at Tom-Su next to me. He had a little drool at the corner of his mouth and turned to me and buckedtooth-grinned from ear to ear. I smiled back. That was before he ever came fishing with us.

When he first moved in, we'd seen Tom-Su around the projects with his mother. They'd moved into the old Sanchez apartment. It was average and graycoated with rough grimy surfaces and grassyard enough for a one-yard run. There were hundreds of apartments just like it in the Rancho San Pedro housing projects. (The Sanchezes had moved back to Mexico because their youngest son, Julio, had been hit in the head by a stray bullet. It had traveled five or six blocks before finally getting to Julio.) Each time we'd seen Tom-Su he'd been stuck gluetight to his mother, moving beside her like some shrunken shadow of a person. It made him seem barely born or as if forever sunlightscared. Sometimes they'd even be seen holding hands, at which point we just knew something wasn't right with the guy. A mother and son holding hands? In our neighborhood it was unheard-of.

"—it's for special cases like Tom-Su," said Dickerson, handing her the note.

"No no," said his mother, "not right school. Please. Tom-Su father no like; he get so so mad."

"I'm sorry, Mrs. Kim," said Dickerson.

That night a terrible screaming argument that all of the Ranch could hear busted out in Tom-Su's apartment. The father mostly lost his lid and spit out one not-understandable sentence after another, sounding like some out-of-control Uzi. The only word we were hip to that came up again and again was "Tom-Su." The mother got in a few highpitched words of her own, but mostly seemed to take the bulletshot sentences left, right, left, right. Whenever she spoke we would hear a muffled wailing cry, too, that pricked every inch of our skin. The cries sounded like a person forced to watch the last of his blood dripdrop from his body. The cries came from Tom-Su. The father must really not've wanted his son at Harlem Shoemaker, we guessed, and must've taken the very suggestion as deeply personal, like it was a nasty negative on his name. Harlem Shoemaker, though, had a huge indoor swimming pool that we thought should've evened things up some. We didn't understand why Mr. Kim had to rip into his family the way he did. Or how his yelling could help any.

On our walk to the Pink Building the next morning we discovered a blankfaced Mrs. Kim and stonefaced Mr. Kim in the street in front of their apartment. Tom-Su stood by the door and watched them with this unshakable grin on his mug. Once, he'd looked our way as if casting a spell on us. Mrs. Kim had a suitcase by her side and a shoulder bag on her arm and spoke quietly to Mr. Kim, not really looking at him but up the empty street. Mr. Kim, though, glared hard at the side of her head, as if he'd wanted to bite her ear off. Then a taxi drove up, which had Mr. Kim grabbing onto his wife's arm and clipping some words hard into her ear as she struggled to free herself. They were quickly separated, though, by the taxi driver, who kept Mr. Kim from his wife as she scooted into the back of the taxi and locked her door. The Kims stared at each other through the window glass as the driver trunked the suitcase, stepped to his seat, and drove away. Mr. Kim watched the taxi head down the street and out of sight. When he walked back to his apartment he stopped at its door and stared his son in the eyes, who for some unknown reason maintained his grin. Together they looked nuttier than peanut butter. Mr. Kim glared at Tom-Su for what had to be a minute, then said one quick non-English brick of a word and smacked the boy on top of his head. Tom-Su bolted indoors. Abuse like that made us glad we didn't have any fathers in our homes. We continued on our walk to the Pink Building.

———

It was the next day that Tom-Su attached himself to us for the first time. We'd stopped at the donut shack at Sixth Street and Harbor Boulevard and bought ourselves a dozen plus donutholes. Then we strolled along the railroad tracks for Deadman's Slip, but after much spotting of Tom-Su sneaking along behind us, derailed ourselves towards the boxcars.

The railroad tracks ran between Harbor Boulevard and the waterfront. The same gray-white rocks filled every space between the wooden cross ties. At Sixth and Harbor the tracks branched into four and on the middle two tracks were the boxcars. Just to our right Beacon Park sat on a goodsized hillside and stretched maybe a ten-block length of Harbor Boulevard. From its green highground you could see clear to Long Beach and beyond. To our left a fence separated the railway yard from the nearby harborwater.

Several times during the walk we'd turned our heads and spotted Tom-Su following us, foolishly scrambling for cover whenever he thought he'd been dialed. Twice we stayed still and waited for him to come out from his hiding place, but only a baseball-cap bill and a small speck of forehead peeked out instead. At the last boxcar we jumped to the side, climbed on its roof, laid ourselves down on our stomachs, and waited to be found. When Tom-Su reached our boxcar he walked to the front of it, looked up the empty tracks, and then all around. Suddenly pure wonder showed on his face. They became air, said his expression. Poof! He turned to look back, side to side, and then straight up the empty tracks again—nothing. Staring into the distance, he stood like a windslumped post. Half a mile of rail and rocks and he waited for a hint to the mystery. Up on the roof I'm sure we all had the same exact thought: Why doesn't he check out the boxcar? Under it, in it, on top of it. It never crossed Tom-Su's mind, though, to suspect a trick. As far as he was concerned we were magicians who'd straight evaporated ourselves! Then, when we started to laugh from up-high, Tom-Su spun around like some onstage tap dancer rooted before a charging locomotive and looked up at us as if we weren't at all real. Once again he glanced around and into the empty distance. We could disappear, fly onto box-cars, and sneak up behind him without a rattle. When he took another look at us, all the wonder had reappeared and poured into his eyes. And a click later he busted into that buckedtooth smile and clapped his hands hard like a seal, turning us into a volcano of laughter. We took him along.

As a morning ritual we climbed the nearest mountain of tarped and twice-our-height fishing nets at Deadman's Slip. The nets usually belonged to the boat *Mary Ellen,* from San Pedro, California. Up on *Mary Ellen*'s nets our donuts vanished piece by piece as we watched straggler boats heading into or back from the Pacific Ocean. All the while the gray-and-orangebeaked seagulls stared at us as if waiting for the world to flinch.

———

The first few days along Tom-Su didn't catch a fish. In fact he didn't even seem to know what it was we were doing. And didn't seem to care either. He just sat alone, taking in the watery world ten feet below the Pink Building's wharf. Meanwhile we cut pieces of bait and baited hooks, dropped lines, and did or didn't pull in a wiggler. All the while Tom-Su was and wasn't a part of the situation. Not until day four did he lower a dropline of his own. And even though he'd already been along for three days, he had no idea how to bait a hook. So we took it upon ourselves to get him up to speed. For the rest of day four, though, nobody got the smallest nibble, which was a very rare thing at the Pink Building. It made us wonder whether Tom-Su was some kind of bad luck. We discussed it and decided that thinking that way was a bad luck in itself. We went home fishless.

The next day we set Tom-Su up, sat down, and focused on our droplines. For a while not a fish bit and not one of us said a word. We didn't want a repeat of the day before. Usually if no one got a bite we'd choose to play those different baits or move to a new spot in the harbor. But a couple of clicks later neither bait nor location concerned us any longer. Our new friend, you see, had finally expressed himself.

Tom-Su had been silent and calm and staring down at the water as usual. Then he got a tug on his line and jumped to his feet, shooting a quick, freaked-out look our way. The next tug threw his rubbery legs off-balance and he almost let go of the dropline. Tom-Su reacted as if something were trying to pull him into the water and became scared of the edge. That's when we yelled for him to start pulling up his line—and he did! He'd understood us. We yelled and yelled and he pulled and pulled as if he were saving his own life by doing so. Suddenly the fish sprang into the air. It was a big beautiful mackerel, which Tom-Su immediately wrapped his hand around, unhooked like an expert, and took straight into his mouth. Before we could say anything we heard a loud and nasty skeleton *crunch* and the mackerel went from a tailwhipping side to side to a stiffcurved dead. Tom-Su then removed the fish from his mouth and spit the bitten-off head to the ground. Some light-red blood eased down his chin from the corners of his mouth along with some of the strandy mackerel innards. Fish slime shined on his lips. Needless to say, our minds had been blown like glass. Tom-Su stood before us lost and confused, as if he had no idea what had just happened or that the faces in front of him had fascinated written all over them, not to mention more than a crumb of worry. Suddenly, though, Tom-Su broke into his broadest, toothiest grin ever. "Dead already," was all he said. It was also the first thing he'd spoken since hooking up with us. Then he started to laugh and laugh and clapped his hands like a seal, and it was so goofylooking that we joined his lead and even got to laughing some ourselves. I mean, if he could laugh at himself in such a situation, why couldn't we join him? Eventually we'd get used to the gore.

The chewed-into mackerel got tossed into the empty bucket and we each headed back to our droplines, but not before we set Tom-Su up at his same old private spot. And maybe it was mean of us, but we didn't bother to put any-more bait onto his hook for the rest of that day. Nobody was in a rush to see another fish at the end of his dropline. Tom-Su sat off to the side and stared at the water as if dying of thirst. Only once did he lift his head, to the sight of two grayblack pigeons flapping through the harbor sky. He wasn't bad luck, we agreed—just a bit freaky.

We caught a good many perch, buttermouth, and mack-erel that day. On the walk to the fishmarket, though, and then to the Ranch, we kept looking over at Tom-Su, expecting him to suddenly do something strange. Like fall to the ground and shake like an earthquake, hammer his head hard against a boxcar, or run fulltilt into the speeding traffic on Harbor Boulevard. But instead he was his usual goofy mellow, though once or twice we could've sworn he'd snuck a knowing peek our way—as if to say he'd understood exactly what he'd done to that mackerel and how badly it'd shaken us. But mostly we looked at him and saw this crooked and dizzy face strolling next to us, not able to speak a lick of English.

So most of our summer was spent fishing the San Pedro wa-terfront and selling the catch at the fishmarket. It was a nice rhythm. During the walks Tom-Su joined up with us with-out fail somewhere between the projects and the fishing spots. On the mornings we decided to head to Terminal Is-land or to Twenty-second Street instead of the Pink Building we never told Tom-Su and never had to. He somehow knew what direction we'd go in anyways, as if he'd picked up our scent. Early on we stopped turning our heads to look for him closing from behind too. We knew he'd find us. And as we met, Tom-Su simply merged with our group without saying a word, checked which of us held the buckets, took hold of them, and carried them the rest of the way. We knew that having a conversation with Tom-Su was impossible, though sometimes he'd say two or three words to a question he'd been asked. Words that meant something and nothing all at the same time.

One day in late July, Tom-Su caught up with us on the railroad tracks as usual. On the right side of his forehead was a red, knucklesized bump. Tom-Su walked with his eyes fastened to every cross tie in front of him. When he saw a few of us balancing eagle-armed on the thin rails, he tried it and fell right to his backside. As soon as he grounded he did that handclap of his and we all broke out in a fit of laughter.

The day after, a Sunday, we didn't go fishing. Instead we caught an RTD bus at First and Pacific for Downtown L.A. At city hall we transferred to the shuttle bus for Dodger Stadium. The Dodgers against the Mets would replace the fish for a day—if we could get the discount tickets. During the busride we'd wondered what Tom-Su was up to; whether he'd gone out and searched for us or not.

Monday morning we ran into Tom-Su waiting on the railroad tracks. He had a black eye and again had trouble looking at us—as if he were ashamed of the shiner. A couple of us put an arm around him to let him know he'd be all right in our company. He might've understood. We did the same a few days later when the forehead bump showed again, along with an arm bruise. As Tom-Su strolled beside us we agreed that the next time pops would pay a price. We became Tom-Su's insurance policy. Pops would step from his apartment one morning and get cracked on both temples with some two-by-fours and then be hammered on for a painful minute or so. In our book, being a father didn't mean he could be as disrespectful as he was. Luckily we saw no more bruises. But compared with what was to come, bruises were less than fleabites on an elephant.

Sometime in the middle of August we sat on the tarped netting as usual. The sky was dull and gray from a low marine layer clinging fast to the coastline. Tom-Su popped a donuthole into his mouth and took in the world around him. At times he and a seagull connected eyes for a very long minute or two and seemed perfectly alone with each other. Then we noticed a figure at the beginning of Deadman's, snooping around the fishing boats and tarps lying next to them. We shook Tom-Su from his staredown, slid off of *Mary Ellen*'s netting, grabbed our buckets, and broke for the back of the Pink Building. Then we crossed the tracks, snuck between some warehouses, and waited at the end of Twenty-second Street. An hour later and we knew he wouldn't find us or his son.

The next morning, though, he came looking again, and again we slid down *Mary Ellen*'s stack and jetted for Twenty-second Street. Pops must've gotten hip to his son's fish smell, we thought, or had some crazy scenting ability that ran in the family. How Tom-Su got out of the apartment we never learned.

The next day we rowed to Terminal Island and headed for Berth 300 where we knew pops would leave us alone. By our third day at 300, though, the fish had thinned out terribly, and because we had to row back across in the late afternoon when the port was at its busiest we needed more time to get to the fishmarket with our measly catches. We'd become frustrated with everything except the highdiving pelicans, though, to be honest, even they'd gotten on our nerves once or twice with all the fun they were having. Plus they were catching ten-to-twenty fish to our one and even the overflow-robbing trailer birds had more success than we did. We decided to go back to the other side.

The next morning pops didn't show himself at Deadman's. After we finished our donuts we strolled to the backmost spot of the Pink Building, dropped our gear, unrolled our droplines, baited hooks, and lowered the lines. The water below spread before us still and clear and flat like a giant lake mirror. Off its far surface you could see the upside down of Terminal Island's cranes and drydocks. Every fifteen minutes or so a ship loaded with autos, containers, or other cargo lumbered into port so the longshoremen could earn their pay. The big ships were the only vessels to disturb the surface that day. As our heads followed one especially humungous banana ship moving towards the inner harbor, we spotted Tom-Su's father sniffing at the entrance to the Pink Building. He hadn't seen us yet. One of us quickly grabbed Tom-Su by the head, shaking him from his deepdown watertrance, and turned it towards the entrance. His eyes focused and refocused several times on the figure at the start of the wharf. In the next second Tom-Su shot down the wharf ladder saying, "No, no, no" until he'd disappeared from sight.

The father's lonely figure moved along the wharf, arms stiff at his sides and hands pushed into his jacket pockets. Even from the good distance between us his neck looked rockhard and ruler-straight and his steps quick and choppy, as if he immediately had to hit up the restroom. We said just a couple of things to each other before he reached us: that he looked madder than a zoo gorilla and that, if he got even a little bit crazy, we'd tackle him, beat him until he cried, and then toss his out-of-line ass into the harbor.

At ten feet he stopped and looked us each in the face.

Another step forward and we'd get up and rush him. But he just stood still. His belly had a small paunch, his jetblack hair was combed back thick and shiny, and his face was sad and mean at the same time, the sadness and meanness seeming to compete with each other for worst possible facial expression. While he stood there his eyes checked around our buckets and droplines like some kind of dock detective. Suddenly I thought that Tom-Su might go into a permanent shock if we threw his pops into the water. Instead, maybe we'd just beat him down and drag him along the ground for a good stretch. We watched and waited.

After he'd thoroughly checked out our goods, he again checked our faces. But we were each calmer than a Buddha statue. Pops then let out a snort and moved sideways to the edge of the wharf, where he looked down below and side to side. When we did the same we saw that he saw nothing interesting. Then he turned and walked towards the entrance—which was now his exit. When he'd finally faded from sight we called below for Tom-Su to come up top, but heard no movement. Again we called and again we heard not a sound from below. When one of us mentioned the word drowned, we all hurried down low to pull Tom-Su from the water. Once underneath, though, and we found him sitting on a plank between two pilings, his back to us. He was bent close to the water. When we moved up from behind we froze at what we saw him looking at on the watertop. Tom-Su's hand traced over a flat reflection it was careful not to touch; a reflection of his own surfacefloatingface that was much more regular and goodlooking than the one looking down at it. As a matter of fact, it looked more like Tom-Su's handsome twin brother than Tom-Su himself. Its eyes showed intelligent and its teeth had none of that serious buck to them. Overall, though, the face was Tom-Su's, but without any of the tilted dizziness eyeing down at it. The face and water and Tom-Su were in a dream of their own that we'd come upon by accident. Suddenly, though, a shipwave flooded in and soaked all of our shoes and pant legs and had Tom-Su pulling his hand back as if from a fire, but then he plunged it into the water over and over again. It was the same crazy jerking motion he'd made whenever he'd gotten a tug on his dropline. When he was done grabbing into the water, he turned to us to see us crouched beside him like so many ocean vultures.

Up on the wharf we pulled in fish after fish for hours. The marine layer had lifted while we were down below, and the sun had bleached the waterfront. Every once in a while we'd looked over at a bloodstained Tom-Su, who was again hanging out with his handsome twin brother. Around him were the headless bodies of a perch and two mackerel that'd briefly bothered their relationship. After we filled our buckets we rolled up the droplines, shook Tom-Su from his stupor, and headed for the fishmarket. On the walk we kept staring at Tom-Su from the corners of our eyes. His bad features seemed ten times more noticeable than before. His teeth were now a train cowcatcher, his eyes two tarpit traps, and his drool a mighty waterfall. At the fishmarket locals surrounded our buckets and after twenty minutes we'd sold our full catch three fish at a time. We split up the money and washed our hands in the fishmarket restroom. Back outside we realized Tom-Su was missing. We searched for him along the waterfront for what felt like a day, but came up empty. We went back to the Ranch.

In the morning we walked along the tracks, a couple of us throwing rocks as far down the railway yard as we could. At the last boxcar we discovered the door completely opened and somebody snoring loud inside it. We peeked in and saw Tom-Su lying on his side in the corner, his face pressed tight against the wall. When we jumped in and woke him he gave us his ear-to-ear grin. Because the same bloodstained shirt was on his back, we knew he hadn't gone home.

The next several mornings we picked Tom-Su up from his boxcar and on *Mary Ellen*'s tarped netting let him eat as many donuts as he wanted. Twice we'd seen pops in the distance, stepping along the waterfront and talking to whatever people he'd bumped into. Tom-Su, we knew, had to be careful. We fished at the Pink Building, pulled in our bucketfuls, heard the fish heads come off *crunch crunch crunch* and sold our catch in front of the fishmarket. We brought Tom-Su some soap and made him wash up at the public restroom, got him a hamburger and fries from the nearby diner, and walked him back to the boxcar. We also brought him a good blanket to use.

Except for him crashing in the boxcar, though, things felt pretty good to us: the fish were biting well in back of the Pink Building and we weren't bothered by anyone from early mornings until late afternoons, when the sky got sleepy and dull. At those moments we sometimes had the urge to walk to Point Fermin to watch the sun ease fiery red into the Pacific, just to the right of Catalina Island. From the harbor side of Deadman's Slip we mostly missed all of that.

One morning we came upon the boxcar and Tom-Su was gone. He wasn't in any of the other boxcars either. We continued along the tracks to Deadman's and downed our donuts on *Mary Ellen*'s netting, all the while scanning the railway yard and waterfront for Tom-Su's gangly movement. When he didn't come we saved his donuts and headed for the Pink Building. Later we settled with the only local at the fishmarket and then stopped by the boxcar on the way back to the Ranch. But Tom-Su still hadn't shown. After waiting until dark we left him the donuts and a few dollars to boot. It was the end of August.

The whole week before school was to start, Tom-Su seemed to've dropped completely out of sight. The donuts and money we'd been leaving him hadn't been touched either. But instead of worrying about it we decided that he'd eventually find us, though once or twice one of us climbed under the wharf to make sure he wasn't hanging with that twin of his. Finally we decided he must've moved in with his mother or maybe went back to Korea where he'd come from.

Sunday morning before school started we were headed to the Pink Building for the last time that summer. The project's streets were completely still except for a small cluster of people gathered right in front of Tom-Su's apartment. From a block away we stood and watched the goings-on. Then a taxi pulled up to the crowd and a woman stepped out. It was Tom-Su's mother, Mrs. Kim. When she walked into the apartment we headed straight for the crowd.

That summer we'd learned early on never to turn around and check for Tom-Su coming up behind us during our walks to the fishing spots. If we did, he'd just jump out of sight and then peek around a corner, believing he was somehow invisible. Or he'd already be waiting for us at the boxcar or netting, hoping to get a bucket inhand ASAP. But he could be anywhere. That last morning, though, after we'd left the crowd in front of Tom-Su's place and made our way to the Pink Building we kept turning our heads to catch him before he fully disappeared. Each time we saw something unusual we'd tell ourselves it was a piece of him. Once he looked like the edge of a drainpipe, another the bumper of a car parked among a dozen others, and yet another a baseball cap riding by on a bus. He was anything but the smaller of the two body bags that'd floated out of the apartment that morning. It couldn't have been him, we told ourselves, because the bag had been way too little between the grown men carrying it out. And when we'd heard the maintenance men talk about a double hanging we were amazed, sure; but as we headed down the railroad tracks and passed the last boxcar, we were convinced he was still hiding out somewhere along the waterfront. Especially since the donuts and money had been taken.

At the Pink Building we'd been set up for a good hour and got not a single nibble. The silence around us was broken into only by a nearby seagull, who then yapped over and over until it rose up and faded out of sight. We stared into the water below and wondered if we shouldn't head for another spot. Suddenly, though, one of us got a bite and started to pull and pull at the dropline with the rest of us yelling like mad, but just as we were about to grab the fish at its end, the dropline snapped.

As the morning turned to afternoon and the afternoon to night we talked with excitement about the next summer.

As the seagulls and pelicans roofed themselves because they'd grown tired of the day we gathered our gear but couldn't speak anymore because the summer was already done. And as the roofed birds called sad and lonely all around the waterfront, a single star showed itself in the everywhere spread of night above. Mostly, though, we just stood at the edge of the wharf and forever looked down at the faces staring up at us.

Violence; ever since five I remember it a problem. That was the first time moms broke through the apartment yelling for us to hit the floor while she shut down all the lights. Since I was in the livingroom, that's where I dropped. Then I heard the *pop pop pop* just outside the door, a wild shouting, another closer *pop,* and finally the fastfooted running across our front yard. For the longest time all we knew was a longdrawn silence.

Because the pops themselves had sounded no more than some gone-off metallicky firecrackers, I asked moms what the big deal was. But she just shushed me quiet, which I stayed, until the red-and-blue police lights finally strobed through the front window and the helicopter up above daytimed up our entire street.

That was pretty much how the drill had gone at least twice a year for the past seven, with the last time two months back a bullet finally coming through the front window and lodging deep into the livingroom wall.

The violence was every time gangrelated.

There was more of it, too, in other parts of the neighborhood. For example the night two lowrider sets went a hellish heads up next to our nursery hangout. By the time the cops had swarmed, four bangers from either set lay paintwisting on the ground from every kind of knifewound apiece. Somehow, though, they all lived. Or the Saturday afternoon a year back when, at the start of our crosstown football game at the Big Park—us, the Edgewater Boys, against them, Thirteenth Street—a beat-up old Ford Pinto of all cars stopped in the middle of Second Street, the driver getting out with the biggest baddest automatic weapon we'd ever seen with which he started spraying an entire row of apartments for one very loud minute. Even reclipped business-as-usual-like while he was at it. Then he jumped into the Pinto and simply sputtered off, at which point I finally checked my teammates to see that every one of them had smartly done like me and hit the grass, whereas Thirteenth Street had had the ignorance to've stood staring a very slackjawed at the whole incident as if watching some happening-right-in-front-of-'em action movie. It was probably one of the reasons why we afterwards rolled all over them 96-0.

By then, though, the violence had mostly become the revenging kind between local sets, or between them and the sets from other neighborhoods like Wilmington, Compton, and Long Beach—each one maybe a five-minute deathride from the next. Because the favorite style of attack was the drive-by, which made the revenging no more than a quick, murderous U-turn away, they were nervous times. Not only couldn't we trust strange people suddenly showing up in the Ranch, we couldn't trust strange cars. At one point the drive-bys had gotten so bad that whenever we walked anywhere in the neighborhood and some not-familiar vehicle came cruising our way up the street, we'd always time that car and ourselves meeting even with a van or truck or telephone pole between us so as to at least have a little piece of protection in case that long-expected gat sprang from one of the car's windows. Luckily for us it never did. But still, you couldn't help but feel that open season was in full effect and that anything on two legs was the prize game.

The most violent thing that'd ever happened to me personally, though, didn't leave a single seeable scar anywhere on my body. A month or so before that bullethole in the wall, I was walking home from school down First Street when, at Mesa Street, an out-of-town cholo came from around the corner and we bodybumped against each other. Before I could apologize the tip of a gun was at the tip of my nose. That's how highstrung crazy it'd gotten. One second you're walking along minding your own business and the next you're staring into the black steel of a guntunnel. Almost immediately I'd lost any and all feeling of myself on that corner. I'd simply disappeared from myself for a stretch, not really knowing if that violentest of deaths—the gunshotblast—had finally claimed me or not. That pointblank guntunnel, I later decided, had somehow sucked me and everything around me right into its deep dark destructive space. How long I was up in it I don't know. Only that when somebody who knew me eventually said a few words that brought me back to my senses, I found the gun gone, the cholo gone, and my whole body shaking as if on-the-very-verge-of-seizure sick. I don't think I spoke to anyone until a solid week later.

The violence supposedly stopped for good two weeks ago. That was when all the leaders of all the gangs in L.A. met to once again agree on what's called a truce. That's like a promise not to take each other out at twenty miles an hour anymore—or at all. The real enemy, they'd decided, was the L.A.P.D., two of whose officers had just gotten off after shooting half-a-dozen ghetto kids playing gangster with toy guns. The shooting struck a nerve all over the city, with the sets somehow feeling responsible as well. Maybe it was the playing gangster that'd brought on the guilt, or that, unlike that lowrider fight, none of the children lived, but either way, at the truce meeting each set leader decided to tie his set's color rag—blue, red, purple, green, and so on—into one long rope that was supposed to mean something like a newfound brotherhood, and then actually *hugged* each other, which was the weirdest, awkwardest thing I'd ever heard of.

Our neighborhood Crips (known as the Second Street Mob) were now supposedly down with all the Bloods, all the Bloods with all the Pirus, all the Pirus with all the Crips, and all of them, believe it or not, with all the lowriders too. Mass peace had hit. If there were any run-ins, the set leaders themselves agreed to do whatever necessary to figure out a nonviolent way of responding to them. Like always, it was broadcast on the late news and everything.

Two weeks later, though, and not a single gangster shot had been fired in at least all of San Pedro. A sort of miracle if you thought about it. But then our neighborhood had its first big problem in the way of Beefy and Monet, which instantly led to its second big problem: how to deal with the first one. And not in a neverending lifetime could I have imagined myself upclose involved in either of them. But I was.

Beefy was this redhead and freckled, chainsmoking sixteen-year-old lowrider-wannabe who could've sworn he was full-blooded Chicano. On top of sporting the lowrider uniform of baggy, creased, down-to-the-ground work-Dickies, extra-long, ten-X T-shirt, color-ringed tube socks, and a rubber-bottomed pair of winos, every sentence he spoke had to have in it at least one lowrider word. "What's happenin', vato?"; "Where you headed, homes?"; "I need me a ruca, ey";

"Símon, homeboy"; "I heard that, ese"; "Órale pues, carnal"; on and on and on. Beefy was so wannabe he even wore the veterano's forehead bandana and got a huge homemade tattoo on his right arm: "El Gordo" it said. "The fat one."

And fat he was. Beefy came in huge meaty sections of body—treetrunk thighs, elephant trunk calves, not-a-swimming-trunk-in-the-world-fitting ass. He was so fat he needed his own zipcode. Each of Beefy's fingers looked like a skinless chicken drumstick, and his neck alone as if it weighed as much as me with a big wet coat on. Not only that, but his fat had flab to it. A simple Beefy arm or leg movement sent a surging swell of skin all over the rest of his body. If he'd have been a balloon he would've looked overblown and underblown at the same time. When Beefy heavied through the neighborhood, you'd wonder how his joints held him at all together, which was probably the reason he'd become knockkneed to the point of his thighs grinding so hard into each other; a grinding that every month wore out a pair of those creased-down work Dickies. To watch the guy move about was like watching an impossible strength workout. *Ba-boom ba-boom ba-boom.* As if he were tied to a dozen staked ropes or was pushing himself against some invisible, but always-in-front-of-him wall.

Like all wannabes, Beefy couldn't back down from anything, especially if that anything happened to be a streetfight. Sure, he'd committed his share of crime, but to go toe-to-toe?—that was his real love. Beefy'd heavy through the neighborhood, skytilted forehead and squaredback shoulders, just daring the world to mess with him. But if it wouldn't, he'd simply change his tactics—like try and catch someone staring at him, for example. And if he did, he'd quickly lock in with a stare of his own until one of those all-out and awkward staredowns thickened up the air real bad. And if the starer didn't look away quick enough, Beefy would bust out those two words that always meant a "let's rumble" whenever he said them, arms halfraised at his sides and hands wide open for a sure-to-be war: *"What up?"* In any other situation "What up?" meant what it always or should've meant. How you doing? How you been? What's going on—with you, your life, the day, your wife? Kind of a strong questioning hello. But said from one starer to another, the words communicated nothing less than a challenge; as if to say: "go for watchya know," "step up, fool," "let's dance, bitch." None being too good an idea when it came to a Beefy who might've moved big and slow while on his skinswelling stroll through the neighborhood, but in a squab was anything but. With his five chicken drumsticks, for example, we once saw him snatch an about-to-land-with-his-jaw punch right out of midair and then proceed to snap several of the puncher's handbones-plus. And once Beefy got agrip of another's body part *it was all over.* He'd just boa constrictor a guy till things started to break or puncture or the scarier-than-a-nightmare blackout came on, at which point, no matter how much the poor bastard cried out or tried to land against Beefy's armorplated skull, it wasn't but a matter of minutes before he'd given up his whole oxygen supply. And being knocked out around Beefy was no way to be in a fight with him.

The neighborhood's lowrider set, the RSP Locos, and their leader, Chuy Lopez, mostly accepted Beefy as one of their own. And why not; they'd all grown up together and, what was more, absolutely knew they could count on him in a pinch. But still, that wannabe tag hung over the guy like his very own raincloud.

Except for his age, Monet was nothing like Beefy. He wasn't fat, flabby, or slow and was definitely not a wannabe. Monet wasn't a wannabe because his foot-shorter, ten-years-older-than-him stepbrother Papa Pierre (one of the scariest individuals you'd never hope to meet, and who'd just happened to run the Second Street Mob) wouldn't have it. Which, if anything, made Monet something of a not-allowed-to-be.

The stepbrothers never really had any parents. Moms had spent most of their lives in lockup, and each of their fathers had been no more than the typical round-the-way stranger. So they had to selfraise themselves, which really meant that Papa Pierre had to fill in as daddy for his already-way-outgrown-him stepbrother. And as such, he had strict rules for Monet. Not only wouldn't Papa Pierre let his stepbrother anywhere near his set, he wouldn't let him get into a single little squab or allow anybody else to mess with him, either, gangster or no gangster. "Too much to lose, boy," Papa

Pierre said to him. "You've got it going on, and if it's up to me, it's staying on." Monet wasn't allowed to fight, gamble, claim to be a Crip, hang out with other thugs, steal, vandalize, and above all, do any drugs. Basically, Papa Pierre allowed his stepbrother no bad behavior of any kind. The two times Monet did mess up—once for sporting a backpocketed blue rag to school and the other for taking a hit off a joint—Papa Pierre locked him in their bathroom for a week straight. (But not before the first time pulling Monet through the neighborhood by his ear, and the second time slapping him upside his head all the way home, both of which would've been highly embarrassing events had it been someone other than Papa Pierre doing the punishing.) Papa Pierre often said he protected Monet because he had high hopes for him.

"He's a wunderkind," he told us one day. "You all know what that means?"

We all said no.

"It means child superstar. That's why he's off limits. He's got a future in front of him. Unlike the rest of the riffraff you see around here."

A child superstar he was. A solid, superyolked sixfoot-four with a vertical leap of forty-eight inches, Monet could reverse dunk a basketball and run a sub-eleven hundred by the *fifth* grade. In high school he was *the* athlete, landing MVP of the basketball, baseball, and football teams. "I'm a man among boys," Monet once told us. In one basketball game alone he had fifty-four points on twenty-seven dunks, in a single football game eighteen passes caught for seven touchdowns and three-hundred-and-eighty-three yards, and in his only track meet broke almost every varsity record on the books—*including* the pole vault. He was athlete of the week every week all year long and made every all-American team in the country. "I shouldn't even *be* here anymore," he once said. "I've *been* ready for the big time." And if you'd have asked any of us, he probably had.

The Beefy-Monet problem happened at the Big Park, one of the only two places Papa Pierre allowed his brother to hang out (the other being their apartment). Monet would return from an afterschool practice and usually just lie on the Big Park grass and stare all silently at the sky until it was time to get himself some food. Besides an occasional comment or two our way, he talked to no one in the whole neighborhood.

On the day of the problems, though, Monet sat elbow-propped watching me and the fellas throw the football around in the parkcenter. Once in a while he said a nice word to a pass we'd thrown or make a you-guys-are-sorry gigglesound. For a child superstar, I sometimes thought, he tended to look real bored and lonely lying there all by himself, which must've been how a person got who was never allowed to get into any trouble. Then, from the direction of the unused jungle gym, we noticed a cigarette-sucking, squabseeking Beefy working a hard and headed-our-way diagonal through the park.

"How you doing, Beefy?" we all said to him when he'd reached us.

"Samo-samo, homeboys," said Beefy all lowrider-like, "samo-samo"—and kept on heavying towards the corner exit near Monet's resting spot, forehead skytilted and shoulders squared back to that rough, tough, and dangerous.

Even though Monet was watching Beefy heavy along, we paid neither of them any more attention and got back to the pigskin. Beefy knew Papa Pierre's younger brother wasn't affiliated and was off limits—just like Chuy Lopez himself had some nonbanging family members who weren't to be touched. And Monet had his own rules to follow. So we started tossing the football around like before. But suddenly that giggle of a laugh sounded from Monet's direction—and loud. Since I'd just thrown this ugly, nonspiral of a pass I assumed it was meant for me. When I looked Monet's way, though, he wasn't looking at me but at a Beefy still on his heads-up heavy towards that corner exit. Beefy, I assumed, either hadn't heard anything or, if he had, was absolutely committed to those off-limits rules. Anyways, we brushed it off and again got to midairing the football. But by the second pass in the same loud gigglesound happened, only this time nastier. When we turned to look it was at the sight of a still-elbowpropped Monet staring dead at a full-stopped-and-glaring-right-back-at-him Beefy. Ten seconds later and we stood as slackjawed as Thirteenth Street had been, believing for sure that yet another truce was already halfway to its grave. And by the time Beefy spit out those two words that only could've meant that one thing, we thought the thing dead for sure. Luckily, though, Papa Pierre and his set were already descending onto the Big Park.

Good and bad news traveled at very different speeds in our neighborhood. Whereas good news took its sweet-old, I'll-get-there-when-I-get-there time in making the rounds like some badly-out-of-shape jogger, bad news couldn't wait to get out of the starting blocks and into a street, telephone, and mouth-to-mouth supersprint. Maybe that was because bad news—in the way of beatings, arrests, and the violent deaths of close ones—was a thing that everyone had to instantly share together because, if gotten in time, might help the getter prevent even more of the bad stuff from happening. Whereas the worst bad news could be some impossible-to-listen-to stuff, the best bad news could be the kind that warned of something *about to,* and *not already* happened, giving some bad news a good news kind of feel to it. If gotten in time, that is. Which was most likely how Papa Pierre understood things when he'd heard that Beefy (a no-doubt-about-it, walking-staring-and-talking mountain of bad news in his own right) had entered the Big Park where his mattered-more-to-him-than-anything-else-on-the-planet younger stepbrother was spending his afterschool.

"Cut that shit out, Monet!" shouted Papa Pierre, stepping onto the parkgrass. "Step back, Beefy! You know you ain't supposed to be messing with him!"

Then from the direction of the jungle gym a quick-coming, Chuy-led pack of Locos appeared too, who'd in seconds collected themselves next to Beefy.

"What's going down, homes?" said an ironvoiced Chuy to Beefy.

"That pinche puta started some shit, ey," said Beefy with a headpoint at Monet, which instantly set off a barrage of fuck yous from the Cripside that only got rightaway repeated by the Locoside, and both of which had me and the fellas in an ASAP backpedal all the way to the parkcenter. No sense getting trampled to death by a soon-to-be riot of feet and fists, we decided—not to mention what might happen as soon as the two-to-three heads who'd suddenly released from each side returned with the youknowwhats at the lockloaded ready.

What'd kept all the fuck yous from turning into that all-out riot, though, were a quickly turned-their-backs-on-each-other Papa Pierre and Chuy Lopez, telling—no, *ordering*—their sets to "shut the fuck up" and "calm yourselves down," which they soon enough did to a man—though you could see in their tight-and-ready-to-erupt bodylanguages how two weeks' worth of truce had gotten everyone involved into the terriblest of tensed-up physical states, making me wonder if it might not've been for the best to just let them get it out of their systems right then and there. Without those youknowwhats, that is.

Chuy then gestured towards the parkcenter and Papa Pierre yessed his head.

"Keep his fool ass away from Beefy!" shouted Papa Pierre to his set as he turned to walk our way. "And vice versa!"

Considering what'd damnnear gone down, the set leaders moved along talking as though some righteously good friends who'd just happened to end up on opposite sides of each other. Twice they stopped, looked our way, said a few things, *chuckled,* and then continued their walk. When they got too close for comfort we made a move to leave, but they immediately called for us to stay. "Say what!" we whispered to each other, not sure what to think of the request. Then Papa Pierre put his hands up as though waiting for a pass, which made me realize I'd been the one left holding the football, which I quickly threw to him. Then they stood right in front of us. Without that football inhand I suddenly felt the worst kind of naked.

It was the closest I'd ever been to either of them and, to my totaldeep shock, we were all the exact same height. Had I growthspurted recently? I wondered. I was sure I hadn't, or the invisible-feeling clothes I knew I sported would've had a sure-enough tightness to them, no? To eye them eye-to-eye felt so strange I could hardly accept it. I mean, we were talking *Papa Pierre* and *Chuy Lopez,* the topdogs of the Crips and Locos; two of the main reasons why moms had run through the apartment for the last seven years, killing all the lights while yelling for me to hit the floor; two of the main reasons for that recently-happened bullethole in our livingroom wall; and two of the main reasons why a helicopter at least two nights a year daytimed up our entire street. Those guys. And we were *the exact same height,* with some of my best growing years still to come. The more I stared at them, the more I started to realize why I hadn't expected our sameheightedness to happen to me: I'd always assumed them bigger because of whatall I'd over the years heard people say about them; about their very violent runins with the rollerboys, about their revenges on enemy gangs, and even about their sometimes terrible handling of everyday residents of the Ranch. Things a lot of the time spoken in such fearing worried voices that they'd even made it many times into my very own dreamworld, a place where a something like height had its own way of being. Where a person might one night be maybe the size of the tiniest of black ants, and another, as tall as an oncoming, sure-to-destroy-it-all-with-you-included tidalwave.

"What happened between them two, little homeboys?" said Chuy to us.

He was looking for fault, and we knew better than to answer him the truth and be forever known around the projects as a bunch of dimedropping rats. Instead we played it a very smooth deaf, dumb, and blind, which quickly had Papa Pierre chuckling as if proud.

"The fifth," he said. "It'll definitely come in handy one day." When he twirled the football some in his hands, I suddenly had this deepdown urge to snatch it away from him. But I didn't dare.

"Me and Papa Pierre, ey," said Chuy, "we're trying to figure out a good way for these little maricóns to settle their petty-ass problem."

"Without 'em really fighting each other, though," said Papa Pierre real quick. "Can't risk my boy's safety. Know what I'm saying?"

We yessed automatic.

"So you eses got any ideas?" said Chuy, looking us each dead in the eyes. We turned to each other as if crime accused. "Something Beefy's got a chance at, ey."

"Which means no football, basketball, running of any kind—"

"C'mon," said a somewhat-offended Chuy to Papa Pierre. "They know what your hermano's good at, ey. Just like they know what Beefy's good at." Then he looked our way again. "Símon?" We again yessed automatic. "Good then, vatos. So give us some ideas. We're not very good at this."

"How about some target shooting?" said one of us, not

sure he should've said anything at all. "You know, at the pistol range by Five Points."

"No, no, no," said Papa Pierre. "Monet can't touch a gun. Not even at a range."

"Plus half the shooters there are cops," said Chuy.

Again they looked at us.

"How about a minibike race?" said another one of us, which lit up Chuy's eyes.

"Naw," said Papa Pierre. "Can't risk an accident."

"You gotta risk *something,* homes," said Chuy to him, "or else the competition means nothing. Sabes?" Papa Pierre looked at Chuy, and then at us. "Your boy's a man. Let him—"

"That ain't gonna be him, dragracing on a minibike," said Papa Pierre. "It's gotta be something safe. Something—"

"How about swimming?" I said suddenly.

Chuy looked at me as if faceslapped, which had me ready to sprint for some impossible-to-find cover. "Yeah!" he said, though. "That's it, homes! They swim it out in the harbor!" He looked at Papa Pierre. "You can't say no to *that.*"

Papa Pierre, though, didn't say anything to anything.

"Swimming!" said the Crips and the Locos after we'd returned to them.

"You're damn straight," said Chuy, suddenly looking at

me. "Break it down, little hombre." And with that, over two-dozen wound-up-and-wondering heads spun my sorry-ass way to wait for the word. "Go on, ey!" said Chuy. "Tell 'em the plan you were telling us." Plan! I thought, looking for a little help from the fellas, who'd suddenly gotten all superinterested in the tops of their shoes or with the watching for birds in a very birdless sky. Papa Pierre, I could see, wished I'd never even existed. "C'mon, vato, break it down!"

In so many stops and stutters I proceeded to tell everybody present that swimming made the most sense for Beefy (who I felt a very deep need to apologize to) because he wasn't as athletically gifted as Monet, and for Monet (who I also felt like apologizing to) because of Papa Pierre's safety issues. Then I agreed with Chuy about the harbor location—"but not the inner harbor," I said, starting to get excited about my idea, "but the outer one. There are no ships, and they could swim from the breakwater fishing pier to the small inner beach. It's not too short, not too long, and all the way waveless." For a good chunk of time nobody said a word. Just stood and stared at this all-too-excited, loud-mouthed intruder among them.

"This shit's ridiculous!" snapped Monet suddenly. "I ain't getting into no seawater!"

"What?" said Chuy. "You worried about big fat Beefy beating you, homes?"

"Hell no!" said Monet as if absolutely insulted. "He'd get worked on or off land. And I'm not your 'homes,' homey."

"What's the problem with a little swim then?" said a

sounding-mighty-up-for-the-challenge Beefy suddenly, to which nobody, Monet included, said a word. That was when a longquiet Papa Pierre stepped in front of his younger brother.

"Ain't no problem," he said to Beefy. "You wanna swim, big boy, we'll swim. Just have yourself ready, you hear?" to which everybody present cheered and gave either Beefy or Monet (depending on affiliation) many backslaps apiece. Monet, you could see, was suddenly feeling downright Crippish, which had Papa Pierre scowling at everything he saw. Especially me.

At first the swim was supposed to go down the very next day, but things got complicated. Beefy said he needed time to get his lungs into shape, and Monet needed "no more than two-three days," as he'd put it, *to learn how to swim.* It was one of those hard-to-believe things, him not know-ing how to swim. All sixteen years of his life spent right along the-size-of-something-like-a-fifth-of-the-planet Pacific Ocean, and he'd never bothered to get in it.

"If his big ass can do it," he'd said all wunderkind-like as he left the park, "it can't be that hard."

So everybody (meaning Papa Pierre and Chuy) agreed to ten days later. Until then, Beefy and Monet weren't al-lowed any contact. If one glimpsed the other somewhere around the neighborhood, he had to make the greatest effort not to get anywhere near him. In other words, Beefy had to stay away from the Big Park like me, who also had to keep well out of Beefy's way, believing as I did that I was in for a hardhanded headslap-plus from everybody but Chuy himself. Luckily, though, Beefy's lung training and Monet's swim lessons were to keep them both off the sidewalks busy for those next ten days.

By day two of those ten, though, some strange unexpected things started to happen around the neighborhood. For one, people were rumoring away about a swimming match between Beefy (representing the Locos) and Monet (representing the Crips), which thoroughly amazed them. It was a buzz that'd just happened on its own. No matter what block we found ourselves on, people couldn't get off the subject. A Crip and a Loco *swimming* it out? The very possibility numbed. A one-on-one on the basketball court, maybe; gloved and swinging in the boxing ring, okay; hell, even a tacky-ass game of tennis sounded closer to home. Well maybe not. But *swimming* it out? In the saltwater ocean? It was all too much to handle. And because Beefy and Monet had already achieved the reputations they had, a great interest was suddenly taken in each and every detail of their lives. "What had been said between 'em at the Big Park?"; "How's Papa Pierre feel about his kid brother representing his set?"; "Whose idea had the swimming been?"; "Where and when are they practicing?"; "How many cigarettes a day is Beefy down to?"; on and on and on. It became so quick so much a surprising soap opera, it caught

Papa Pierre and Chuy completely offguard, making them appear as if repeatedly shot at. What'd started out as a kind of harmless joking lesson on their part had overnight turned on them into this unstoppable grapevine gossip. Next thing, both set leaders became so deeply involved in their swimmer's progress you just knew all the attention had gotten them thinking that the swim would be a serious statement on themselves and their sets. Like who was really topdog of the topdogs? You could almost see the word written in big block letters right across their foreheads: P-R-I-D-E. When by day four Monet hadn't even learned to dogpaddle, Papa Pierre actually hired a real-live swim teacher to show him how.

(On the side, I became known as the boy who pushed Beefy and Monet into the sea.

"Little big man," someone said to me.

"Congratulations, son," said another.

"You did good!"

And, "You've got *some* nerve, young man.")

It was also too much to handle.

Another interest the competition kicked off was in gambling. Four different bookies suddenly had pools going that everyday jumped a good chunk higher *and* started betting lines with every-hour-adjusting odds. Day one opened with the all-American-in-all-events Monet a twenty-to-one favorite, and closed with him and Beefy even on the strength of the "breaking" news that Monet hadn't even known how to swim. Needless to say, me and the fellas had quickly slapped together whatever money we could muster and already locked it down on Beefy the underdog before that Monet-couldn't-swim-a-lick news officially broke. Not that we had any faith in Beefy's ability to beat the wunderkind, we just couldn't pass up the fact that our twenty-nine dollars down meant a possible four-hundred-and-eighty-dollar payday—if it did indeed pay out. It's sad, but that kind of lumpsum payment had a way of making a young guy wish the evilest of evil on a person. For example, every day until race day came one of us never failed to bring up the possibility that a crippling cramp could hit Monet in midswim. And to be terribly horribly honest, some even prayed for such a cramp to definitely happen.

Since we suddenly had an investment to consider, we decided it was best if we kept a tighter tabs on what was happening with both of the swimmers. I, for one, couldn't live on grapevine alone. So we headed to Cabrillo Beach where Beefy'd set up training camp, and what we saw on arrival boggled: Beefy, sandsitting like a beached, redheaded hippopotamus in a black, ten-X wifebeater and cutoff Dickies. His arms hung meatybig at his sides and two lowrider girls massaged each of his massive shoulders while a third held a sodacan to his mouth. Just past them, along a short stretch of the beach, four Locos stood almost the same, as-if-duncepunished distance apart. They were smoking cigarettes and talking. Then we saw Chuy near the beach entrance conferencing with some handholding, touristdressed man and woman. We headed over to them.

"But I don't see the cameras," said the man.

"That's because they're underwater cameras, ey," said Chuy, as if he'd done so a dozen times already.

"But isn't he a bit big to be a movie star?" said the woman, looking at Beefy.

"It's a comedy, ey," said a quick-on-his-feet Chuy. "An underwater comedy." Then he saw us next to him. "These are his costars."

"Really!" said the woman. "An underwater children's comedy!"

"Yeah really," said Chuy. "Now we've gotta get back to work or Hollywood'll get pissed at us, okay?" The couple frowned but then turned around and slowly walked away. "Please come back next week!" yelled Chuy after them. "Romantic pendejos. Why can't they walk in the goddamn park or something? Visit family." Then he looked at us again and said, "What do you vatos want?" which instantly had us holding our breaths, which he rightaway saw. "C'mon! Don't be so serious, ey. You're at the beach. Enjoy yourselves a little." We sucked in some air.

———

"Why wouldn't you let those two onto the beach, Chuy?" one of us said finally.

"They mess with Beefy's concentration, ey, when they stare at him," he said. "You know how it gets when people stare at him, and we need the vato to focus."

"Why're the Locos standing like that?" said another.

"They're being markers, ey," he said. "See where the first two vatos are?" We yessed. "That's how far Beefy swam his first time in. And so on and so forth. It's a real team effort."

"But they're only fifteen-twenty feet apart."

"Yeah, I know," said Chuy. "But he just busted about a twenty-five footer, homes, and by race day he'll be doing a mile." He looked Beefy's way. "He's resting now, ey, 'cause his chest hurts. Still muy malo." Then Beefy slowly got up and started to heavy for the water. "C'mon, vato!" shouted Chuy, jogging after him. "We can't let those Crip putos get over on us. You hear me, Gordo?"

"Yeah," said Beefy all serious and determined. "I hear you, homes." Then he was in the water.

"C'mon, big boy!" yelled Chuy. "Show us what you got!"

"C'mon, Beefy!" yelled the Locos and their girls, to which Beefy swam a hard parallel to the beach, but so slow as to barely move.

We walked up to Chuy. "C'mon, Beefy!" some of us (or that four-eighty back) shouted along.

Finally, after maybe another twenty-five feet, a suddenly-greenfaced Beefy came to a stop, stood up, and staggered out of the water and back to his resting spot, too tired to even notice me and the fellas standing next to a suddenly-worried-looking Chuy. Then Beefy plopped himself down.

"Just between us, vatos," whispered Chuy our way, "but we're gonna need a good tide, no? You guys know anything about that?"

We noed our heads.

Chuy thought some. "By the way," he finally said, "how's Papa Pierre's boy doing? Can he swim any yet?"

We all shrugged.

"Well, you never know," he said, holding up two fingercrossed hands. "He could catch a cramp, ey."

The handscribbled sign on the front door to the Peck Park pool read, Closed to the Public—and this means YOU! But we opened it anyways and headed through a dark empty locker room till we reached the poolside door, where we waited and listened, not wanting to step out until we knew for sure that Monet wouldn't notice us.

"This time really try to keep your arms relaxed," said a peppyvoiced man on the other side of the door. "And try and breathe *easy*. Okay?"

Next we heard what only could've been an injured seal or drowning seabird beating a wild flipper or wing against the watersurface *Splat! Splat! Splat!* We eased through the poolside door as nonchalantquick as possible, only to see something that made my whole system ache—not to mention send a guilty-as-charged pang through my taken-aback heart for ever having suggested a swim-off in the first place. In the shallow end of the pool, and though stomachpropped by the swim teacher's hands, a stiff-bodied Monet's arms windmilled in some frantic, I-don't-wanna-die mode, spinning so fast around I expected both of them to any second pop out of socket. Suddenly, though, and for some awful, uncontrollable reason, seeing him splash away as he did made me want to laugh out loud.

"Slower, Monet, *slower*," said the teacher. "Please try and relax. And *breathe*. I've got you!"

But instead of relaxing, his stiff arms continued to windmill wild until one of them suddenly smacked the teacher hard against the jaw, making him let go of his student, who instantly sunk stonehard right to the poolbottom, from where a splitsecond later he sprung out of the water coughing like a long-not-used waterhose. That was when Papa Pierre waved us over to him and the Second Street Mobsters, all sitting around in poolside beachchairs. Next to them was a table with a big jar of peanut butter, candy bars, and bags of potato chips on it.

"You looked better that time!" shouted a chip-eating Papa Pierre to his younger brother. "Keep it up, keep it up!"

Monet, though, to our relief, didn't look Papa Pierre's way, but continued to cough a good amount of poolwater into his hands while the swim teacher felt around his jaw for any sign of broken bone. Eventually, they'd both huddled up for another attempt.

"What's up with all the junkfood?" said one of us to Papa Pierre.

"Swim instructor says Monet's lack in bodyfat's hurting him flotation-wise," he told us. "So we gotta fatten him up a bit." Again the drowning bird went off, which had several of the beachchaired set wincing hard in its direction. "You wouldn't know it by his behavior, but he's already learned how to tread water pretty good. He'll just forget to do it when he needs to most. It's all still too new to him for it to come naturally." Then the wild waterbeating stopped to a suddenly-secondslong silence, only for another round of coughing to kick in.

"Damn," said Papa Pierre, looking towards the shallow end. "I wish he'd calm his hyperactive-ass down a click. Between us, fellas, I had someone make him some swim shorts out of this special flotation foam."

"Why's he sinking then?" said one of us.

" 'Cause he ain't got 'em on yet," said Papa Pierre. "I mean he did yesterday, and they worked like a charm, but he said they felt and looked like diapers—which they kinda did—look like them, I mean; *I* ain't never had the mother-fuckers on. Anyways, I'm having 'em thinned out some as we speak. I figure if Beefy can have all that bodyfat of his, Monet should be allowed a skimpy pair of custom-made swim shorts. Am I right, fellas?" he said to his set.

"You're right," they all said together, bored but loyal.

Then Monet started climbing out of the pool, which was our signal to immediately bail. We turned for the exit door.

"Hold up right quick, fellas," said Papa Pierre, standing up and walking up to us. "You know anything about Beefy's situation?" he whispered so his set couldn't hear him.

"Like what?" we said.

"Like how his lungs are doing? You know, his health and stamina?"

We looked at each other, then shrugged Papa Pierre's way.

"Nothing, huh? Damn," he then said mostly to himself. "I'm gonna have to get me a spy. How've I overlooked that? Any volunteers?"

We quickly noed our heads.

"We're gonna get paid!" said one of us as soon as we exited Peck Park's front door, to which we all jumped around like Olympic gold medalists.

"He looked *sorry*, didn't he?"

"From superstar to fallingstar."

"Like his ass was having fullbody cramps."

"Can you believe that diaper-shorts business?"

"It's a damn shame, embarrassing him like that. His own kid brother."

"Wait up. Monet got *himself* into this mess, starting that nonsense with Beefy."

"Starting trouble *with* trouble."

"Maybe Papa Pierre should've just let'm throw down in the Big Park like they'd wanted to."

We looked at each other with that four-eighty flashing on our brains.

"Hell no!" we all said together, and laughed like a pack of already-got-away-with-it robberbandits.

Back in the neighborhood people had gone betting crazy. Welfare checks, food stamps, rolls of piggybanktaken coins—you name it and it was put down on one or the other swimmer (which, when we'd thought about it, neither could really be considered yet). But anyways, whenever we saw a television or radio being carried down the sidewalk we knew it'd soon be collateralled at a bookie's for so many dollars this way or that. Events had gotten so out of hand, the gambling germ even infected the much-despised L.A.P.D., who'd not only put down healthy sums of their own money but, as a supposed goodfaith gesture, guaranteed the crowdcontrol at the race itself as a way of protecting everybody's investments. (In every third apartment window, by the way, homemade signs had gone up with things like "Make my day, Monet" and "Don't hit a reefy, Beefy" written on them. The lines, it seemed, had already been drawn.)

But the best and craziest thing of all was that the truce had stayed in effect. Every day that clicked by was another record set for a shot not fired, be it from a car, a sidewalk, or an apartment window. And with all the attention the swim was getting, who among the sets had any time to remember their old revenging hates? Besides, busting constant back-and-forth caps couldn't have been as big business for as many people as the Beefy-Monet battlebuild had become. Sure, half the neighborhood would lose some money, but half of it would *make* some, too. Whereas when the guns had steadily blazed all you had was loss: in the way of medical costs, funeral costs, loved-and-known-ones costs, etc., etc. But in the end, the swim had given up gain in the simple and beautiful way a person was free to stroll down a ghetto street, which had, in a sense, given those swimbuilding days something of the nonstop springtime to them.

It was a very good thing that we'd once again decided to visit the training sites the day before the race, since doing so most likely spared us a nasty little heartattack apiece. In the nine days that'd passed, each of the swimmers had made some seriously respectful progress; progress damnnear as respectful as the first-visit lack of it had been disrespectful. Monet, for example, was now managing several speedy back-and-forths at a time—and without being stomach-propped and then drowning within point-five seconds either. He just zipped from poolend to poolend as if he'd been doing so his entire life. And at first glance we started to worry. But what'd finally given us a heap of hope wasn't only that he still badly beat his arms against the watersurface, but that, by lap three or four of his swim, he'd start in on his usual sinking action.

(Papa Pierre, by the way, told us he'd decided against those foamy swim shorts, which did and didn't disappoint us some.)

Meanwhile, over at Cabrillo Beach, Beefy, though not nearly up to that mile Chuy'd hoped for, was managing maybe one-hundred-foot stretches whenever he entered the water. A four-to-five-times improvement from those earlier sessions. Sure, on the downside his tempo was that of a floating tree and his chest would get to aching hard with those rest-and-massage periods longer than before, but on the upside he'd stayed cigarette-free since the Big Park run-in and now had the lungs of, say, a way-less-unhealthy sixteen-year-old. *And* he'd lost a few pounds.

"He's really grown as a person, ey," said Chuy to us that day, quickly laughing at how he'd done so. "I didn't mean that as no joke either, vatos."

Race-day morning came along oceanswim perfect, with the air sunnywarm and only a small on-and-off wind breezing up the streets. As I headed to the Big Park to meet up with the fellas, I nearly tripped a dozen times I was so anxious about the swim-off ahead. The sidewalks, I noticed, were active with lots of other people too, who were all moving in the same direction as me. In fact, it seemed the whole neighborhood was headed to the Big Park, where this everywhere-respected streetlord named Earl the Grizz had promised to have a half-a-dozen fifteen-seater vans ready to shuttle whoever needed a ride to the swim site.

"First come, first serve, though, fellas," the Grizz had said. "I'm a community man providing community service."

At the Big Park I spotted the vans, sure enough, but along with what had to be three hundred locals trying their utmost to tunacan themselves into them and any other vehicle arrived to load up racegoers. People crammed so hard together a couple of fights damnnear broke out, the second one between two women known to've been good neighborly friends their whole ghetto lives. Foodstamp investing, crossed my still-anxious mind, seems to've brought out the dead serious in folks. When someone said the women should swim against each other as an undercard, the whole crowd started to laugh.

Besides Monet sneaking a quick, on-and-off peek Beefy's way, the swimmers fully ignored each other. Next to them, the crowd had positioned itself along a long, manmade strip of boulders that separated the outer harbor from the Pacific Ocean. On the boulders, which ran parallel to the race course and clear to the finish-line beach at the end of it, the crowd looked like an army of Beefy-Monet-siding rock-crabs. Here and there were some of those homemade windowsigns, while mixed into the crowd itself were several just-happening-by tourists and fishermen, windsurfers and beachwalkers, and whatever other looky-loos a good-weather day had angled to the coastline. The rollerboys, as promised, had crowdcontrol perfectly in hand.

Beefy sported the same kind of black, ten-X wifebeater he wore at his workouts, which perfectly hid his skinfolds, toiletbowlsized bellybutton, and always-weird-to-look-at man titties the way a lightercolored wifebeater wouldn't have done. On top of that he wore a pair of those trusty cut-off-at-the-shinbones work-Dickies. All in all, he sat there waiting for the race to start looking like some lowrider Buddha with attitude.

Monet on the other hand sat without any of the calm Beefy showed. On top of that occasional sidepeek Beefy's way, he checked out the crowd whenever his name got shouted, flashed it a helpless-sheepish-toothy smile, and bounced his legs a constant up and down. Monet sported a blue-and-gold silk robe with a hood attached to it—the kind a boxer would wear right before a fight. Because we thought the robe a strange touch, we got to wondering whether Papa Pierre hadn't changed his mind about those flotation diapers after all. Suddenly me and the fellas wished that we'd brought a just-in-case-he-had camera along.

———

"Bee-fy! Bee-fy!" shouted half the crowd.

"Mo-net! Mo-net!" shouted the other half.

Then they were calfdeep in water. While Monet (who was definitely diaper-free) inched himself into the water over a two-minute, toothchattering span that even had me chilled when it was over, Beefy simply rolled the rest of himself in no different than a waterwanting sea lion. Insulation, I thought, has serious advantages. After the swimmers lined up to face the finish-line beach, the Grizz suddenly showed on the rocks right above the swimmers, a snub-nosed doublebarrel in hand that got a stadium roar out of the dying-with-excitement crowd and not the smallest of eyebrowraises from crowdcontrol, and angled the snub-nosed high over the Pacific-Ocean sky. That's the Grizz for you, crossed my mind—*and* the L.A.P.D. Then the Grizz shouted a "Ready! Set!" and dropped the hammers on both airtearing barrels: *kaboom!* The swimmers were off.

Well, *Monet* was off—and like some kind of clumsy waterrocket at that. Just as in the Peck Park pool, his arms chopped and windmilled at the watersurface as if they had a deepdown hatred for the stuff. While he chopped to the insane-sounding crowdroar, Beefy, already a good thirty feet back, slowarmed it after him as he watched Monet's part of the crowd separate from his own in order to crabscramble after their superswimmer. "Pick it up you fat bastard!" yelled some woman in the Beefy crowd suddenly, which instantly got her a rude round of fuck yous from the worried-to-death Locos (Chuy included). Lucky for her, I thought, that she wasn't a man or else she might've been regaining consciousness the next night sometime to find out about the happened-long-ago race results that way. Beefy did all that he could do, though, to keep up with Monet, who continued on his man-gone-mad windmills all the way to the halfway point—which was also the moment one of us mentioned that, "oh well, it was only twenty-nine dollars we'd put down on him, anyways," to which the rest of us quickly and murderously told him to shut his dumbass up or get forced for a harborswim he hadn't planned on taking that day. "He still might cramp up!" one of the true believers told him hard.

"Suck it up, Gordo!" shouted Chuy. "You're still in it, homes! Just don't give up! Comprendes?"

"Yeah," said Beefy between armlifts.

"Atta boy!" cried Chuy. "You're a warrior! You got the bigger heart!"

Monet, I could see, had slowed up some but still moved good enough to wrap things up in the next minute or two. Distancewise, the gap he'd managed had to be a solid hundred feet. But then a very expected-unexpected thing started to happen. Monet's body began to be less seeable. He wasn't necessarily sinking, but that wild hydroplane he had going just a few seconds before wasn't what he was about either. Then his windmill chop was happening half underwater, which all of a sudden slowed him like a car on fumes. And as soon as the up-ahead, Monet-sided crowd started in on its "Oh noes!" and checked back to see where Beefy was, Chuy went crazy.

"He's dying, Gordo!" he screamed. "You see that! Go after his ass, Gordo! This is our chance! Heart, heart, heart! You gotta have the bigger heart!"

Somehow the words gave Beefy an energy boost, because he shifted into a not-at-all-expected second gear and was maybe even looking for a third. Half a minute later and that hundred-foot gap had been halved.

With no more than a quarterways to go, Monet now dog-paddled for the beach for everything he was worth. "Boy, don't you stop!" shouted Papa Pierre. But except for the about-to-merge-with-each-other crowdhalves and a Beefy closed to within five-to-ten feet, the old progress was hard for him to come by. Then, just as Beefy's side of the crowd got its loudest, Monet's suddenly went a cold cold quiet.

Then the swimmers were even.

I wish I could say a lot of good things about that exact moment. Like how, when I listened and looked around, I for the first time in my life felt a part of a big beautiful fearless family that was itself a part of something bigger and beautifuler and more unafraid than we were; or I wish I could say that those of us who won their bets took their winnings and treated the losing half of the crowd to the biggest baddest all-you-can-eat restaurant meal ever ordered; or that, because of the swim, the truce had lasted for years and years to come, and then forever and ever after that. At that moment they were even I wish I could've said all those things and more. But I couldn't. I couldn't because even when the altogether happiness was at its topmost level, the notforgetting part of me couldn't manage to remember away all the fear and worry that'd come before the sets had once again decided to go a supposedly-permanent nonviolent. Even if I'd double-and-triplestrained to wish all that the same way Monet had strained himself for the beach during his sad-to-see dogpaddle, I knew it wouldn't have done any good. In that way, that exact moment had made me feel over a-hundred-years old already.

Up to ten feet past, Beefy had showed not a sign of letting up on the now-fulltreading Monet, until a hard-to-believe second thing happened. In the middle of one of his just-got-into-third-gear strokes, Beefy seized up cold. Just like that he went from powerstroke after powerstroke to a chestgripping stop, and then rolled onto his back. Needless to say, the Beefy crowd seized up as well.

"Does he need an ambulance?" a suddenly-there L.A.P.D. asked Chuy.

"Nah," said Chuy with disgust. "It's only this chest cramp that he sometimes gets. Pinche pendejo!"

The L.A.P.D. stepped back.

As he gripped at his chest, the floating and skystaring Beefy moved ever so slowly away from the beach and towards a barely-treading and tired-to-death Monet. The tide, it seemed, was on its ebb. Then, at a couple of feet apart, a now–damnneardrowning Monet quickly reached an arm out to grab onto one of Beefy's own. Beefy gave the grabber a sideways glance and, thinking nothing of it, turned his eyes back up to the sky.

For the longest stretch not a single person in the whole bunchedtogether crowd said a word. Not the fishermen, the sets, or any of the locals who'd put down bets. Nobody. They just watched as the failed-to-finish swimmers ebbed and bobbed on the gentle harborswell. Then an older woman said, "Well well, will you *look* at this," which somehow sounded so dead on funny that, one by one, and then bunch by bunch, the whole crowd started laughing as if underarmtickled by a thousand invisible fingers—set leaders included. That's all it did was laugh and laugh at the silly-seeming sight in front of it. And as it did, Beefy and Monet continued to float and float ever further away from the rocks. I tried to imagine what they might've been saying to each other, but couldn't. They'd have been some words I'd have loved to've dropped in upon.

The next day Chuy was shot to death while making a telephone call up at Mundo's Liquors, instantly sending bad news on another one of its hundred-meter supersprints all through the projects. Any other day you'd have said it an extremely careless thing for him to've done, walking up to

Mundo's unarmed alone as he was and offering his back to whatever violenceminded thug (in this case a cholo from Ghost Town in Wilmington) who came along to do him some harm. But to understand that carelessness, all you had to've seen just the day before was Chuy's face at that moment Beefy had evened things up. It wasn't the sureness of a win that'd lit it up sunshinehappy, but something of the caught-up-in-it-all converted that had him, Chuy Lopez, believing that none of all that beforehappening violence had ever really happened, or ever really would again. It had to be the same foolish high he'd been on while telephoning that day. I don't know; maybe that kind of thinking would always make him a fraction of an inch taller than me—no matter how many years of growing I hopefully still had in front of me.

Later on, we got mean without knowing it.

In late October, for example, one of us kicked a cat, *hard,* and for no good reason. The cat was just on a nice fourlegged sidewalkstroll when, *blam!,* one of our shoes came out of nowhere to send it smack against a car window. Sure, it was close to Halloween, and sure, we'd heard the stories about what some of the older heads had done to the very backsides of the animals during Halloweens past with M80 cherry bombs, but as far as I could remember none of us had ever so much as pet an animal too hard before. But then there was this cat flying against a car window.

We got mean in other ways, too.

In early November, for example, we were all after school headed home to the Ranch when we came across this little kid standing in his yard and looking at us pass. He was maybe two and in these raggedy-ass diapers and just staring at the lot of us, which somehow got on all of our nerves at once. We stopped, and the more we looked at him, the more he stared us up and down as if some strange alien creatures. And that's how it went for the longest awfulest time until, not able to stand it anymore, we all looked around and, seeing not a single soul in sight, had one of us walk up to the kid and push him straight to the ground. He screamed and screamed and we took off topspeed for the not-too-far-away-from-us housing projects, worried that a whole pack of his family or possibly even a squadron of L.A.P.D.s would run us down like dogs and beat us a very welldeserved dark black and blue.

At the schoolhouse itself we kept Lowrider Louie damnnear everyday busy by starting one fight after another with him. We didn't just jump him or anything, but simply spent our entire recesses walking through the schoolyard until we found him, and then sent an always different one of ourselves in his direction to make him pay the price for having messed with us one too many times in the past. By Christmas vacation we'd worn Lowrider Louie down like some just-about-to-badly-hole-up socks.

But the main way we got mean was with a guy named Skeeter, who lived just around the corner and down the street from Tom-Su's old place.

We'd rarely thought about messing with Skeeter, but when we did it used to be fun to watch him step from his front door and lose it. He had a crazy temper, and usually after we dogged him we stayed far away from his apartment for a good couple of weeks—the amount of time we needed to fully forget his terrible self-abuse—until the last time, that is, when things with the man got so completely out of hand we decided to promise each other never, *ever,* to mess with him again. Especially since we'd heard the ridiculous-ass rumor that ever since his recent madhouse release he's been strolling through the housing projects with a baseball bat in his grip asking all around for us. Of course we knew the rumor not to be true, but, then again, it had this special kind of seriousness to it that could give a young guy doubts. Luckily, we told each other, our neighborhood was like a maze with block after block of apartment complexes that we could zigzaggedyzigzag through just in case we had to keep a badly-bent-on-payback individual like Skeeter well off his balance.

Skeeter was a grown man who supposedly lived alone with his mother in a small apartment on the corner of Third and Beacon Streets. The apartment had no plants on its front porch and the windowroll was always drawn down, which gave the place an old thrownawayforgotten alleybox feel. In all the time we'd lived in the Ranch, never once had we seen his mother. In fact, nobody'd laid their eyes on her in something like twenty years, and only a few of the older folks even remembered her, walking as she did along Beacon

Street each Sunday morning from her apartment to the Baptist church two blocks away and back, or sometimes to the farmers' market a block further than that. The older folks had also seen her gathered with relatives on her front yard for barbecues, just sitting around talking. The last time they'd seen her, though, was on the day they'd buried her oldest boy. And at some point after that she disappeared for good. But like Skeeter and that baseball bat, there were rumors.

For example, some people believed she'd lost all interest in life after her oldest died and didn't have the strength enough to any longer face the day. Some believed she'd become bedriddenparalyzed from a stroke of some kind and couldn't leave the apartment anymore. And still others believed she'd long ago moved back to the state she originally come from—Louisiana, I think it was. But mostly people believed she'd already died a natural, middle-of-the-night death and was given a quick and private family-only funeral and that ever since Skeeter had been living all alone off her Social Security checks. From all the errands that he ran, though, it seemed as if an army was staying in the apartment. Skeeter shopped until he dropped for groceries of all kinds and did uncountable household chores. Every day, for example, you'd see him taking some laundry to be washed or mowing and watering the front and back yards or putting out a full bag of trash. Whenever he did these things you could tell he enjoyed doing them because of how he strutted while he worked. Skeeter seemed to enjoy the routine of keeping up a home; of being the man of the home.

Skeeter did two other things outside the apartment that caught your attention because of their regularness. Every day at exactly ten a.m. he came outside, his thick bottlebottomed bifocals and flipfloppity flipflops on, with a metal bucket, soap, and washrags in hand, all of which he'd place on the sidewalk. Then he would unroll the waterhose, put its end into the metal bucket, and turn on the water pressure while adding the soap. After the bucket was full he'd slosh one of the rags around in it and leave the others to the side and dry.

Next to the sidewalk sat Skeeter's pride and joy: his Mini Cooper. If there was a smaller lighter car anywhere in the world you could've sold it in supermarkets. No higher than a kitchen counter, no wider than a twinsized bed, and no longer than a laid-onto-its-side refrigerator, the Mini was painted a very dark green that shined for days. The chrome bumpers had not a single scratch, letting us damnnear see ourselves in them from a half-a-block away, and during highnoon they could reflect a razorbeam sunlight they were so well, so thoroughly, so lovingly polished. And you couldn't tell the Mini Cooper had windows either, because of Skeeter washing and polishing them to the point-of-disappearance well. Sometimes when we looked into the car we expected the interior to be ruined from a rain or wild wind blowing through it too, but instead it'd be a spotless shinyclean, the seats, dashboard, and headliner looking nicer than any livingroom furniture we'd ever laid our eyes upon. With so much attention paid to it, it wasn't any wonder

Skeeter's Mini Cooper was as sparkling beautiful as it was—like a midget Rolls-Royce.

Skeeter spent two full hours a day loving that car. First he hosed it down real steady and nice. Then he took the slopped-around washrag from the soaped-up bucket and eased it along each inch of the not-too-many-inches-having body: first the hiphigh rooftop, then the thighhigh windows, then the kneehigh hood and doors, and finally the grill and the tires. The car was so small you'd have thought it washable in a single swipe, but not with Skeeter's TLC. He would ease the washrag with one hand and then with the free one feel from behind to make sure that no dirt and only smooth smooth surface remained. Ease and feel, ease and feel, with every once in a while reslopping the washrag until the whole of the little car had been covered and rinsed.

When Skeeter dried the Mini his face got so close to the car you'd have thought he'd leave his very eyes, nose, or lips somewhere inside the paintjob itself. At the facelooking headlights and grill he sometimes actually got to talking to the Mini in these secret whispers, like the ones that people used who thought a plant grew and got happy if you said a few wonderful things to it everyday. Maybe Skeeter saw his little green ride as his own little garden or something; one that would grow high and happy too if he spoke some beautiful words to it.

The other thing Skeeter did when outside was walk in squares. Most people we'd seen who had lost their minds tended to walk in circles, pace back and forth, or wander all the hell over the place, sometimes even forgetting who they were or where they'd started from. Skeeter, though, walked in squares—and only at night all night. At Third and Beacon he'd walk from his, say, northeastern corner, cross the street to the north*western* corner, cross the street again to the *south*western corner, to the southeastern corner, and then return to the northeastern one. A full square. He stepped from corner to corner to corner deep into the night and always turning a left left left. Whenever a car came along, the squarewalking Skeeter never saw it but just kept on stepping, disregarding any of the honks or shouts coming from inside of it. To our surprise he'd never once gotten hit.

At first we tripped seeing Skeeter do his squares all night long, looking as he did like some wigged-out windup doll. Where did he get the energy, we wondered, to every night march from dusk till dawn only to wake up the next day to do those many chores and errands of his? After a while, though, we decided to forget about the freakiness of the thing and instead told ourselves that it wasn't really Skeeter doing the squares, but someone else using Skeeter's body. A someone we'd eventually called the night-Skeeter. You see, the real Skeeter to us was the loving-up-that-Mini-Cooper-so-much day-Skeeter, especially since the night-Skeeter was nothing about love and everything about shermstick—or PCP-dipped cigarettes—also known as angel dust—a drug wellknown for giving the taker this almost-superhuman strength. Night-Skeeter was like Dr. Jekyll's Mr. Hyde, his daylife full of chores and errands, his nightlife filled with senseless squares and sleeplessness. Senseless, we thought, until that last time he'd lost it, which was also the moment we'd realized finally what it was that'd kept his sanity/insanity side by side next to each other: that Mini Cooper. I mean, sure his squares looked no more than a nervous drugged-out paranoia. And sure, he marched deeper and deeper into the night like some gone-mad-for-good laboratory experiment. But not until it was too late did we finally understand that he'd been smoking the shermstick to keep himself up all night to guard his ride. Skeeter's problem, though, was that when the shermstick high evaporated, he'd have to leave his little ride solo and alone for a few hours to give in to some sleep. And every few weeks he'd step from his front morningdoor to see the Mini not the way he'd left it and *snap*.

This was how we'd usually done the Mini Cooper: a good bunch of us would creep up to it an hour or two before its ten a.m. scrubdown. We'd get behind and in front of the Mini and in the deadest of deadquiets grab onto those chromybright bumpers, yes each other our widegrinning heads to the count of one two three and *lift*. Once we got the Mini over the sidewalk the frontyard was only a couple of feet away. With all of our straining strength we'd shuffle the car sideways until nothing but the wellmown yardgrass was under our shoes. Then we'd lower the midget ride very slow and gentle until all four of its donuts were down and sprint half a block away to kill the time playing blackjack or talking a distracted nonsense until the man himself finally stepped from his apartment door, metal bucket, soap, and washrags in hand. And next we'd be on our hands and knees laughing ourselves weak.

Our typical reaction to seeing Skeeter lose it was the same as when we'd witnessed him doing his squares: it amazed. He'd notice his yarded Mini and stare at it in a deep and manyseconded disbelief, as if to think: how in the world could this have happened again? Then he'd start in on a few simple cusswords like shit, goddamn, and sonofabitch, only to build to the uglier nastier ones. As Skeeter approached the Mini his whole body'd tighten as he softscreamed the cusses without all the way opening his mouth; as if he were trying to keep them down in his gut; or as if their very badness and not him was doing the cussing, with him just hoping to take some big-enough bites out of them as they made it to his lips. Then he'd quickly search the street for any witnesses to his nuttiness, but, at a half a block away, had no chance of spotting anyone through those very thick bottlebottoms of his.

A good ways into the nastier cusswords, Skeeter'd start to circle around his Mini and fake fast and furious kicks and punches at it, sometimes getting within inches close to the body, but always stopping just before some damage was done. The fake kicks and punches would go on for a good tenish minutes and, after dozens of those trips around the car, Skeeter'd make as if to walk right back into the apartment, leaving all of his washing goods outside, but would freeze up just as his hand had made it near the doorknob. He'd just stand there like that with his hand about to grab for that doorknob, which had us dying even harder with laughter. His hand, though, just couldn't seem to latch onto it. Then he'd sometimes spin around, look over his yarded ride again, and actually do one quick and frenziful trip along his square route: corner one, two, three, and home.

That last time we yarded the Mini Cooper, though, Skeeter did a few things different. After the fake kicks and punches, he removed his bottlebottoms all matter-of-factly, folded them into a pantspocket, and commenced to punching himself in the face. *Hard.* To actually see such a thing not only amazed, it shocked. Righthand up at the eye, lefthand to the nose, righthand, lefthand, rightleftright, till he was all a badlyblooded mess. Skeeter tried to scream like always, but because he couldn't find any volume something like a raspy-crampy laryngitis came out instead. It was a terribly disturbing thing to see, a grown man trying his damnedest not to lose his mind.

Blam! Blam! Blam! he continued to whale on his mug, the blood flowing heavy down his cheeks. Though his silly hurtinghimself fascinated, we winced and cringed with every blam. There was no doubt, I thought at the time, that the shermstick highs had had everything to do with it. Anyone knowing anything about a drug like that had to know that a good dose of it stayed in the system long after the high had gone, only to kick back into the bloodstream on maybe a too hot an afternoon or maybe when the adrenaline got to pumping too hard and out of control. At the time we thought that that kind of thinking explained Skeeter's actions to a tee, and simply did what anyone else in our neighborhood would've done: laughed it off. Sure we knew it was not a laughing matter, but just the same, we really couldn't help ourselves. It was one of those hard-to-explain reactions you sometimes got to the outright misfortune of another. (Like Monet back in that swimming pool.) Then Skeeter did something else. He picked up his metal bucket and cracked himself knockouthard over the head with it, the tinrattley contact sounding for blocks and blocks around. Instead of blacking out, though, he simply cracked himself again and again until his face looked a thoroughly redpaintdipped. Needless to say, our laughing stopped forever and a day.

The rollerboys can do some of the strangest shit. As soon as Skeeter noticed the L.A.P.D. squadcar rolling up he sat down on his porch and, without flinch or blink, eyed it as it came to a stop. The rollers just sat in front of his apartment most likely, we thought, to scheme up an offense against the man. That's how they worked. I mean you'd think for sure that they'd radio for an ambulance to deal with Skeeter's full-headed bleeding or even get out of the car themselves to administer some first-aid, but they never budged or got on the mike. For five-plus minutes they sat there in their squadcar staring at the guy until Officer Shotgun finally opened his door, stepped onto the street, and headed into Skeeter's direction. In his hand was a single slip of paper. Instead of approaching a sitting-and-waiting-for-him-to-get-to-him Skeeter, though, Shotgun walked up to the Mini and put the slip of paper right underneath one of its windshieldwipers. Not too legal to have your car up on your yard in the housing projects, we decided, no matter how small it was. Shotgun then turned to go back to the squadcar.

Skeeter, meanwhile, got up, stepped to his Mini, took the ticket off of the windshield, looked at it, and immediately turned his attention to a Shotgun already taking his seat. Skeeter then quickwayed over to the squadcar just as it started rolling off. "Hey!" he said, to which the squadcar instantly braked to a stop and both rollerboys turned their heads to the sight of a bloodyfaced and marching-as-though-on-a-mighty-mission-towards-'em Skeeter.

"Wh-wh-why am I getting this ticket!" he stutter-shouted at them. "I didn't do nothing wrong!"

Shotgun slowly rolled his window down and mouthed something out to him. Most likely some sort of rude explanation because Skeeter suddenly balled up the ticket, stuttered a loud "Fu-fu-fuck you!" at Shotgun, and actually *threw* the ticket into his window, hitting him dead on the forehead with it before it bounced back out of the car and onto the street. That was when we hurried towards the action.

By the time Shotgun and his partner had jumped from their squadcar, Skeeter was back on the sidewalk in full furious sprint, while a handful of his neighbors had gathered in every other apartment door. When one of his flipflops came off, he stopped, picked it up, and threw it too at the hardcharging rollerboys. His brain, one of us mentioned, must've gotten broken during those bucketblams. Finally at his front door, Skeeter went for the doorknob as usual, and just as usual came to a stop right before the grab. While he stood there you could tell he thought powerfully hard about turning it to enter the apartment, but instead turned his body around just in time to be snatched off his feet by four angry hands attached to two rabid rollerboys. And to our amazement, a suddenly-custodied Skeeter had about as much surprise on his face as some not-very-interested-in-the-happenings ragdoll. But then he quickly came back to life and, possibly because of that PCP, powered himself rollerboy-free and, for no sensible reason at all, did a somersault over his whole car, landing a horrible facefirst on the sidewalktop. His brain, we all agreed when we'd seen it, had gotten much more than broken. It'd gotten annihilated.

While Shotgun kneed Skeeter chestfirst to the sidewalk, his partner radioed for backup when he saw us gathered just across the street. The rollerboys always instantly did that when they felt themselves outnumbered by a bunch of twelve-year-olds. With his face pressed to the concrete, Skeeter again started in on those uglier nastier cusswords, splattering a deepred spit all over the place. We could see that his eyes had redlined too, and that his front teeth had chipped up bad from the end of that came-completely-out-of-nowhere somersault. After both of his arms got twisted behind his back, his wrists were brought together and hand-cuffed. Finally, Shotgun lifted his knee and snatched Skeeter up off the sidewalk and sat him on his porch.

In the next few minutes the street filled with seven more squadcars and door-to-door locals. One of the newlyarrived rollerboys picked up the guttered flipflop with a pen and dropped it into a plastic bag that he closed up with a twisty, while another suitwearing one stood over Skeeter with a clipboard in hand, scribbling away as he checked him all over. Then he hounded around the yard and sidewalk for anymore evidence, like maybe some toothbits or something. Most of the rollers, though, did exactly what they always did during an arrest in the Ranch: stood around by their cars staring hatefully at the locals around them, who stared a not-so-friendly-like back at them.

Because the sight of Skeeter jacked by the rollerboys had suddenly hit us with an ill and awful shamefulness, we decided we had to do something to help him out. So we shouted for the rollerboys to let him go; told them that he hadn't committed a murder or anything; that he'd only thrown a ticket and a wild flipflop at somebody. But we quickly gave it up. We knew that a simple-ass tickettoss was more than enough to have the whole Los Angeles Police Department converging on the neighborhood, batteringram and all, to beat some ass and take names later. In their book, a paperball tossed at a rollerboy's face was an unforgivable act against all of life that'd ever been—such an act also being one of the speediest paths to the deathworld to boot. I mean the last thing an L.A.P.D. needed was an excuse to shoot someone dead—especially a ghetto-ite like Skeeter—which we were all probably shocked hadn't happened yet. Hell, some L.A.P.D.s were known to give themselves secret award medals just for having taken a person out for the fun of it, no matter the innocence or guilt.

Suddenly two of the rollerboys approached us to ask if we'd witnessed any of the ongoings, to which we made all of our noes sound like one no-doubt-about-it HELL-motherfuckingno. The rollerboys walked away.

That was when the brokenbrained Skeeter figured it out. How he figured it out we still don't know. Maybe he'd recognized our voices from a morning we'd giggled or spoke too loud while dogging his little ride; or maybe those bottlebottoms he sported had had more of a range to them than we'd given them credit for; or maybe he'd even faked his sleep one morning and saw us messing with his ride. It was impossible to tell. What we do know, though, was that when he stood up, searched in our direction, and dove right into the ugliest nastiest cusswords yet, that those cusswords were absolutely meant for us. And he completely shattered his own record he cussed so hard, making us all at once take several mightylong steps backwards in the process. The suited rollerboy quickly grabbed Skeeter by the arm and tried to sit him back on the porch, but Skeeter just as quickly swung his right knee around smack into the suited's groin, which had him crumbling to the grass as if made of some very ancient writing paper. "You did this!" screamed Skeeter at nobody but us, grabbing his metal bucket with his cuffed-behind-his-back hands. "Not me! You!" By the time he'd reached the sidewalk, though, he was surrounded by two-dozen rollerboys, guns drawn long. They warned him to stop and drop to his knees, and Skeeter did the stop all right, and even put the bucket back down, but he remained a deep and angry on his feet. The only reason he hadn't continued forward, we knew, was that he'd suddenly lost us when the rollerboys had scampered all around him. Again they yelled for him to kneedown, and again he stayed standing.

When the tazer finally hit Skeeter he did like a just-landed fish for a stretch and then was out. Afterwards he got uncuffed, strapped, and recuffed, wrists and ankles, to the gurney of a finallyarrived ambulance, which sped off and out of the Ranch with him with its lights and siren in a fullscreaming flash.

For the next few minutes all we did was sit and wait for the staring-at-us rollerboys to leave, which, except for Shotgun and his partner, they'd soon enough done. Shotgun's squadcar just sat in that same exact spot it'd braked in earlier while he and his partner both scribbled something on their clipboards. Then, just as they'd started to roll off, they came to another stop.

Shotgun got back out of the car and picked the balled-up ticket up off the street, slowly unrolled it, walked it over to the Mini Cooper, and put it under the same windshield wiper it'd been put under earlier. Then he got back into the squadcar and it finally drove off.

For the rest of that morning and into the afternoon time passed without hurry. When the sun had been high overhead for awhile we stood ourselves up and started crossing the street. On the yard we got in front and behind the Mini, gripping the chrome bumpers for that fullstraining lift. We placed it in exactly the same spot it was in before ten a.m. It felt good to've put it back; as if we'd almost righted things with a simple reverse move. Looking at the Mini on that once again quiet corner, it started to seem as if nothing had happened at all. Not the ticket or the cusswords or that ending-things-in-a-hurry tazerblast. But then we noticed them all over the bumpers: greasy, grimy, and smudging up everything: our fingerprints. We just stared and stared at them as if badly joked against until, from a shameful kind of instinct, we one by one took off our T-shirts and polished at those bumpers for all we were worth. But no matter how hard or long we did so the shine, that superamazing Skeeter shine, just wouldn't return to them. Knowing it made us feel the worst kind of worthless.

Єl Niño (meaning "little boy" in Spanish) hammered down hardest from mid-November to mid-December. To us it was as if the heavens had taken it upon themselves to wash down the Mini Cooper while its owner was busy in some mental-health facility just outside Los Angeles somewhere. The mostly-nonstop downpour was so bad it had people not only not talking drought for the first winter of my life, but had them absolutely panicked to death that their whole city might get permanently waterdunked or pushed into the sea there was so much furious flooding and mudsliding going down, with everyday another person getting swept away with some wild and wicked stormwater.

So mainly we hung indoors in our own cribs, waiting for the waterlevels to get back to normal. And being house-ridden wasn't such a bad thing either, so long as it was only me and my moms in the apartment. I'd mostly hang on the couch and read some of a good book to whatever classical music she had flowing through the speakers. In the last few months she'd in fact become crazy about the classical stuff to the point of even taking a few singing lessons on the very little to no money we had. She'd even memorized all these opera lines—in Italian, at that. Some of them had something to do with butterflies, I think. Her favorite singer was a woman named Maria Callas, who moms thought had such a big beautiful voice she told me she'd one day fly herself straight over to Italy just to hear her singing in person. (That was before she found out that Ms. Callas was dead, though, at which point she decided a grave visit would do.) But the way I tried to look at moms and her singing lessons was that, though we barely had a nickel to our names, it was a nickel that could've gone to some very different things, like all the drink, drugs, and cigarettes that so many of the other mothers in the Ranch depended on. But it didn't.

Something else that moms had gotten crazy about lately was this new guy she'd been seeing named Goldie for the fat gold tooth he sported in the toprightcenter of his grille. Goldie had this spent-much-time-in-the-jailhouse-for-many-a-violent-crimes look written all over him, which moms either didn't notice, didn't care about, or wasn't very much interested in. They'd met at the tailend of the summer and, as it'd happened several times before, the meeting had moms living as if on one continuous cloudnine ride ever since. Which would've been fine if it hadn't've been for Goldie starting to spend more and more of his time at our crib, until finally a young guy couldn't make a single move without that fat gold tooth getting in his way. And not only that, but Goldie'd developed this really bad habit of asking a person for a-hundred-and-one favors a day, and always with a "right quick" thrown into the request. "Toomer," he'd say, "couldn't you get me a cup of coffee, *right quick?*" or "Toomer, couldn't you run to the store for a pack of smokes, *right quick?*" or even, "Toomer, couldn't you maybe go for a walk, *right quick,* so's me and your mother can have a private minute together?" A go-for-a-walk-right-quick favor?—and in a fullblown El Niño downpour, at that! Moms, I kept telling myself, sure knew how to pick them.

Then, in late December, one of the fellas named Richard started dropping by the crib. At first it'd been for an hour or two in the evening, and then from the late afternoons till the late-at-nights, until finally he was crashing on our livingroom couch until the following mornings. It wasn't till week two of him dropping by that I realized that he'd most likely been doing so because his moms, Dee Dee, had a very ugly toe-to-toe going with her live-in boyfriend, the Grizz, a man Richard had always had this closest of connections to, which must've made the inhome toe-to-toe a very hard thing to take.

When in early January El Niño came to a manydayed stop, me and Richard decided to spend some of our time around a certain parking lot up on Second Street, me doing so more for Richard's sake than my own. Then I don't know if it was the man just being tired of us around him so much or of him cold knowing that we had no other place to be, but we were made an offer that we just couldn't refuse.

"You guys know how to drive a car?" said the Grizz in his big husky animal voice.

"Yeah, Grizz," we said, lying through our teeth.

"Then it's time for you two to get mobile," he said. "A man without a car isn't anything but a pair of feet in my book." He reached into the chestpocket of his staple silk dress-shirt and brought out a ring of keys. "Consider it a chance for you bucks to get out of Dodge for a bit."

Me and Richard took a good long look at each other, which was sometimes our way of agreeing that a very strange thing was going down, and saw pure confusion looking back—which, of course, the ever-alert Grizz instantly picked up on.

"It's a cherry of a car," he said, "parked in the alley behind Mundo's Liquors. You do me one favor—a very important favor—while I'm out of town this weekend, and the car's yours for keeps." Again me and Richard traded those looks. "I got the pinkslip, the keys, *and,*" the Grizz reached into his back pantspocket, "a *gas* card." Then he said to Richard, "Your mother knows nothing about this, you hear?" to which Richard quickly yessed his head. "She would eat me alive."

The Grizz was really Earl the Grizz, Richard's recently-kicked-out-of-the-apartment stepdad, and the man who'd blasted that shotgun at the swim-off. Unlike wannabe Beefy,

I wouldn't say the Grizz was fat; he was much too big for that. And I especially wouldn't say he was fat while in his company; *I* was much too small for that. But I would say the Grizz was always everywhere there; meaning: if he wasn't in front of your eyes but just around the corner somewhere else, like inside an apartment or even in another part of town, you couldn't help but feel the man's presence or think about him. And if anything troubled a person the most about the Grizz it was exactly this everywhereness. At six-footsix, fourhundred-plus pounds, he still managed to take up more invisible than physical space. And along with his size and everywhereness, the four guns he constantly carried around damnnear overhelped him (along with Papa Pierre's assistance) hold down the whole stretch of Second Street between Beacon and Mesa Streets, including the parking lots and playgrounds, which he altogether ran like the whalesized landshark that he was. And as a landshark the Grizz only bit down when it was absolutely necessary to do so, which was nothing like the gangs, who'd often do their damage for damage's sake—which, when it wasn't another payback revenge, was mostly a kind of bloodbragging act.

Anything meaningful or dull, though, that happened in the Ranch—stolen merchandise, drugs, gambling, etc.—the Grizz got a cut. The Grizz claimed never to have stolen a thing, bought or sold a drug, or ever been arrested in his whole entire life. He said he was mainly around to protect people from people because, as he'd once put it, "you know how nasty some of them can get." Everybody got along with the Grizz too: blacks, whites, Mexicans, Crips, lowriders, rollerboys, you name it. Not that there was much choice in the matter. But still, the Grizz could be a regular Santa Claus when he wanted to be, one time giving an old woman an air conditioner in midboiling August, for example, or a child some kind of just-happened-to-be-his-or-her-birthday toy. Public relations, he called it. "It's the little things that matter the most to people," he'd once told us. "Like, say, me wearing this imported silk instead of an average cotton." And about his guns the Grizz merely said, "I've only used 'em but a handful of times. They're mainly for show." Like his shark teeth weren't.

Though they'd recently lived together, Richard wasn't allowed to be around the Grizz anymore. "Beware of that man," said his moms Dee Dee, a round ranting fearless-eyed woman. "He takes *too* many chances." Which must've been true, because even the Grizz himself had once or twice said to us that, "Risk, fellas, is the lifeblood of living. You've gotta risk something to get something." So Dee Dee was at a hopeless crossed odds with the Grizz, which upset Richard plenty. What she said she'd finally tossed him from her apartment for was habitgambling and a dangerous overeating (cheeseburgers morning, cheeseburgers afternoon, cheeseburgers night) that'd eventually added an extreme amount of poundage to his already-oversized frame. Dee Dee'd wanted the Grizz away from the streets too, and working a much more regular job. "And you could also use some churchgoing in your life!" we'd even heard her tell him. Richard, though, said the regular job talk was mainly so the Grizz could get himself some health insurance, which Dee Dee felt he needed more than anything else. According to her, the man was recklessness in the flesh, which, no matter how you looked at it, was a hell of a lot of recklessness. But the Grizz just couldn't or wouldn't change his ways, so she finally decided she couldn't have him around her or her son anymore—the final verdict being that the Grizz had become a very bad role model—and threw him onto the street. The last straw had been when the middle-of-the-night L.A.P.D. had once again knocked on her door. According to Richard, the Grizz and the L.A.P.D. had a constant secret sidebusiness going. A business Dee Dee wanted to keep way outside of her home. Richard, though, never questioned the Grizz. If anything, he looked up to the man.

As soon as the Grizz gave up the car keys, me and Richard fastwalked all the way up Second Street to the alley behind Mundo's Liquors, turned right into it, and came to a deadstop. The car was less a cherry and more a big purple lemon that'd been squozen and resquozen to a very juiceless pulp. In fact, it barely even looked like a car; more like a rolled-into-the-ditch-a-few-dozen-times junkmobile. Two crooked fenders, a missing headlight, a smashed rightside of windshield, a badlybent hood, and a meteorsized hole in the trunk—from some kind of explosion, I thought—the car was a far-from-pretty sight to take in. To top it off, it had an awful kind of multi-lean effect going on, which we quickly realized had to do with the tires each being a very different size from each other. Needless to say, we stood perfectly paralyzed. And not until we'd gathered enough nervestrength to put one foot in front of the other did we take a closer look. And luckily we found a couple of pluses hidden behind all the damage. The interior, for example, was in excellent condition and the motor looked ready for Indy—not that we knew anything about motors, that is. But at least all the parts and wires weren't hanging all-over-the-place loose with holes in them. When I turned to Richard, I saw the car keys extended my way.

"Me!" I said. "I can't drive." Richard's eyes got instantly concerned, and then he started to laugh some. "Damn. You can't either? Well we better not tell the Grizz or he might take his offer back."

"Sure enough."

Richard got behind the wheel and I slid in next to him. Just sitting like that in the alley silence, we felt plugged into a wall. Richard then keyed the motor, which immediately onned to this smooth muscular purr of an idle, and jerked the car forward through the alley. He jerked it forwards and backwards, backwards and forwards at least twenty times until he finally got the hang of it pretty good.

"A lot like a bicycle," said a full-of-concentration Richard. "Just different handlebars and pedals." Then we pulled out of the alley and into the street to head for the projects just a blockaway.

I sat back and relaxed. We damnnear own a car, went through my head. As Richard drove into the neighborhood, it'd become a different place to me; a new place that I felt we were visiting for the first time. And it also felt like we were gliding in in some kind of rare steel animal. No one in my immediate family, I suddenly realized, had ever owned a car before. At twelve I could become the first proud owner of an automobile. Well, co-owner, that is. I looked at a still-concentrating Richard working the steeringwheel and believed we'd come up in the biggest of ways. As we moved down Second Street I saw some people smiling our direction, which made me feel like waving at them the way the grand marshal of a parade would do. And I did. I waved and smiled as if the grandest of grand marshals ever, and as though the parade were being held especially in our honor for having landed our very own Swoop d'Ville. A no-doubt-about-it automobile, I thought once again, making the word automobile last as long as possible in my mind. It was instant status. If this is what having one's own ride is about, I'll never goodfoot it again. Then I saw two younger women staring at us with their hands over their mouths. They seemed to be laughing into their palms. Then a lawnchaired old man started pointing towards our car. And he was laughing too. Others looked at us with these badly horrified expressions. I could've sworn one woman even scooped up her child and ran into her apartment at the sight of us driving by. Suddenly I remembered: we were inside a rolling joke. Again I felt the lopsided tirewobble I'd felt earlier in the alley and I slowly slunk myself towards the floorboard to hide behind that shattered-to-a-glass-cobweb windshield. Forget about rain, my parade had been ruined by the clear and visible day. When I turned to Richard, he was already giving me a disgusted-with-it-all look himself.

" 'A cherry of a car,' " he said, as if Earl the Grizz was a madman liar who'd never spoken a more dishonest sentence in all of his overeating life.

After Richard made a wobbly turn into the Grizz's hangout lot and killed the engine, we got out of the car and stalked right over to an-already-looking-at-us Grizz, who was sitting on a low wall with Waldy and D-Dan, a couple of the older fellas, and his so-called street assistant, Puppet (who, because he had the mind of a child was, in Richard's personal opinion, more of a taken-care-of pet than any kind of street assistant). In other words, Richard didn't care much for Puppet.

"What kind of a bucket are you trying to push off on us, Grizz?" said Richard all upset, and with me very glad that the man was sitting so down as he was.

"What's wrong with the car?" he said, faking seriousness.

"You said a cherry, Grizz. That," said Richard, pointing to the lopsidedlooking thing in the parkinglot, "that's a big beat-up grape."

"Grape!" said the Grizz. "It's a Ford Torino! A collector's item. Am I right or am I right?" he said to Waldy, D-Dan, and Puppet, whose full-of-shock attentions were still all over our mess on wheels. *Well?*

"Oh, he's right all right, fellas," said a quick-on-his-toes Waldy.

"Couldn't be righter," said a just-as-fast D-Dan.

"That's right," said a deadheating Puppet.

"A collector's item," they said all together.

"What'd I tell you," said the Grizz grinning big. "You guys are in the possession of an absolute cherry and don't even know it."

"You're damn right!" said Puppet, suddenly enjoying the show.

"But it's got a Nike stripe from front to back," I told the Grizz. Which it did.

The Grizz, though, just laughed his big animal laugh. "I'll tell you what," he said, trying to recover some. "Come by tomorrow morning before I leave on my trip to Vegas and we'll work something out, okay? I'll have four new tires slapped on the badboy and then you'll do me that favor I mentioned earlier. That all right with you?"

New tires! The words had filled us with so much soaring joy we even forgot to look at each other.

"Yeah, Grizz." "Thanks, Grizz." "Tomorrow morning then, right, Grizz?" "By the way, you did say *tomorrow* morning, right? That's what we thought: tomorrow then. All right; we'll see you tomorrow morning then, Grizz. Till then."

"Richard," said the Grizz with a suddenly-sad voice. "Tell your mother that I miss her, all right?"

Richard slowly yessed his head. "Sure thing, Grizz," he told him. "As soon as I walk through the door."

For the rest of the daylight and into the night me and Richard both got the hang of the car pretty good. When it'd gotten dark we wedged and taped a heavyduty flashlight into the missing headlight slot. It worked perfect. Then we mainly drove around on sidestreets and some goodsized parkinglots for the rest of the night.

I went to bed that evening with a very different feeling about myself. Like grandmarshalling that parade was a definite go again. When me and Richard hooked up the next morning both of our hands ached terribly from having gripped at a steeringwheel for many hours for the first times in our life. Richard even had this knucklesized blister.

"Hollywood!" we said.

A cheeseburgermunching Grizz was headed to his own car, a long white Lincoln Continental, with us and Puppet walking tight behind him. He popped the Lincoln's trunk, which was full of all of his traveling gear, and took out a black, mediumsized duffelbag.

"I want you to take this bag to a guy in Hollywood for me," said the Grizz as he chewed the cheeseburger. "You do that and I'll new up the whole damn car for you. Not just the tires, but everything. Headlights, windshield, paint job, all of it."

"And the fenders?" I said. "You'll new up the fenders too?"

"Them too."

"And the hood and the trunk?" said Richard.

"All of it," said the Grizz. "You'll be rollin' sevens every time you get into the damn thing."

I don't know if it'd been being joyed up so high by the thought of our own car redone with a new paint job, windshield, fenders, etc., but we hadn't even bothered to ask the Grizz what the duffelbag had inside of it. I mean it'd crossed my mind to *wonder* what was in it, but to actually think of asking the Grizz didn't happen. Not that I would've if it would've come to mind. You see, if a man like the Grizz opens up his trunk to give you something to deliver for him, then that, in a very strong sense, was all you needed to know about the matter. You didn't pry into his affairs with any suspicious-sounding questions, making him maybe wonder if you were up to the job or not or had the proper amount of trust in him. Even Richard, who could claim a kind of family status with the man, understood the no-questions-asked nature of neighborhood business. After all, if someone like the Grizz could claim to have anything, it was his own private reasons for doing what he did, when he did it, and how. Period. And if he'd have wanted us to know about anything, he'd have told us. It was that simple.

As we all went back to our car, the Grizz let me and Richard know what San Pedro garage to go to to get those new tires and then gave us a sheet of paper with the name

Bruno on it, an address, and a telephone number. On the back of the slip were the directions to Hollywood.

"This stuff strictly belongs in the hands of an Italian and this guy's just the man for the job," said the Grizz, finishing off his cheeseburger. "He does the best work in the city. Anybody else might botch it. And Earl the Grizz can't and won't risk a botched job. In my line of work it'd flat out make me look bad." He put the bag into our backseat. "He's expecting you sometime this midafternoon." Then the Grizz stepped back and looked at the car he'd given us. "And if you can, park this thing around the corner from his place. We'll have it cherried out as soon as possible."

The last thing the Grizz told us was not to come around looking for for him for three-to-four days; he'd be in Las Vegas, he'd said, for some badly needed R and R; said that the Ranch was wearing him to the ground with all his "community responsibilities," as he'd called them. And that was that. He was off to roll a few dice and we were headed to Hollywood with a black duffelbag to meet up with some Italian guy by the name of Bruno.

After getting the new tires we went for gas and, to our straight-up surprise, filling the tank was trickier than we'd expected. For one thing, we didn't know which one of the three kinds of gases the car had to have, so we did the only intelligent thing to do: put a little of each in the tank. But actually figuring the gas gun into the carside, and then getting the gas to flow right, wasn't so easy either. There were levers to lift, buttons to push, gas counters to eyeball, and guntriggers to hold. Not to mention having to guess how much of each octane we'd have to give the tank. By the time we finally finished we'd spilled enough gasoline on our shoes for a whole second tankful of the stuff. But we grinned at each other like lottery champions anyways.

"Now we can go for hundreds of miles," said an all-revved-up-excited Richard before he pulled out of the station. That parade, I thought, could be a very very long one indeed.

We followed the Grizz's directions north along Gaffey to Five Points at the far edge of San Pedro, and readied to run the car up Western Boulevard like a pencil along a twentyfivemilelong ruler. As we left San Pedro I got the feeling that a truly great thing was happening. No longer were we nailed down to the place we'd grown up in all our lives, with only the Rapid Transit District, or RTD for rough, tough, and dangerous, to take us out of Dodge for a stretch to visit other L.A. places like Long Beach, Santa Monica, and Dodger Stadium. (Plus the RTD had always meant countless stops and starts and hours of pissyleather riding just to make it a couple of miles from the neighborhood.) But now we had a car, with one of us sitting strong behind the steeringwheel and facing nothing but endless streets and avenues. It was like learning to walk, run, and fly all at the same time. And after our errand was done we could take any of those streets and avenues we wanted, to any parts of Los Angeles we wanted, and at any time of day or night. When I felt the gas card snug inside my pantspocket, my imagination suddenly caught me up in this brandnew surge of thinking:

To freedomfly didn't really mean you had to leave the ground and get all airborne. It could also mean something like never getting a flat tire, or never running out of gas, or simply never losing a car key. Wings, I thought, staring at the cityscene pass, didn't really have to be wings either, but something a lot like wings. Like a steeringwheel or a gas pedal, for example. I mean, why couldn't our made-it-out-of-Dodge-with-style freedomfeel be the same as the one a bird could know while on its smooth soaring fly through the sky? Or even the same as one of them just perched real comfortable on a treebranch, rooftop, or telephone wire, knowing in its heart that it could move up through the air anytime it wanted? That's how moving along in our Swoop d'Ville felt. Like having a bird's simple winged ability always along at hand. I wasn't sure what was at the very true middle of my thoughtsurge, only that I didn't want the freedomfeel in my system to go away anytime soon. Or ever.

Those first several miles out of San Pedro we stared out of the windows without saying a word. We just stared and grinned out of them as though on some galaxycruising spaceshiptour, with each passing block a new planet, each new neighborhood a solarsystem, and all of it together the newestborn galaxy out in outer space. Any vehicles we passed were suddenly fantasticlooking spaceships themselves that, when they stopped at a redlight or stopsign, did nothing more than follow spacetravel rules.

As we drove through South Central, L.A., I counted the churches and liquor stores we passed. Never in my life had I seen so many of either clustered so close together for so many blocks on end. Churcheswise, there were Baptist, Methodist, Unitarian, Pentecostal, Presbyterian, and Muslim ones set up like so many booths at a Sunday afternoon fleamarket. I couldn't believe that I'd bused it along the same parts of Western Boulevard in the past and hadn't noticed them. Like Second Street the day before, it'd become a strange, new, unfamiliar place to me. On one block alone I counted four churches and three liquor stores one right after the other. It had to be the case, I thought, of the congregations being constantly drunk or the drunks being a very high holy. Here and there mostly-cornered men and women sat along both sides of the boulevard guzzling out of paperbags. Obviously, I said to myself, we were passing through one very sad solarsystem filled to the brim with alcoholic believers.

Then I noticed an RTD pass in the opposite direction and turned to watch the awful giant thing from behind, but stopped when I noticed it on our backseat: the duffelbag. Suddenly I remembered Bruno the Italian waiting for us and his special delivery like some ugly alien creature at the end of the universe. When I looked at Richard, I saw he'd lost a good amount of the excitement he'd had earlier too and was pressing his blisterfinger hard against the steeringwheel without even knowing it. And it was a pressing that suddenly bothered me terribly.

"Ain't this a bitch," said Richard into the rearview mirror, though, which I instantly knew could've only've meant one of two things: that a major part of our car had just fallen off, like the whole rearend, for example, or that a rollerboy had added himself to the parade. When I one-eightied my head again, I sure enough noticed the pop and the blitz of emergency lights and then heard the loud tinny sound of a police mike.

"Pull your vehicle to the side of the road!" said the mike. "Do it *now*!"

"What should we do with the bag?" I said quickly.

"What do you mean 'do with the bag?' " said Richard back.

"I mean, what do you think is in it? And should we try and get rid of it?"

"*I* don't know what's in it," he said. "Only that it's gotta get to where it's gotta go, period." His voice was suddenly very business. "Too late to get rid of it anyways."

"But what do you think is in it?"

He glanced at me annoyed. "It's impossible to say not having opened it. I didn't lift it either, and when the Grizz did it didn't seem to be that heavy."

This didn't mean much to me since the Grizz was probably strong enough to lift our car with us inside of it if he'd felt like it.

"Think it might be counterfeit bills? Or jewelry? Or guns?" I said.

"I wouldn't suspect the Grizz to have us moving anything illegal for him, would you?"

I didn't answer, though, because I'd started to think about Dee Dee's strong opinion of the man. That stuff she'd said about his recklessness. I could tell I'd gotten Richard a bit nervous with my questions. On top of seeing the Grizz behind Dee Dee's back, he was suddenly running a who-knew-what-kind-of errand out to *Hollywood* for him too. And then driving there himself! If she ever found out any of it, who knew what might happen to her boy. Maybe he'd end up way out on his backside like her habitgambler had.

"The Grizz isn't stupid," said Richard suddenly, to which I still didn't say anything. "He wouldn't put us in a bad situation . . . would he?"

"You know him better than me," I finally told him. Richard said nothing to me, though. "It's this Italian business that's messing with my head." I stole a look his way. "Why would the Grizz of all people ask *us* to do something this important for him; I mean something worth a whole car, no matter how ugly, and having to do with a no-doubt-about-it, mob-involved Italian?"

"I can't say," said a suddenly shoulder-shrugging Richard, who had these red and blue lightflashes splattering onto his forehead from the rearview mirror. Then I could immediately tell what he was thinking: put the pedal to the metal and don't stop till we've outrun the backside roller or completely run out of gas. It was one of the naturalest reactions a person could have on knowing an L.A.P.D. was at their back. And I knew Richard had it in him to take off too; but more than that, I knew our car, new tires or no new tires, wouldn't have an outside chance against even a standard rollerboy issue.

"Pull it over, Rich," I told him.

"Yeah," he said, starting to do so. "Moms is gonna murder me."

After he'd eased us to a stop, we waited with our hands flat on the dashboard. The rollerboy hadn't miked us to dashboard our hands, it was just another one of those natural-like reactions a young guy developed growing up in the housing projects. Like I said earlier, the last thing an L.A.P.D. needed was an excuse to shoot someone dead in the head, however innocent or guilty.

Then there were footsteps, followed by a voice.

"Both of you out of the car and put your hands on top of the hood."

We slowly did so.

"You know why I pulled you punks over?" said the rollerboy, whose nametag read Roberts.

Neither of us answered.

"You have no idea?"

Still we didn't answer.

"I thought I had a runaway vehicle!" he said all angry-sounding. "Not until I got close enough to barely see the tops of your heads was I sure that this travesty of a vehicle wasn't going to plow into any pedestrians or devastate any head-on traffic." Then he looked at Richard. "How old are you anyways?"

"Seventeen."

"Bullshit!" said the rollerboy like some kind of drill sergeant. "You're no older than twelve; thirteen max." Then he looked at me. "And you? How old are you?"

"Fifteen," I said with a deeper-than-usual voice.

"Double bullshit!" he said. "I'm writing you up *and* hauling your asses into the clink."

Next he piled traffic violations on us like a starving man would've done a plate of food. No license, no registration, no insurance, a threat to public safety, joyriding, on and on and on. He called us a menace to society and an even bigger threat to ourselves. But one good thing, he said, "the *only* good thing," was that the car hadn't been reported stolen. Otherwise, he said, we'd have been kissing everything we'd ever known a bitter goodbye for a while. Then, superviolations and all, he let us completely off the hook to continue on our way. Told us that we had more problems than we could handle and that he had more important things to do than to take a piddlyass pair of joyriding offenses into juvenile court. There were murderers and rapists to catch, he'd said to us, and real car thieves. *"Bank robbers even."* "Go home," he finally said to us with a wink, "then park the car and wait about five years before getting into it again." Just like that he'd gone from asshole to angel, got into his squadcar, and drove away. The L.A.P.D., I thought as we'd watched him vanish down Western Boulevard, more sinful than all the devils in the underground. I thought it not to be ungrateful or anything, but because in the end it was the Grizz who we really had to thank. You see, when the rollerboy named Roberts had snooped into our backseat and noticed that black duffelbag on it, things immediately changed for the better.

"What's in it?" he'd said to us.

"We don't know," we'd told him back.

"What do you mean, 'we don't know'? It's in your car, isn't it?"

"Yeah, but it's not our bag."

"Then whose bag is it?"

"Big Earl Buckley's," said Richard suddenly, to which I'd immediately shot him a look that demanded why he'd just blurted the Grizz into trouble and us right into a pair of good-to-go, tailor-made coffins. Unless, that is, the Grizz didn't have us cremated on the spot first.

"Big Earl who?" said Roberts, checking us out a little closer.

"Buckley," said Richard all confident. "You know who I'm talking about."

Then Roberts eyeballed Richard only, as if he were trying to place his face. "Oh, yeah," he said all slowbrained then. "Big Earl Buckley. Now I remember. Big mountain of a guy, right? How's he doing anyway?"

"Busy," said Richard. "Very very busy."

"Of course," said Roberts as he flashed a look back to the duffelbag. "Come on you guys," he suddenly said all buddybuddy-like, "I know you know what's in it. Why don't you tell me."

"We don't," said Richard a pointblankbold. "So we can't say."

"Then you won't mind if I take a little look?"

"No problem," said Richard. "But we would have to tell Big Earl about it."

Roberts then stared at him. "Of course," he finally said, closing up his ticketbook. "Good footsoldiers, huh? I had no idea that the Grizz was using children, er, I mean young boys, to do his work for him these days."

"For all we know," said Richard, "all that bag's got in it is dirty laundry."

" 'Dirty laundry,' " said Roberts with an out-of-nowhere laughseizure. "That's a good one," ha-ha-ha. " 'Dirty laundry.' Do me a favor," he said, trying to recover some. "Tell Mr. Buckley Roberts says hello, okay? And that I think of him every once in a while. He'll know what that means." Then he got back into his squadcar and, still laughing and muttering to himself about that dirty laundry comment, drove away.

"What in the world was he trippin' off?" I said after a bit.

"Shit, you know you've gotta be a good amount loony to become an L.A.P.D.," said Richard.

"True," I said with a head-yes. "And sinful too."

Before we stepped back into the car, me and Richard agreed that the Grizz had more pull than a fullgrown rhino. Then behind the wheel, Richard propped himself up on two cushions we'd found in the openair trunk and once again we were on our way to worldfamous Hollywood. Somehow the parade was just meant to continue.

"How'd you know to tell him the Grizz's name?" I said another bit later.

"He looked familiar," said Richard. "Then I remembered that he was one of these rollers who used to come by the apartment a while back. They had something serious going with the Grizz at that time. But Moms had hated him. He must've gotten transferred out of San Pedro."

"Big Earl Buckley. That's his real name, huh?"

"Just Earl Buckley," said Richard.

"Well if I had to call him just *Earl* Buckley," I said, "I'd probably piss all over myself. Earl the Grizz is just fine with me. Sounds cuddly even."

"Yeah, and you sound stupid."

To the right we saw downtown L.A.'s great buildings standing like some tall glass suns all over the planets below. Never had we seen anything beautifuler in all of our days. Twenty, forty, eightystory buildings seeming like an end-of-the-rainbow city of some kind for the way they kept staying the same exact distance away from us. If we'd have wanted to, though, we could've driven right for all that big glass beauty; right between those tall shiny buildings, even if just to simply hang our heads out of the carwindows to get a quick whiff of that downtown cityair. But instead Richard busted a left onto Wilshire Boulevard to continue in the direction of Hollywood.

Several miles later we checked out the big and white

blocklettered HOLLYWOOD sign squatting high and bright on a hilltop to our right.

"I bet it's seeable from space," I said as we stared at it. "Like that Chinese wall."

"I doubt it," said Richard.

"But we can see it all the way from San Pedro," I said. "And that's a good twentyfive-thirty miles from here."

"Yeah, but space is millions of miles away," he said. "Just the moon itself has to be many thousands of miles out."

"That's the moon, though. Space—as in *outer* space—that starts just a few miles up; a little past where the sky ends."

Richard gave me one of those you-better-check-your-mental-health-right-quick looks.

"Don't believe me then," I told him. "But let's swoop up and check out the view anyways. See if we can see back to San Pedro from it. Maybe even the neighborhood. We can kick it on the Ls and the Os."

Richard's face, though, had suddenly gone a very serious with worry. The Grizz and the delivery, I could tell, once again weighed terribly on his mind. I decided to change the subject.

"How we doing on gas?"

"The needle just went below the F," he said as I watched the Hollywood sign fade high behind us, "but we still have hundreds of miles left in the tank." At the steeringwheel a seriousfaced Richard suddenly seemed like the captain of some ship, working the dials and instruments, watching for icebergs, and even ready to shout out some seaman stuff like "land ahoy!" and "aye-aye, matey" so as to get him, cargo, and crew safely to port. Then we turned right and headed for Sunset Boulevard, where we made another left. On Sunset we passed dayshift prostitutes (women, men, and those inbetween), limousines limousines and more limousines, giant guitar shops, a lady in a tight pink plastic dress, tourists tourists and more mapreading cameraclicking tourists, and the down-and-out homeless, and all of it was along the maybe filthiest ugliest streets we'd ever seen in our lives.

"For a worldfamous place," I said to a shocked-to-see-it-all Richard, "Hollywood's kind of lacking in the hygiene and beauty departments, no?"

"You said it," said Richard. "I'll take San Pedro anyday."

Just as the Grizz had said to do, we parked the car around the corner from the Italian's place, which turned out to be a very small sleepylooking house in an even sleepierlooking neighborhood just four blocks off of Sunset. A nice nonchalant front, we decided.

"I'll stay with the car," said Richard. "In case we have to make that getaway." I looked at him damnnear insulted.

"I know how to drive this bucket, too," I told him. "So I can just as easily be the pedal." For a good stretch we stayed in the car quiet. "Look, the Grizz wouldn't put us in harm's way," I finally said. "You even said so yourself. What, you doubting the Grizz now?"

"I guess I am," said Richard, looking down at his leg.

"All right then," I said, "if one goes in, the other does too. Cool?" Richard yessed his head. "I'll handle the bag."

"Is it heavy?" said Richard as we headed for the corner.

"Nah. It's actually kind of light. Really light."

"See, I knew it couldn't be guns."

"It could still be counterfeit bills, though. But not too many of 'em."

"Depends on the denominations."

"True."

At the front door we caught our breaths and pushed the buzzer. Instead of a buzz going off, though, we heard a churchbell clanging go all around through the inside of the house. Before it ended the door was opened up by an old, peachfuzzmustachehaving woman in a long black dress, like for a funeral. Me and Richard gave each other those wondering looks. Then the woman smiled and called behind her in Italian, and as soon as this graysideburned, mostlybald-headed man came to the door, the old woman left. The man had on black slacks, a black Grizz-like silk dress-shirt, a silver watch, two very knobby gold-and-diamond rings, and smelled like a whole garden of fresh flowers. Not only that, but he looked fitter than a Hercules; as if all he did alldaylong were push-ups and sit-ups. Then suddenly a high-pitched machine kicked in somewhere in the background that whined and hammered as it sped and slowed, sped and slowed, which instantly had me and Richard checking towards each other again, with his look saying, *"Bet I'll beat your slowrunning-ass to the car!*" and mine quick answering, *"Bet you won't!"*

"Can I help you gentlemen?" said the man at the door then in a very strong Italian accent. The machine behind him had gotten an even faster kind of furious.

"Yeah," I said, barely holding back a stutter. "We're here for Bruno."

"I am Bruno," he instantly accented back to us, which actually made my skin jitter. I couldn't believe the guy was sporting a flowersmelling perfume.

"The Grizz sent us," said Richard to him then.

"The what?" he said.

"Earl Buckley," said Richard. "We—"

"Ah yes," said Bruno, suddenly sounding a lot like Roberts had. "Mr. Buckley. *Bene-bene.* And where is the bag? Mr. Buckley said you would have a bag for me."

"It's over here," I said, walking to a nearby bush. I'd hid it just in case we really had to bail the scene ASAP.

"Strange place to put a bag, no?" said Bruno with an eyebrowraise. The backroom machine slowed, then kicked in again in the same furious way.

"Can never be too careful," I said to him.

Bruno, though, made a notunderstanding face at me and called to the back of the house in Italian. The machine stopped humming. Again that mad dash for the car dominated my mind. Then the old woman reappeared at the door and Bruno said a few more Italian somethings to her and again asked me for the bag. I handed it to him and watched him as he transferred it to the old woman, who then told us a *"chow"* and toted the bag away as if it held in it nothing more than some very old underwear.

That was when we realized a strange man was standing right behind us. He had a gray suit draped over his arm, fidgeted nervously, and had come absolutely quietly out of nowhere. Because his right hand was hidden under the draped suit, I could only think of a single thing. *Handgun.* When I glanced at his face I noticed two dark and heavy bags under a set of very washedout eyes. Our escape route had been slyly and smoothly snatched away from us.

A stranger, I thought, getting angried up inside; how could the Grizz let a stranger decide our life and death? Not that a familiar face would've made me any difference. But somehow, at that very moment, him being a stranger had bugged the shit out of me. Maybe a halfminute went by without anything said between anyone of us.

"Is there anything else you'd like to say?" said Bruno finally, making me wish that I myself had done maybe a little more churchgoing in my life.

"Yes, is there?" said the man behind us in an irritated tired voice. "I'm in a hurry, if you don't mind."

Bruno waited. "No? Good," he said. "Tell Mr. Buckley to come by in one week. No sooner. As you can see, I am a very busy man. And tell him that he can pay me then, as usual."

"He's just gonna let us go?" I said with a headpoint about the guy behind us.

"I don't see why not," said an again-confused-with-me

Bruno. "Are you going to let them go?" he said to the baggy-eyed man.

"Not if they make me late, I won't," he said, to which we instantly busted for the sidewalk and then the car that was around the corner past that.

"That guy behind us, he was a hitman, wasn't he?" I said as Richard wheeled the car back onto Sunset, our adrenaline all over the place.

"Hell yeah he was a hitman," said Richard. "Hitmen all look like that: cheap suits and messed-up eyes. I've seen it time and time again in the movies."

"And that guy Bruno, he had a sweet front, didn't he?" I said.

"That old lady," said Richard, "she's probably the Godfather's very own mother. They're not beyond using their own mothers for their business."

"And what about that machine?" I said with a nervous relieved laugh. "Scary as hell, no?"

"I heard that," said Richard, giving me a quick wildeyed look. "There was no goddamn *way* I was stepping into that crib. It had *Scarface* written all over it."

Chow, we decided, must've been some Italian code word that the Grizz'd forgotten to tell us about.

————

For the next three days all we did was drive. Wherever we wanted to go, we went. Downtown L.A. to see those giant glass buildings, Chinatown, Sunset Beach to bodysurf and lie in an unexpected sun, then bodysurf some more, and Venice and Santa Monica to hang out with all the freaky people along the boardwalk and pier. San Pedro alone we crisscrossed maybe eighty times. All we wanted to do was drive drive drive our very own car and nothing else. For two back-to-back nights we didn't even go home; just slept in the front and backseats. Richard's blister, by the way, popped by day two.

On the fourth day after the delivery we checked Second Street for the Grizz like he'd asked us to, but he was nowhere to be found. We checked the parks and parkinglots, his main cheeseburger connection, Spiro's Burgers, in and behind Mundo's Liquors, you name it, but we found no sign of the man. Finally we ran into Puppet sitting on a Pacific Avenue busbench. He looked a terribly shaken up; lost even.

"What's happenin', Puppet?" we said to him. "Where's the Grizz?"

He looked at us as if the very words had permanently offended him.

"The Grizz ain't in town," said Puppet all full of mope, "might never be back neither." His eyes started to tear up some and his head started to droop.

"Why not, Puppet?" said Richard, suddenly alarmed. "What's happened to the Grizz?"

"He's in a hospital in Las Vegas," said Puppet. "That's all that I can say, 'cause that's all that I know." Then he got up off of the busbench, ran across the street, and disappeared from sight.

As we drove for the next few hours things just faded by the carwindows in one long notnoticeable blur. When we finally snapped out of it and spoke we decided that something very very crazy must've happened between the Grizz and Bruno, and suddenly got to hoping our delivery hadn't messed things up. And since they'd seen our faces, we also hoped that Bruno and his baggyeyed hitman wouldn't come looking for us.

So we just kept driving. Our thinking was, if we simply stayed a constant mobile, we at least wouldn't be some stupid sitting ducks when they finally did come around the Ranch for us. In the next few weeks we added thousands of miles to the distancecounter and got to know almost every part of Los Angeles as good as our own neighborhood. Gas station attendants in Riverside, Carson, Long Beach, and Westwood all knew us by car and name. We even drove deep into the desert to Palm Springs, down to Tijuana, Mexico, and up the coast to Malibu for yet another bodysurf session. Fifteen hours a day we drove drove drove till one day the gas card completely tapped out; just like that some gas station attendant in Pasadena for the very first time denied us a taken-for-granted tankful. An hour or so later, we barely made it back into San Pedro.

That day we parked the car where we'd first picked it up, behind Mundo's Liquors, and then walked ourselves home on the funniestfeeling legs of all time; we stepped along as if the sidewalks were bobbing on water. And a few days later our car was gone. Towed away impounded. Another name for car arrest. The gas card, though, I kept as a souvenir.

One Sunday afternoon a few days later, me and Richard, glad to finally have our landlegs back, were strolling through the Ranch when we noticed someone waving us down in the Big Park. Puppet, who we hadn't seen since that busbench, was sitting next to him. We headed over. The closer we got to them, though, the slower we walked. Puppet, you see, had the grin of a circusclown going because sitting right next to him was none other than a very-happy-to-see-us Earl the Grizz Buckley, or, part of that person anyways. The man had dropped serious weight! In fact, compared to who he'd recently been, he'd gotten downright skinny. His pants were much too big and baggy and his silk dressshirt draped over him like some oversized parachute.

"*Grizz . . . ?*" we said as if talking to some grasshugging cloud.

"How you fellas doing?" said the old booming voice, though.

"All right/Okay," we said, still shocked into a long and low slackjaw. It was impossible to figure how he could've shrunk so much.

"You dying of something, Grizz?" I said, not sure I should've asked it.

The Grizz, though, just laughed his big strong animal laugh while Puppet noed his head with the proudest of happy grins. If Puppet had a tail, I thought, it would've wiggled him dizzy. "No, no, no," said the Grizz. "I've got much time left in front of me, fellas. Hope to outlive you two."

"But what happened to you, Grizz? Did Bruno poison you or something?" said a still-not-believing-his-eyes Richard.

The Grizz, though, wrinkled his nose and foreheadskin. "Bruno? Poison me?" said the Grizz all awonder. "Nobody did nothing to me, man. Nobody except my very own heart, that is. Rolled an upfront seven with twentythousand down. Greatest moment of all of my life, snuffed out by cardiac arrest. It's what I got for not listening to that beautiful mother of yours."

"Cardiac arrest!" we said.

"Yeah!" said the Grizz. "A heartattack! Cheeseburgers and stress'll do that to a person. Besides the heart surgery, the doctors had to staple up half of my stomach and cut out something like eight feet of intestines. Then they put me on these pills called diuretics, right, and a strict low-sodium diet. Hell, I'm not even allowed to look at most foods now and've already lost damnnear a-hundred pounds." Then his eyes shifted over towards Second Street. "So, somebody's out to get the ol' Grizz, huh fellas?"

"No, well, what we thought was that maybe you and that Bruno guy had some kind of falling out," Richard said.

"And that he'd tried to kill you," I said.

"Me and Bruno?" said the Grizz, again getting all confused with us. "A falling out?"

"Yeah," said Richard. "You remember: Hollywood; the stuff in the duffelbag?"

Suddenly the Grizz eyed us in an unbelieving wonder, and then once again roared his big booming laugh, but this time coughing some.

"Have you guys lost your minds? Bruno's my tailor, man!" he said, to which me and Richard gave each other these ridiculous-ass looks. "He does my dress-shirts for me." Again the Grizz roared out laughing. "Now, about that gas card, fellas, because. . . ."

But we missed the rest of his sentence for the simple fact that we were headed in a full oppositedirectioned sprint through the park. That laugh, though, it was an impossible kind of thing to outrun.

Richard was lucky to have a guy like the Grizz around the neighborhood. A guy who not only said he considered Richard a part of himself, but who'd many times backed up such talk with plenty of proving-it action. On top of getting Richard and a friend a car (with gas card), for example, he at the every start of a schoolyear copped Richard a decent set of clothes to wear, every other week stuck a little chumpchange into his always-empty pockets, and made it a point to ask him the sincerest of questions, like "How've you been doing lately?" or "Why do you have that long-and-wrong face on today?" and then, if Richard felt like answering him his mind, the Grizz would actually stop whatever he'd been doing to long enough listen, and sometimes even give back some advice. It was a lot of little stuff like that that'd made the Grizz as special as he was.

But in another sense, and even though she'd bumped the Grizz from her crib, Richard was lucky he had Dee Dee for a moms too—no matter how wellknownfamous she was for taking certain things to the edge of extreme—like those antigambling beliefs, for example. In her own way, Dee Dee could be a person's very worst nightmare. But me and the fellas, we knew she mostly did and said what she said to make sure that her boy was AOK when in and out of the apartment, which was mainly something a person had to respect her for. You see, Dee Dee wasn't the kind of woman to lose sight of those close to her just because she'd met some supposedly very nice new guy, no matter how taken-in impressed she'd become with him. I mean, she'd booted *the Grizz* of all people, because she thought that doing so would actually keep her kid all right. Do you think a woman like that capable of walking with her six-year-old son three miles to some bum-and-dealer-infested, ten-o'clock-at-night downtown-L.A. park, where she'd all along planned to meet up with some not-having-told-you-about guy, get into his car, and tell you from the driving-away carwindow that you'd manage just fine hoofing it back to the apartment all by your very lonesome? Or do you think a woman like that would've just as quickly faded from your presence whenever her latest so-called boyfriend asked you to get him something from the store, for example, or maybe take another one of those right-quick walks *right quick*, just so he could lock you out of your own crib for half a day or sometimes deep into the night past that and think nothing of it? Or, do you think a woman like Dee Dee would've the very morning after such a lockout session suggested something crazy like, "Really,

Toom, you should listen to so-and-so every so often," to yet another favor asked? "He really is a good man to have around, you know. Someone you could benefit from."

The more Goldie hung around the apartment, though, the more I thought about a certain surprise telephone call that'd happened to me back on September Twentyseventh. That was before the El Niño rains that'd kicked in hard again in late January just a few months back had ever even started. The call was from my pops, Alonzo Toomer, a man I'd never met and had only talked with once before three years back when I was only nine-years-old. All I remembered from that first call were two things: first, him telling me over and over again, as if needing to excuse himself for something bad about himself, that his father, named a Hanno Toomer, had been a mean and always-drinking old man, and that second, the telephone call itself had been much too short, with the telephonetone coming much too fast.

But the September Twentyseventh call had been very different. That was the time he told me that he'd just moved from New York City to one called Cleveland, which he said was a mostly frozenovergray, and how much living there had made him deeply miss the island he was from in the Bahamas, a place he said he'd tell me all about when he finally visited me sometime during the winter. *What!* flashed through my mind. I couldn't believe I'd heard him right. Visit me? In the winter just to come? Without ever having had to figure out a way to ask him myself, which I'd mostly felt like doing during our whole telephonetime together, he'd up and offered to visit me all on his very own-some. It'd been too much to listen to. But then a full-of-El-Niño November and December, and then a January and February came and went, without so much as a peep from Alonzo Toomer. Not a telephone call, a letter, or even a pennypriced postcard. Nothing. For the longest while I told myself that he'd probably managed not to make it to L.A. because the Cleveland airplanes weren't allowed to take off or land on always-frozen runways or because El Niño had shutdown all the L.A. airports.

When El Niño had started up again in January, it did so without any quit clear into March and the first few days of Easter vacation. In fact the storm had gotten so violently vicious it'd punched three giant holes smack through the harbor's supposedly-unbreakable breakwater, tossing its fifteen-ton granite blocks around like so many styrofoam cups. That was the stretch when Goldie'd become his locking-me-out-of-the-apartment terriblest too. At one point he'd even stopped with the rightquicking favortalk to finally flat out tell me things like, "Three's a crowd, little brother, out!" as he held the exitdoor wide open, always sure to throw in an "I need to walk around the place naked for a bit," comment or two just to mess with my mind. Moms, of course, would be nowhere to be found, hiding as she'd be behind her fullblast classical music and a very locked, only-Goldie-was-allowed-to-enter-into-it bedroom, pretending that things in the crib were a yankeedoodledandy. To be honest, though, I'd gotten as glad to be asked out of the crib as they'd been happy to have me gone. Just one of Goldie's trips through the livingroom, you see, had become enough to tighten up the apartment air for several hours on end, or just a single favor asked enough to have me once again hoping hard for that long-overdue visit from pops to happen just so he could do with Goldie what Dee Dee'd done with the Grizz. Meaning throw him far out on his needing-to-walk-around-the-apartment-naked ass.

But anyways, instead of standing out in the windywet weather myself, I'd head straight for the only place I knew of that'd let a person hang out until nice and dry, and up until a ten-o'clock closingtime past that, no questions asked: the San Pedro Public Library; a place where the workers actually got completely happyfaced at the sight of a young guy like me walking in through the door.

"Can I help you find a book?" one of the older volunteer women had asked me in the warmest friendliest voice as soon as I'd for the first time sogged into the place. "Or maybe a newspaper or magazine? What are you interested in, young man? Fiction? History? The sciences? Geography?"

Geography! That was when I'd suddenly realized how little I actually knew about my pops's islander life. I mean moms had shown me a bunch of these old photographs of him that she wouldn't return after they'd split up. In most of them the young Alonzo Toomer was right around my age and was fishing or swimming or eating off a wooden plate with his feet buried in a creamygold beachsand and, except for this one kind of family-portrait photo with his mother, brother, and baby sister around him, he's always got a never-ever-smiling Hanno, his mean-and-drinking-father, right at his side.

Suddenly, though, I had a tabletop full of books with all the detaily stuff a person could want to know about a place like the Bahamas, like the food and flowers, the animals and weather, and just by thumbing through them all the young Alonzo's story came to me all on its very own.

On a good map of the Bahama Islands, Little Inagua is nothing but a speck in the Caribbean Ocean, and on a bad map is so small that it doesn't even show up. But I can't really blame the bad-map makers for not specking Little Inagua in where it should've been, since it really is so small in all that bluecolored water. On the bad maps you'll see the places called Cat Island, Castle Island, Mariguana Island, and Great Ragged Island—even a Great Inagua Island—but not the just-too-little Little Inagua. But believe me, it's there.

One day in the middle of all that mapblue emptiness the young Alonzo Toomer was looking out of his family's shack-window. What he was doing was watching the ground in front of the shack move by as if by magic, always coming up from the beach towards the shackside, and then up the goodsized bump of hill just behind it. It wasn't really the ground that was moving, though, but the shelltops of thousands of on-the-go soldiercrabs who scraped along because they knew that another storm was coming. And even though the air outside was still and thick under a bigclouded sky, it didn't mean the storm would be another hurricane, but it also didn't mean a nice soft rain either. Maybe something right inbetween. When the young Alonzo Toomer looked at the closeby ocean, he noticed how large the swells had grown too. We have to be careful, he thought. I have to tell Hanno about the skiff. But when he did, his lying-in-the-corner father looked at him with the same meancreased eyes he'd always looked at his son with and said, "It'll be gotten when it's gotten," and rolled himself facefirst to the corner and laid there like some just-sickened-up animal. Alonzo returned to his window.

When the storm finally slammed the island, bending and bowing the tall palmtrees, the young Alonzo Toomer went back to his father, who'd already so fullblanketed himself that not an inch of him showed. Under the blanket the old man shivered hard to every palmbending wind, and when the young Alonzo saw it, the same heartleeching feelings as always filled up his chest; feelings that meant that his father was really a deepdown coward. Before the young Alonzo Toomer got any angrier, though, he stepped out of the shack and into the strong strong siderain, only to see that the oceanswells were hitting harder than before and that all of the soldiercrabs had already disappeared wellbehind the shack. Quickly he grabbed the skiff and dragged it a foot at a time away from the beach and, after a good hour or so, had it all the way uphilled, roped and superknotted to a very thick palmtree whose coconuts on and off groundthudded right next to the young Alonzo Toomer like the very deadliest of natural bowling balls. When Alonzo finally finished treetying the skiff he ran back down to the shack to be with his younger brother and sister. Once inside, though, and he again saw the blanketshivering lump that supposedly was his father and automatically spit right onto the shackfloor. It was the only way he had of getting some of that ugly ugly word coward just a little out of his system. Then he pulled his brother and his sister tightinclose with him and listened to and looked at the storm happening hard just outside their shack. And it was a beautiful storm the whole time it lasted.

The storm had actually been a lot like an El Niño. Or like a very smallsized hurricane even. There were brokensplintered palmtrees, beachscattered driftwood, and this all-around shoreline damage, but like always, the island had made it through to once again show its afterstorm beautiful. Butterflies and hummingbirds were flapping and fluttering about as if in some firstborn spring, and wherever the young Alonzo Toomer looked, a came-back-to-life frangipani or morning-glory or passionflower looked him right back. If I could just go out alone today, he thought as he took in the once again perfectlooking island, I could have maybe the best day of my life.

Alonzo pulled the skiff back down to the beach and laid his sling and speararrow next to the fish and conch sacks, crabbox, big bottle of rum, baitknife, and the hooked-and-leadered droplines. Then he waited for the badcoughing Hanno to climb one slow leg after another into the skiff, waited for him to sit in his usual spot, and finally jumped in himself to row them both a goodways into the calmed and easy seawater, which Alonzo steadily checked for fish, except, that is, for the quick one time he sideeyed Hanno, who, with no tophair and only some short white templescruff, simply sat and stared at the faraway horizonline while somehow looking older than the world itself. Hanno's skin had this darksalted driftwoodcolor and his cheeks were covered in these small brown spots with thin red zigzaggedy lines all around them. Toothswise, the man was missing them all, and his two gray oceanbottom eyes had a way of reminding a person of the very nervous Gogoleye fish or even the easy-to-spear Passing Jack. But what was strangest of all about Hanno's eyes was that by every sunset eve they'd completely lose their color, going from that oceanbottom gray to a kind of nightmatching black. As long as his son could remember Hanno's eyes had done that.

One thing the young Alonzo Toomer never sideeyed, though, was that big bottle of rum. If he got caught doing so he could expect one of Hanno's easily-given roughpalmed slaps ASAP—the slaps and the rum being two of the things that Hanno was best at. But no matter what Alonzo did, by the time the skiff was headed back to the beach the roughpalm had been given many many times and for almost any reason at all, like, for example, the young Alonzo Toomer not swimming fast enough or for him not having found the choicest of fishschools or even for him not rowing them in or out hard enough. The roughpalm, though, made Alonzo glad that he had the fish to dive after. So when once in a while a local reminded him of an island superstition like, "To dive is to kick our God in the face," or, "The creatures of the ocean are thirsty for the blood of man," the young Alonzo Toomer didn't listen to them or care. Otherwise there was only the skiff and Hanno and nowhere for him to go, which maybe would've let those heartleeches get the too much better of him for way too many days in a row. No; he'd stay in the water alldaylong and only swim to the skiff when he absolutely had to, to put a sack of fish or conch in it, or maybe even an octopus or a turtle he'd snatched up off the oceanfloor. Even then, though, Hanno would sometimes look into a sack, take out maybe a conch, and throw it at his son. "We need more fish!" he'd shout at him, to which the young Alonzo Toomer would rightaway grab his sling and immediately dive back to the bottom until a good twenty-plus fish had been caught and hopefully even some blue or white crabs to boot. The heartleeches, Alonzo would tell himself when he'd later row them back to the beach, they won't beat me today. And they won't beat me tomorrow either. I'll beat them all until the day that I am free.

———

The first mile on the road to Animal Bay was the white mile from the shoreline sand having steadily pushed its way towards the middle of the island. The second mile was the red mile that was everywhere the color of blood. It was along the third and black mile, though, that Hanno always came to his fullstop to watch the early-evening sun ease a hotfierygold right behind the horizonline, and where the young Alonzo Toomer sometimes watched the sunlight colors changing on the old man's lostsomething face. He used to wonder what it was that made Hanno stare so deep and long at that slowly-going sun. Maybe Hanno imagined the places it went while it lit up the rest of the world, or maybe he tried to remember what it might've looked like back when he was himself a boy, or maybe he simply believed it the beautifulest thing to keep happening and happening all throughout his life. Only after the sun had fully gone would Hanno come back to his senses and continue along the black mile, which, if it wasn't for a fullmoon sometimes lightbulbing up the land to show an on-and-off-again lizard or flamingo or some other kind of island animal, could look to have not a lick of life left on it.

Years back, you see, the black mile had had enough vegetable farms to feed several islands around. But then a superstrong hurricane, the strongest to ever slam into the Bahama Islands, destroyed every tomato and shaddock, brown sapodilla and yellow jujube planted in the ground, leaving behind only a black black mile that, even in a not-too-hot-at-all sun, could easily smell of a badlyrotted land.

Another thing that Hanno was good at was fastwalking to

Animal Bay. By the time the skiff rum had faded he was always so into his bentforward, doublelimped stride that the young Alonzo Toomer always had some trouble keeping up with him because the roadcart that he pushed with all of the fish and conch and other things on it was so heavy. Except for that single sunset stop, Hanno was all about making it to the Green Turtle Market-Bar, where he'd every night meet up with the other men of the island—men who mostly worked in the salt works—for that never-to-be-missed first round of drinks. To miss that first round was to Hanno worse than missing a hundred blackmile sunsets. And if he ever did, Alonzo was sure to get himself a doubledose of roughpalm just out of frustration.

The Green Turtle was always busy with people buying, selling, and trading not only seafood but mangoes and purple seagrapes, tamarinds and scarlet plums, sorrels and soursop, limes, pawpaws, mammees, green sugar apples, and, of course, those everybody-eating bananas and plantains. Once there, Hanno always met up with the Green Turtle's owner, who I think was named Nestor, to show him the cartload of catch that the young Alonzo Toomer had already piled onto the long wooden market table. Nestor, as usual, eyeballed everything close, scribbled a number on a piece of paper, and handed the paper to Hanno, who always frowned at it as if banditrobbed, but then headed straight for the bar and the rum it had inside of it anyways. Then Nestor'd bring out a bowl of "Nestor's Famous Green Turtle Soup" with peas, rice, tomato salad, and some Johnnycake bread, and give it all to the young Alonzo Toomer, who always instantly dug right in. And by the time he'd finished eating, the buying and selling would usually've ended, the market closed, and the only nightsounds alive would be coming from the drinkingbar itself. Then, after sitting alone for some long quiet minutes, Alonzo would slowly get up and move the empty roadcart next to the bardoor to wait for his father Hanno to drink his fill of rum.

Since the time he could walk pretty good, the young Alonzo Toomer's life went this way. He'd in the morning ready the skiff to row it out to sea, dive for whatever in the water sold the best at market while an upabove Hanno slowly but surely drained his bottle of rum, and then pushed that catchhaving roadcart to Animal Bay where he'd finally eat his food and wait for old Hanno to rumstumble out of the bar itself. Oh, and he'd get that daily, all-upside-his-head dose of roughpalm. But believe it or not, and except for all that roughpalm business, the young Alonzo Toomer didn't really mind his island routine that much. He didn't mind all his time in the saltwater sun or the everyday trips to the small hustle-and-bustle of Animal Bay or especially not the very long waits outside of the drinkingbar itself, which a lot of the time had the most interesting thing of all: drunken men who conversationed on about anything and everything that popped into their ever-more-tipsy heads. Sitting outside the bar, the young Alonzo Toomer sometimes believed he was learning more about his life on the island than if Hanno would've let him stay in school like he wanted. Take the weather, for example. Alonzo learned that hurricanes had their very own seasons and reasons for hitting the Caribbean and America so much of the time and not the other parts of the world. According to one of the bar conversations, every hurricane had in it the spirit of a dead slave that'd gone shipoverboard during that great shameless slave trade that he'd heard so much about. The slave spirit, they said, was angry and revengeful for having been taken from its land and left in the middle of all that Atlantic water and so came back as a destroying-everything-in-its-path hurricane. Sitting outside the bar, the young Alonzo Toomer also learned about a Morton Salt company that'd once wanted to move all the people of Little Inagua to another island so as to turn the whole of their own into one big salt factory—a thing that all of the men, and most of all Hanno, had at the time been absolutely upset about and which had scared Alonzo terribly whenever he'd afterwards thought about it. Luckily for everyone it didn't ever happen. Other things he learned about were sports and fishing and wives and children. But what was talked most about was money, a subject that instantly heavied up voices or would make the men so all-of-a-sudden quiet that you could feel them saddening right into their barstools. "I work all day and for so little pay," one of them once said, or, "I would like to one time, *just one,* buy my wife a beautiful dress like they sell in Nassau," or, "I have no sons, so how will I live when I can work no more?" It was sometimes an awful thing to have to hear the men talk about, money. But they just couldn't help it, and only Hanno alone didn't complain. Instead, he said something like, "So long as you have your money for rum, you have money enough," in a voice so flat and hard it pushed all the other voices right up against the barwall. "There's more to life, Hanno," said one of the men all testydrunk recently, though, "than all of the time rum, rum, rum." "Like what?" said Hanno. "Like the rest of the world." "The rest of the world . . . ," said Hanno back you're crazy-like. "This island is your world, so don't bother about any of the rest of it." But all of the men at the same time disagreed. "Where then?" said Hanno all mean, to which the men altogether said "New York City!" as if they'd practiced to answer him that way every hour of every day since they'd been alive. "There we can make real money, Hanno"; "And have ourselves a future"; "And send enough back for our families to live and then later follow us." Hanno, though, just laughed. "You know what New York City is?" he said to them. "It is eighty blocks of eightystory buildings, that's what. The water around it is so dirty, you cannot even put a foot or finger into it without needing to see a doctor. There are *ten million* greedy people living right on top of each other and always more coming. And everyone of them miserable! Believe me, you will each go crazy, die, or kill someone in a place like that. I know!" Then, before any of the men could argue back, Hanno suddenly coughed real hard into his handkerchief until a small spot of blood was on it, and for the longest time nobody said a word. "They are getting stranger, I tell you," Hanno finally said down at his lap.

"What are getting stranger, Hanno?" said one of the men all secrety quiet.

"The sunsets," said Hanno with a slow headlift, and as if he was seeing right through the barwall and up against that eversetting sun. "They have a very violent burn that they've never had before."

"That's because the summer is coming."

"No!" snapped Hanno in that sunsetseeing voice. "They are different! I have been watching them very very closely. They burn more violent, I tell you, and fall to the sea much faster than before."

"Yes, Hanno," said another of the men then, "and maybe when they're high overhead you sit under them for too many hours each day," which got a small rolling chuckle from the others in the bar.

"Okay," said Hanno to the men, though, "go and laugh. But I am telling you, something very bad is going to happen on this island soon; something much much worse than the great hurricane; and it worries me."

"Then maybe it is time for us to go," said one of the men. "And maybe time for you to come along too."

" 'Come along'?" said Hanno in that still-off-over-the-ocean-somewhere voice of his. "Where are you going?"

"To New York City!" he said, and all the men started to laugh and laugh like never before. Outside the bar, though, the young Alonzo Toomer could only hear how unhappy old Hanno had been.

———

Hours later, Hanno stumbled through the bardoor with his nextday's rum bottle in hand as usual. He climbed onto the roadcart, laid on his back, and instantly fell asleep, his arms sprawling wide and his mouth open up enough for a very small star to plop right into it. Then the cart was in motion, with Hanno jiggling around on it all the way to the shack.

The young Alonzo Toomer slept not a wink that night for two different reasons. He couldn't stop thinking about that place that Hanno had talked about with its tall tall buildings that went on for so many stories and blocks. Not that he knew what a block was, but he guessed it at least as long as the white, red, or black mile, or maybe even the roundtrip row out to sea and back. But a story he knew about from the time Nestor had talked of building the drinkingbar on top of the market, but didn't. That would've been a second story, he remembered Nestor saying, and those two times forty more were way too many for the young Alonzo to imagine just going and going up, up, up and never falling down. Then he wondered what it must feel like being with ten-million people in such a tight and built-up city, and all of them all the time working, working, working for nothing but money, money, money. Maybe like a human kind of hurricane, he thought.

The other thing that kept him awake was Hanno, who nonstop coughed until the early-morning sunrise came.

One day the young Alonzo Toomer was diving for fish as usual when a big white boat showed on the sea. It was headed towards the skiff where Hanno was sitting with his bottle of rum and dropline and Alonzo started to swim that way. The closer he got to the boat the more he saw a man and woman and boy and girl standing on the deck. They had on the most-expensivelooking clothes Alonzo had ever seen; clothes he was sure even the business-owning Nestor couldn't afford to buy. When the boat got close enough, the man, who had some binoculars hanging around his neck, said, "Hello there," to Hanno, "we saw you not far off and thought that he," he being a pointed-at Alonzo, "should know that a pretty-goodsized hammerhead is scouting these waters not more than a quartermile out."

"Thank you very much," said Hanno to the man in this suddenly superchildish voice that'd completely surprised Alonzo when he'd heard him use it, making him rightaway realize that he'd never even seen Hanno speak to a non-Inaguan before. Hanno had even done a kind of headbow when he'd thanked the man.

When the young Alonzo Toomer looked back at the big white boat, a strange suspicious feeling about the people on its deck suddenly curioused up his mind. He didn't know what it was exactly, maybe those clothes, or the woman's necklace, or even their sunglasses and hair, but he thought he sensed a special kind of something about them.

"Where are you people from?" he suddenly asked, which got him a quick and fullhating glare from the gladly-out-of-range Hanno.

"New York," said the woman, which didn't surprise Alonzo at all.

"Is that the same as New York City?"

"Why yes, I'm sorry, New York City," said the woman. "Have you been there?"

Alonzo noed his head, and inside was very surprised to notice not a drop of misery on her face.

"Please excuse my son," said a childishsounding Hanno again, and with that same silly headbow to boot, "but he is young and—"

"What's it like?" said a butting-in Alonzo, though, which made Hanno's face so angry, Alonzo could already feel the roughpalm to come. But at that moment he didn't care; for some strong reason, you see, he had to know what New York City was like.

"New York, how do you explain it?" said the woman to her family. "Impressive, I guess."

"And fun," said the boy.

"And exciting," said the girl.

"And exhausting," said the man.

"The best and worst of everything in the world is in New York," said the woman, who then looked at the island and the sea and the sky all around her and sighed. "Except for this."

"Isn't everybody in New York greedy and miserable,

though?" said Alonzo, which suddenly made the man and woman laugh out loud.

"Some, I suppose," she said, with another look at the man. "We're greedy in a way, aren't we, Henry?"

"Only out of necessity, dear," said the man back to her. "Only out of necessity."

"And of course there's misery," said the woman. "Often lots of it. But for the most part people seem okay. Don't you think, Henry?" Henry yessed. "Misery, though, you can find everywhere," she said, and again took a look all around her. "Well, except here maybe. Do you have any misery here?"

While the woman waited for his answer, the young Alonzo Toomer tried his hardest not to look Hanno's way, but just couldn't help himself. It was really only the smallest of small sideglances, but had been to Hanno many times worse than if Alonzo had stared straight at his rum bottle alldaylong.

"Sometimes," said Alonzo, looking away from Hanno. "We can have very bad storms that can last a very long time."

"And sharks," said the man, ready to work the boat-wheel again. "Do beware of the sharks. Especially hammer-heads. The one we saw looked very big and *very* hungry." Then they all said goodbye and the big white boat headed back to the blue and finally disappeared around the island.

The next few days the roughpalm was terrible. "You like to embarrass old Hanno, do you?" *(Slap)* "You think a tourist woman knows better than Hanno, eh?" *(Slap)* "You want to go to New York City now, do you?" *(Slap)* "Let us starve!" *(Slap)* "He wants to be a bigshot now!" "In New York City!" "Alonzo the bigcity bigshot!" *(Slap, slap, slap)* "Over my dead body! From now on Hanno will keep a very close eye on you."

For the whole week after the big white boat had gone, the young Alonzo Toomer dove very close to the skiff. He didn't like not swimming as far as he had to to spear for the good fish catch, but to be stuck all alone with a big hungry hammerhead for company wasn't what he had in mind either. Instead, he took more conch than usual from the oceanfloor, and a good amount of sponge too, and no matter how much Hanno yelled to him to catch them some more fish, Alonzo just wouldn't do it.

Every day that'd passed after the big white boat, Hanno had coughed a lot harder too. The coughing at one point got so bad he even started to buckle over and lose his balance and breath. And then there was that also-getting-worse-than-it'd-been-at-the-bar handkerchiefblood that'd gone from small spot to very big blot. Finally, after the young Alonzo Toomer couraged himself up for it, he said, "Maybe I should get a doctor for you," to which Hanno snapped, "So you can sneak off to New York City while you're at it? To be a bigcity bigshot? *No!* I know your tricks and I'm not letting you away from my sight!"

In those badcoughing days Hanno's eyes had gotten darker, too, and his cheeks had sunk in so deep you could see the sharp-edged facebones just underneath them. On the walk to Animal Bay his gotta-get-myself-to-the-drinkingbar stride wasn't the same, either, making him miss that never-to-be-missed first round of rum five days running. Then one afternoon, Hanno raised his arm as usual to give the young Alonzo some of that everday dose of roughpalm, but no longer had the strength enough to unload it. It was from that point on that the young Alonzo Toomer knew that something terribly permanently was wrong was the case with the man.

And a week later, and on a day that had to be the strangest one to ever happen in the young Alonzo Toomer's life, Hanno suddenly died.

That day the island calm was so quiet you'd have thought the world in a badlyneeded oversleep. The birds didn't chirp, the sea didn't splash, and Hanno'd illed up-to-the-point-of-coughlessness sick. Out next to a small and fish-schoolbusy reef, Alonzo dove around for some fish, caught a bunch, took them to the skiff as usual, and then returned to the reef for the fifth time that day. After hunting around for a goodlong stretch, though, he noticed that all of the fish were suddenly gone. Just like that they'd disappeared. When Alonzo finally looked up, he noticed the skiff was gone too, which rightaway made him want to go for the watersurface.

But he didn't. Alonzo, you see, had been diving long enough to know that if a whole entire fishschool suddenly up and disappeared, as well as Hanno in the skiff, then a not-so-very-good thing had to be happening in the water somewhere near him. So he stayed close to the reef, checking around and wondering what it might've been that could've chased a whole healthy fishschool off so quick, and then, just as he'd figured it out, he saw the nastylooking answer moving right by him a very big and slow and very deadlyeyed. The hammerhead.

After it'd passed around the reef, Alonzo bolted for the straight-up-above-him air, all the while searching around for shark. But he saw none. At the surface he sucked in deep one, two, three times for air, and then checked around for Hanno and the skiff, which he noticed already rowed a goodways to the beach. That was when he saw the not-so-far-away-from-him waterbump wave right for him along the oceansurface. By the time the young Alonzo Toomer got into his full-stroking swim mode, the shark had closed the gap to maybe half of their old distance. Keep your arms and legs moving, Alonzo told himself. If the hammerhead wants to get me he'll have to grow an extra fin. When he neared the skiff, Alonzo saw how Hanno's eyes had feared up large from the sight of the hardcoming hammerhead just behind him, and that way knew that the shark had gained some more. With maybe ten fullswim strokes left for the beach, though, Alonzo suddenly slowed from his fullswim to look back at Hanno's stillfearing eyes. What keeps me from just stopping cold? he wondered as he slowed. I don't have the same kind of worry old Hanno has, do I? The same cowardy shaking because of a storm coming? My hard swimming doesn't mean that we are the same exact people, does it? Scared of a simple little sunset. Do I really fear like he fears? Then, at a single strong stroke from the beach, Alonzo suddenly saw nothing but wideopen, ready-to-lunge-for-his-leglows sharkmouth rise way up out of the water and all on their own his arms pulled as hard as they could while a sharp sharp pain hit his right foot just as he made it to beachsand, where his acting-automatic body went from the endswim to a fastcrawl to an even faster footrun in one singlesmooth motion, until finally he'd dropped to his knees and then his stomach. Alonzo felt the sun very hot on his back as he breathed in the saltwater air while waiting for the strange footpain to go away. But it didn't. When he finally got up and looked to his foot he noticed the pinkietoe completely bitten off and the red red blood running out from the wound like rain down a windowpane. Some of my life is gone, Alonzo simply said to himself, only to realize he was laughing maybe the hardest he'd ever laughed in his life, and that he'd been doing so ever since he'd seen that fearfilled look on Hanno's face from the sight of that hammerhead cruising mean and lean by his skiff side. Those eyes, thought the young Alonzo Toomer as he laughed and watched that red-ness flow heavy from his missing toespace, they were the eyes of the smallest child. To match that voice of his. All this time, he laughed to himself, Hanno's been nothing but a cruel cruel child and I didn't even know it. And he laughed and laughed at that thought as if badlygonecrazy.

When he finally turned to the sea, Alonzo discovered an incredible thing: the hammerhead, so greedymad for a good taste of him, had run itself completely out of the water and all the way up the beach, leaving a deep and wide sandgroove behind it. How was it possible for that shark to be so hungry for me? Alonzo wondered. Then he saw the paddling-in-on-him Hanno and immediately spotted the best-sized heaviest piece of driftwood he could find, picked it up, and fastwalked it back to the shark, which was bigeyeing the world as if notunderstanding how it'd come to have the not-so-familiar, out-of-water view that it had. Then, standing over the shark but looking straight into Hanno's eyes, Alonzo said a quick, "I'm sorry, my friend, but you've tried your very last sharkattack," and lifted the driftwood high up in the air and slammed it down as hard as he could on the hammerhead's skull. The big fish shivered, bodybent, and shook, and then finally laid a very fulldead on the sand.

Hanno got out of the skiff, walked up to the shark, and meanfaced his son to say something, but could only stutter. When he managed to up his hand to give Alonzo a slap, he froze this time not from any sickness of his, but from the never-happened-before sight of Alonzo's also-lifted, home-runcocked piece of driftwood. "I dare you to, old man," he warned his father cold. "Just know that I will strike back hard," to which old Hanno started to tremble all over as if back beneath that stormblanket, and as if Alonzo had become the terriblest scariest manmade hurricane he'd ever had to upclose witness in his life. Slowly, Hanno dropped his hand and turned around for the shack. Looking at his back, Alonzo could feel that laughing want to grow very strong inside of him again, but instead calmed it down to feel those heartleeches one by one go far outside of his body. "Never again will I let them get in," he promised himself. "Never."

An hour later Hanno came out of the shack a different-behaving man. For one he pretended his son was nowhere near to being on the island with him and refused to even glance at the boy's bloody foot, and for another, he was in this out-to-prove-a-point, don't-need-a-lick-of-help-from-anybody mode. He tied a very thick longrope to the roadcart's frontend and all by himself pulled it down to the shark, where he tilted the cart down onto the sand. After many impossible solo tugs, though, Alonzo decided to help old Hanno out, and after maybe fifteen more minutes of lifting, yanking, and ropegilling the rubberskinned beast, they together had it stretched flat and firm on the cartsurface. Then Hanno grabbed the longrope and pulled the cart as if into the strongest stiffest stormwind ever and, only after Alonzo had started to push real hard from the backend did the cart finally begin to move off of the beach and onto the white mile.

He'd never seen Hanno work so hard in his life, he

thought. By the end of the white mile the old man was such a sweatdrenchedwet, you'd have thought him just climbed out of the sea. Not only that, but his lungs heaved for every ounce of oxygen they got. A couple of times he'd even tripped and fallen to his knees, only to pull himself back up again by the very longrope that he pulled with. For a sick old rumdrinking man, thought Alonzo, Hanno still had a serious energy to him. Near the end of the red mile, though, and the roadcart started to slow down some, and by the start of the black mile it barely even moved, no matter how hard they pushed and pulled. Then Hanno saw the redgold sun already fattened and wide near the horizonline. Rightaway he stopped his pulling, let go of the longrope, coughed real hard in his hands, and turned himself towards that soon-to-be-suneating sea. When it'd dropped to its oceansurfacelowest, Hanno stepped to the roadedge as if to follow after it, but instead stopped and looked at it as if unsure what it was anymore. His shoulders sagged heavy and his mouth hung open wide as if desert thirsty. Suddenly he coughed again and brought a quick hand to his mouth, at which point a sharp pain seemed to hit him in the chest, which he rightaway grabbed with both of his hands. Then a few seconds later his arms dropped to his sides.

After the sun had finally gone, Hanno still stayed completely silent as he stared and stared at the horizonline. He didn't make a move; just stood and stared at the everywhere leftover light as if frozen into place by it. After maybe ten minutes of waiting, Alonzo finally said that they should continue for Animal Bay or Hanno'd once again miss that first round of rum with his friends. But Hanno didn't say a word and just stood and stared some more at that getting-darker-by-the-minute horizonline. Finally Alonzo stepped in front of Hanno to again let him know how it was time for them to go, but suddenly stopped cold when he saw Hanno full in the face. What Alonzo discovered were these openstaring eyes and an openthirsty mouth that had not the smallest bit of life left in them. Alonzo waved a had-to-be-sure hand in front of that face, but after it didn't flinch the slightest reaction back, he knew for sure that his father was dead. For the longest time Alonzo just stared into that deadawful face in front of him and wondered if he should finally give it a slap or two. Not hard, mind you, but not so soft that he wouldn't feel it on his hand either. Then he saw the roadcarted shark and thought of all the credit it would bring him at Nestor's. Maybe even enough for a ticket off of the island; to New York City. Instead of taking it along, though, Alonzo headed for Animal Bay alone, leaving the shark on the cart with Hanno standing on the roadedge a very stonedead in the getting-darker dark.

"I need a shovel," said Alonzo to Nestor. "You can take it from our credit."

"Sure thing, Alonzo," said Nestor, who went to the back of his store and returned with a shovel inhand. "Where's your father and the fishcart tonight?"

"It was a bad day for fish," said Alonzo, "and Hanno, he's gotten very sick."

"Too sick for rum?" said Nestor all surprised. "That is hard to believe," to which Alonzo said not a single word. "Come to think of it, though, the old man has been looking a bit off lately, hasn't he?"

"Yes he has," said Alonzo.

Then Nestor handed the shovel to him. "By the way, Alonzo, what do you need this shovel for?"

Alonzo stared into Nestor's eyes for a reason to tell him the truth. But he found none. "To dig a hole with, of course."

"You are becoming a farmer then, huh?"

"Something like that."

"Well good luck," said Nestor, "because you know how bad the weather can get around here, right Alonzo?"

Alonzo slowly yessed his head. "The days after can be very beautiful, though, can't they?" he said.

Nestor smiled deep and wide and looked around at the night. "Yes they can, Alonzo. Yes they can."

Hanno stood just as he had left him, openeyed and staring at the mostly-pitchblack horizonline. As Alonzo dug and dug, he started to think about all that other death that'd already happened along the black mile and about how the main things about a person's life must suddenly've changed forever after that terrible storm had hit. When the hole was big enough for Hanno to fit in, Alonzo kept on digging. He dug deeper and wider and longer until the earthpile next to the hole almost spread clear across to the other side of the road. After he'd finished, he climbed out of the hole, went over to Hanno, leaned him back into his arms, and drug the old man backwards to the hole edge. Then he slid him down into it. Next Alonzo went to the roadcart, pushed it too to the edge of the hole, and with the every bit of strength that he had tipped it onto its side. The shark slid off so rough and fast it landed a very sloppyhard right on top of Hanno. Seeing them down there together, Alonzo knew he'd maybe done a very disrespectful thing, and most likely a thing against another one of those island superstitions at that. But deep to his tiredfeeling bones he just couldn't seem to care. Hanno, he thought, should always be in his death the way he'd always been in life, and the shark along for company would always remind him of how exactly that was. Then Alonzo filled in the hole and headed for his home.

Tomorrow, he thought, will be a big and different time for me. I will have a very new life to live. But first I must go home and rest. And then tomorrow I'll have a brandnew day.

"Nice pants," said this richboy to me day one in lunchline.

I looked at the faded brown corduroys I had on a full up and down and then at him and the three looking-just-like-him friends he was with. At the new junior highschool I attended his type seemed to be everywhere. They were the sons of longshoremen mostly, along with those of other excellent-moneyearning waterfront workers. "What's wrong with 'em?"

"You shouldn't be wearing them, that's what," he said, as if holding nothing but blackjack. "And you shouldn't be wearing the belt and shoes you have on either."

While those eight full-of-judgment eyes grilled me all over, my mind quickly backpedaled to try and remember exactly where the pants, belt, and shoes I had on had come from. After what'd felt like a reverseful hour, though, I gave it up, knowing damnwell that the richboy was telling me the ninetynine-percent truth of the matter. Nevertheless, I couldn't just agree with him. To do so would've branded me the worst kind of pathetic scavenger to've to ever lived on the earth. And on day one of school at that. "If they're not mine, whose are they then?" I said to him, suddenly groaning inside for having foolishly opened a door for him.

"The city's," he said all matter-of-fact. "That's who usually gets what I've thrown into the garbage." When some sudden gasps and laughs kicked in from the side, I turned my head to see a good dozen-plus students already gathered as-though-me-and-the-richboy-were-gonna-start-to-fight tight. And they all looked just like him too. That was when the redhot shame started to push its way right through my face.

"What I have on," I said in a surrounded-by-the-enemy, wobblyweak voice, "my moms bought me."

"Your 'moms,' " said the richboy then. "What the hell is a 'moms'?"

"Don't lie!" said some damnnear-screaming-at-me girl before I could answer him, though; a girl who I swear I'd never seen or laid an eye on before. She wore these braces and had the hatefullest face you'd ever seen in your life. Possessed even. I had no idea how, not ever having met the girl, I could've offended her so bad. But I had. "I saw you and your mother digging through peoples' trashcans one night! You guys even took a fishtank that our nextdoorneighbor threw out. I saw you take it!"

An hour later my brandnew principal, a Mr. Cepeda, suspended me for a solid week-and-a-half. Not for having gotten busted sporting some trashtaken clothes to school, mind you, but for having coldcocked a fellow student while in lunch-line—the student being that loudmouthed, embarrassing-me-for-no-good-reason-at-all girl.

The trashdigging was moms's trip. It was her out. Going on the constant digs was like her very own security blanket. If people hadn't put their unwanteds on the sidewalks, moms might've gone mad a while ago. On trash nights it was like she had these unbreakable appointments, and since the stuff was sidewalked twice a week she'd be out twice a week, no fail. And I'd be right there with her: digging.

It wasn't only my clothes that came from the sweeps we did, but damnnear everything in the apartment. The living-room sofa, for example, we found on Mesa and Santa Cruz Streets, the kitchen table a block away from there, and the livingroom carpet way up on Sixth and Center. I remember exactly where those had come from because of how long they took to get home. Other things we'd personalized were our beds and blankets, a turntable plus nineteen LPs, and a matching set of forty office chairs we'd come across behind the going-out-of-business-for-good Pacific Trade Center. Oh, and that fishtank.

To get the chairs to the apartment, moms had actually begged me into making nineteen-and-a-half ten-block roundtrips with them, which'd kept me up all the way through the night. At some point during those nineteen-and-a-half back-and-forths I believe Mosley, a neighborhood porchwino I'd every time passed with two chairs at a time at the corner of Third and Palos Verdes Streets, went crazy. After maybe the fifth roundtrip, you see, and who knows how much taken in wine later, Mosley's "déjà vu" turned into a "déjà fuckin' vu" that'd by roundtrip number eight or nine turned into a "déjà *mother*fuckin' vu!" When I saw the guy a few days later his head was still moving side to side as if watching this neverending, make-believe tennis match, with him every once in a while throwing in that still-surprisedsounding "déjà *mother*fuckin' vu!"

One late night moms almost got herself a washing machine too, but we couldn't seem to get it all the way home. To be honest, we couldn't even get it off of the block we'd found it on. Whenever we'd pushed and pulled it along, it'd made the terriblest, as-if-scraping-the-concrete-right-off-the-sidewalktop noise. After just a quarterblock of struggle, *I* knew the mission hopeless. But because all we'd ever done was sink-and-bathtubscrub our laundry to death, moms had wanted that washing machine in the worst possible way. Every ten feet or so, though, someone somewhere screamed at us to let the thing be, but moms wouldn't hear of it and kept pushing along while all the while telling me to pull my heart out, until finally this old, bathrobewearing woman actually came outside to stroll up to us to very politely explain how truly badlybroken the washing machine was. "I'm the one who put it out," she'd said in a nice soft voice, the whole time looking right at moms's desperategotten eyes. "It's motor's completely worthless, young lady, and would cost a fortune to fix. I'm back to using my hands myself." Moms, needless to say, went home a very blue blue.

Sometimes I resisted going on the dig, but moms would every time talk me into it, especially if she wasn't hooked up with another keeping-her-in-the-apartment-all-day guy of some kind—like Goldie. "C'mon, Sunny," she'd say all chummy to me, once again using my first name in hopes of getting something out of me. "I'll be too lonely without you," or, "You know I'm not strong enough to carry anything (meaning maybe a fullsized piano, I'd think) home by myself," or, "What if I run into someone dangerous? How would you feel then?" And like always I'd always give in and tag along. But even then, the first few blocks into the dig I'd mostly have this funkyawful upsetgrumpiness in and all about me, while thinking something like: of all the parents on a planet of five-point-something-billion heads, why'd I have to end up with the one that absolutely positively has to go through other peoples' overflow for a hobby? I mean why couldn't she be interested in another something normal, like those singing lessons she'd started to take? Or why not maybe painting or camping or quilt quilting even? Hell, habitgambling à la the Grizz sounded better than *trash*digging!

The upsetgrumpiness would hit me for another reason too: I didn't want the fellas to spot me out on the dig once again—and especially not on the way *back* through the projects with maybe another exercise bike or headboard in tow.

If so, it'd always be a thing I'd have to hear about not only then and there but for days and sometimes even weeks after that—depending on the goods carried by of course, which could sometimes be the worst kind of ridiculous.

Check this out: one night moms had me carry home three mannequins that we'd come across in front of this women's clothing shop up on Pacific Avenue. Two of them were lying facefirst on the sidewalk while the third stood a very skinnytall against this batbusted parkingmeter with her right hand sticking out as if hoping to hitch a highwayride. They were all three a very assnaked and, for some crazy reason, moms immediately had to have them. "Why!" I said to her all disbelieving. "Why do I have to explain it to you?" she said back, though. "I just want them, that's all." And with that she drooped right to her knees and got to tying the two on the ground together with these badlyfaded T-shirts we'd found earlier on the dig.

Watching her at work, I suddenly had this very ugly urge to dropkick every parkingmeter in sight, and then even her after that. It was the kind of behavior that just made me want to forever walk away from her. I mean, if we'd had a bus or a van of some kind, I could maybe've gotten hip to her sudden need to own a tossed out triplet of lifeless women. That way we could've at least snuck our ridiculous-ass cargo back through the Ranch a very wellhidden from any possible out-and-abouters. But we didn't. Then the more that I watched her tying those two grounded mannequins together, the more I realized I could never've left

her an all-alone exposed to who knew the kind of mean re-
marks she was sure to run into. I'd have to stay with her to
the last man, I told myself, knowing that if I did, one-hun-
dred percent of any and all attention would come my way,
not hers. Especially since I'd be the one carrying her newly-
gotten goods.

Before we entered the Ranch with those mannequins
the last thoughts I had were, one, how featherlight they all
three felt in my hands, and two, that please, god, *please,* don't
let any of the fellas be along our returnroute home through
the neighborhood. But as always there they were, laid out
long along the grass as if just waiting for me and the crazywoman known as my moms to come strolling by. Right
when I'd spotted them, each of the mannequins instantly
sagged heavier in my arms than the longest, brokendown,
filled-to-the-brim-with-ten-of-the-deepestasleep-over-
weight-winos-ever Cadillac you could imagine. And as soon
as the fellas saw how I was coming along, they deadstopped
whatever their conversation had been to gawk, giggle, and of
course, cold cold comment on my latest of conditions.

"Introduce us to your friends, Toomer," said my supposedly good friend Richard.

"Why're you treating your girls like that?" said Will
Man.

"Yeah; why don't you leave us one, homes," said another. "Don't be greedy."

Ha-ha-ha-ha-ha, they busted out.

Ha-ha-ha, I thought back at them, trying my hardest to

grin-agree, but instead feeling a very angryfrustrated. Even moms had a goddamn laugh going about it all, seeming not to feel a crumb of shame about our situation, which instantly turned me to a badlybubbling boil that had me hoping for nothing less than to get back out of sight ASAP, and then forever after that.

It was one of the reasons I'd spent so much of my recent time at the library and not at any of their expected-you-to-hang-out-at-'em apartments. To get away from all that teasingtension like the trashdig that could so quickly and easily build up in our tightest of livingspaces. I mean, if you'd been feeling as raw as I had during those early El Niño days with a Goldie always smack in your face about something, the library quiet and not some constantly-jabbing-at-you friends would've made the most sense to you too. Not that I could've told it to the fellas like that. When they'd discovered I was hanging out at the reading room, for example, they just couldn't figure it.

"Why would you wanna be spending your days in the library?" one of them said to me.

"Yeah," said another. "We ain't good enough for you anymore, or what?"

"It's not that," I told them all. "Up at the library they've got all these sports and fishing magazines that break down everything you'd wanna know about the stuff."

"Magazines? Who needs a magazine when we've got the Pink Building and Big Park to hit up?"

"Yeah, but during El Niño?" I said. "When you can't

even see ten feet in front of you? All you guys do is watch television."

"What's wrong with that?"

"Nothing if you like commercials," I said. "They make me crazy, though."

None of them said anything for a stretch.

But then, "You wouldn't be sneaking in a book here and there, would you, Toom?" said one of them then, which had them all microscoping me like some madlymad professors.

"A book!" I finally said, though. "What in the world would I want with a book?"

"Just wondering, Toom. Thought that you were maybe trying to improve your grades or something, that's all." They all started to laugh, with me joining in on the third or fourth ha.

"Why do you always have to laugh along with people who're laughing at us?" I first thing around the corner said to moms.

"What?" she said back, though, all I-don't-get-your-reaction like. "C'mon, Toomer. It was kind of funny how you were carrying all those tiedtogether mannequins like that."

"If it's so funny, then you carry 'em past those idiots," I told her, even more aboil than before.

"Don't be so serious," she said all above-it-all then. "They're *your* friends; and anyways, what they say shouldn't bother you so much."

"It's not what they say that bothers me," I told her. "I just don't like being laughed at. By them or anybody else. And I especially don't like us being laughed at together! It embarrasses you, doesn't it?"

Then a longdrawnquiet happened between us. "All right, all right," she finally said. "I won't do it again, okay? I promise."

Bullshit, I rightaway told myself. I knew better.

For weeks all the fellas asked me about were the "girlies." They wanted to know which one I was crashing with; was she good?; did she have bad breath?; a nice backside?; firm titties?; ha-ha-ha-ha-ha—for *weeks.* As if they'd ever been with any girls themselves. As they say, though: same old flies, different shit, right? Hell no, because both of them are a bad thing to swallow.

Meanwhile, moms had the mannequins standing in her bedroom in this perfect, leaning-against-the-wall row, just staring out of her viewless window assnaked as ever. Lined up that way they looked like three dizzystiff, lonely, nowhere-to-go people. Then one day she actually started to play lifesized dolls with the poor things. First came the mascara, nailpolish, and lipstick, then the wigs and wardrobes. I couldn't believe it. Like a crazywoman's slumber party. If she starts conversationing with 'em, I told myself more than once, all three of them are going straight into the harbor—maybe moms included. But then she finally met another guy and decided to throw them out on her own.

"Making your ass carry mannequins through the neighborhood!" said a finally-serious-again, just-the-two-of-us-on-the-cornergrass Richard. "Like some goddamn circusprops. No disrespect or anything, Toom, 'cause you know I'm down with you and all, but moms is absolutely trippin'."

"Whose isn't?" I said to him all defensive-like.

"You know what I mean," said Richard, though. "The woman's messing with your head."

"And you guys aren't with all that hilarious bullshit you talk."

"That's just clownin' around, Toom," he said. "Just think how bad it would've been if all we'd done was sit around quietly while you carried your girlies, I mean mannequins, past. We were just trying to keep things loose, that's all. For everybody's sake."

I thought about it and agreed that a stonecold silence might've been just as badfeeling as the laughs had been, and then laughed about it myself for the first time in what had to be a month.

"But seriously, Toom, what could moms have possibly

wanted with some goddamn mannequins anyways?" Richard finally said.

But since I was as puzzled as he was I had no way of answering him back, which, like that lunchline situation, was often how moms's mad behavior had left me around others. No matter how hard I thought her actions through, time and time again the questions couldn't find the answers. Take her relationship with Goldie, for example. Even though the man had lately shown some strong signs of a deepdown dangerousness—for example, he'd one day in all deadseriousness told some person on the telephone that he was going to break their doublecrossing back that very night, and on another day came into the apartment with a fistful of bloodshredded knuckles from having punched at someone through a moving carwindow—moms nevertheless continued to have this kind of reckless lovesickness for him. I don't know what it was about her, but nothing let her judge the guy right. Not even after I'd finally secretly told her whatall had happened on the day I'd come into possession of this big gold necklace that Goldie'd damnnear killed a guy over. Even then, she just wouldn't come to her senses.

Sleep had me deep and good when the loud aggressive yelling started just outside my secondstory window. One look around the room and towards that window said it wasn't morning yet, and except for the weak creep of the just-off-the-corner streetlight, darkness had me surrounded. Way back, I used to worry in that lightcreep because of how it made the night barely seeable. My attitude had been, either light it fully up or keep it fully dark, but none of that inbetween nonsense that made you invent strange stuff around your room.

Again the yelling sounded loud. Just lying there, I knew the situation by heart: Goldie was squabbing with somebody. As I got out of bed, I halfasleep wondered how it was that their voices could travel through stone and glass, hard objects you couldn't hardly get through with even your hands and feet without messing them up real bad. But their voices did just that, and then even managed to dig deep themselves into my dreamworld to pull me up out of it.

I slid the curtain aside and saw the two on the frontyard below. They were fists up, toe-to-toe, and looking for an opening to swing through. And though the one guy had a serious size advantage, I instantly knew that Goldie would win. His unfearing face and firm-and-steady fists, you see, had this nasty incontroledness about them that the other, already-looking-as-if-to-capsize-to-the-ground guy's didn't.

It's weird, but during a squab I've never really wanted to see a next punch thrown. But once I've gotten fixed on the dance nothing could make me turn my head away. It's like I've become brainchained to the circumstance. Then I always get to rationalizing the situation in front of me. It all boils down to this anyway, no? I mean anywhere in the Ranch you go, anything you see, anyway you are, it's always the same toe-to-toe, head-to-head, fist-to-fist run-in. There's always and forever some kind of fight ready to jump off just around the next corner, or the one after that. Then, while I'm watching those two grown fools below, I'm suddenly trying to remember my dream. Because of how fully I'd sunk into sleep, I assumed it to be a good dream. But the more I tried to remember it, the more nothing came back to me. Remembering had become a frontyard struggle itself. Right in my own head, my mind was suddenly going toe-to-toe, snake and mongoose, just like the heads on the frontyard were doing. I'd get a nibble here, an odor there, and maybe a flavor somewhere else, but never the straight-up dream that I wanted.

They could've been differentsized twins, I finally realized, the main difference between them about *gold,* of all things. Goldie, of course, had that shiny gold tooth in the toprightmiddle part of his grille, while the other guy had this big gold necklace around his neck that was thick with quartersized goldpieces connected one to the other all the way around. The necklace had to be two feet long and weigh a good fifteen-to-twenty pounds too. And it wasn't only gold either. At its very bottomcenter it had this blood-colored jewel in it that was way thicker than any one of the quartersized goldpieces. More like a quarter fivestack.

Suddenly Goldie stepped with a leftfooted plant and released a speedy rightcross that connected with nothing but jawbone. The other guy's eyes instantly lit up, his knees buckled in, and he crumbled a very heavyhard to the ground. Goldie then jumped on the guy with uncountable lefts, rights, lefts and rights, beating him down for a long terrible minute until he himself had tired to the point of collapsing onto the downed guy's chest. After he'd caught his breath, Goldie removed the necklace from around the guy's neck and stood up with it. Then he pulled a handkerchief from a back pocket and cleaned and polished the metal until it looked ready for a shopwindow. "Home sweet home," he said to himself as if holding up a no-longer-kidnapped, made-of-the-purest-precious-gold newborn ever. "Home sweet home."

At first I'd assumed the too-big-to-be-true necklace a fake. Around the Ranch you forever had an uphard trying to talk you into buying this or that "fourteen-karat gold!" ring, watch, or necklace from him. And to find out if it was the real Don Steel or not, all you had to do was hit up the closestby available car, pop open its hood, uncap the battery, and stick whatever said-to-be-gold merchandise into the battery acid for a stretch. Then, if the ring, say, was plated and not real, you'd supposedly know it by this flaking or col-orchanging that was supposed to happen as soon as you pulled it out. But then again, I'd lately heard that the battery-acid test was only part of the scam; that battery acid could barely remove the dye off of an Easter egg. Nevertheless, you could never trust a "14K" knocked onto the metal itself.

But the Goldie necklace I believed to be real. I mean, who'd try and kill another person over imitation alone? Plus, when Goldie had removed the necklace, it'd hung in his hands like the heaviestsagging rope I'd ever seen. No, it was real all right. Not only that, it looked more expensive than every car, television, and stereosystem in the neighborhood combined. The necklace, I told myself, had to've come from someplace way outside of San Pedro. Maybe it'd been stolen off of some docking-in-the-harbor touristship—with possibly some superrich queen on board! Yeah, I thought; only a queen could own and sport a necklace like that! Goldie pridefully looked at his property, then at the guy on the yard. "Next time," he said to him, "I'll kill your punk-ass. You hear me? I'll kill anybody trying to claim my mer-chandise. You no good. . . ." and kicked the guy so hard on the temple that his head whipped even harder against his opposite-grounded shoulder. When a police siren sounded from maybe a block away, Goldie, in a quickmoving flash, took off up the street.

It was kind of my fault that moms and Goldie had hooked up. You see, I was the one in the apartment who'd usually done all the grocery runs, but while I was off with Richard back on that manydayed drivingspree, I hadn't been very available. So moms did them on her own. And it was while she was returning from the market one day, shoppingbag big in arms, that Goldie'd first noticed her and offered to carry her goods for her.

"Christ, was she a looker," he'd later said to me. "Beautiful, kneehigh dress, offblond hair pulled into a perfect little ponytail, enough sashay to make you wanna pray, and showing not a care in the world. When she told me she had a son back at home, I couldn't believe it. That body! I said to myself, has had a child? She had had to be kidding."

But the fact was, it'd always been easy enough for a man to involve himself with moms if only he could manage himself into her orbit somehow, which was mainly her rarely-left apartment—front and back porches included. That was how she'd at various times and intensities come to be involved with a Mormon missionary, for example, one of our mailmen (which is no kind of joke), a housing project's maintenance man, a rookie rollerboy (which not only thoroughly disgusted me the most, but had been one of the hardest things I'd ever had to keep a secret from people), and two or three just-strolling-through-the-projects-and-happened-to-be-lucky-enough-to've-noticed-this-very-attractive-woman-on-her-porch-one-day pedestrian types like Goldie. Luckily, none of any of those ever lasted. With moms, though, it was all about the luck of access, which, in a very strong sense, seemed her only true requirement for ever having hooked up with a single soul in the first place.

Back in bed, I stared at the ceiling and replayed the entire situation in my head. Who was the guy on the ground, I wondered, and how had he gotten hold of Goldie's necklace? Part of me believed I'd just seen a man executed, with the kick itself sending a powerful kind of electric shock through my system that'd damnnear paralyzed me in my heart. And all over a necklace too, I said to myself. But a queen's necklace, I suddenly corrected. What was one of those worth? I wondered, and instantly decided an amount too incredible to think of. Then I felt myself diving down again towards that place where my hard-to-remember dream could maybe hopefully finish itself if necessary. Up on the ceiling the red-and-blue rollerboy-and-ambulance lights popped and blitzed like mad, but no matter how crazyfast they did they couldn't stop my eyelids from closing me back into that deepdown darkness I'd so loudly gotten shaken out of.

The morning hit like a month later, and for a long lazy minute I had no idea what exact month I'd woken up in. Sun and white day flooded my eyes to the point of almost lifting me off of my bed. And when I finally did sit up I'd never felt more rested in all my life. A strange strength and energy filled up my arms and legs. Suddenly I remembered the middle-of-the-night happenings and stood up and headed for the window. Pigeons, the ugliest birds anywhere, sat on the across-the-way rooftops and telephonewires damnnear staring right back at me. Below the pigeons, a stray mutty dog wandered from car to car sniffing at all the tiresides. Then my eyes locked onto the frontyard grass. In an all-by-themselves daze, they searched around the yardgrass for any signs of a streetfight, but found none. No blood, no gold, not even the big guy's bodyprint. It was as if the squab had never happened. And maybe it hadn't, I thought. Maybe a nonstop-around-our-apartment Goldie was starting to mess with my dreamworld the way Papa Pierre and Chuy had done for so many years on end. The very notion of the guy tampering around in my deepasleep suddenly had me shivering in a chickenskin. Goldie in my deepasleep! In my very private dreamworld! I wanted nothing to do with it, but felt as trapped as some stuck-in-a-spider's-web housefly. The schoolhouse!, suddenly shot through my mind. I've got school today! I threw on some clothes, grabbed my backpack, and bailed from the room, somehow feeling absolutely saved by the soon-to-be-going-off schoolbell.

Down in the kitchen I saw a not-usually-up-so-early moms with her coffee. She sat at the table and mostly had her back to me, her dirtyblond hair hanging halfwaydown her spine. Around her the kitchen was the typical mess: piles of dishes, laundry, and leftover food. I was about to tip out the door when I stopped, walked around to the front of her, and said, "Where's Goldie this morning?"

Moms, though, just looked at me as-though-not-hearing-what-I'd-said-to-her strange, held the look for a long click, and then pushed it to the side of my head, as if a terribly trippy thought had landed itself on my shoulder. She had a beautiful expression on her face; the kind of expression that for a wonderful splitsecond made you feel that your life with her was going to be all right; that most of your days together would start to have more good than bad in them. I'd seen the expression before and called it her morning beautiful. Moms's eyes would go soft, her cheeks would relax, and she'd look ten years lighter than usual, which rightaway had me wishing she could always have whatever thoughts or feelings were behind that look. Instead of spoiling it I decided to change the subject.

"What are you doing today?"

"Goldie and I are having an afternoon date," she said, though, watching her coffeesteam rise hot from her cup. Then her eyes did a quick focus on me. "You don't mind me and Goldie going on a date, do you, Toomer?"

"Mind?" I said, surprised at the question. "You've got your own life; you know you can do what you want with it."

"Good," she said. "Just wanted to see if you were jealous or not."

"That's the stupidest thing I've ever heard," I told her all offended-like. "You know dirtyblondes aren't my style. And the dirtier the aren'ter."

"Is that right?" she said all fake-offended herself.

"That's right," I said, sounding more than sure of myself. It felt good to be joking around with her a little. Something we hadn't done in something like a year.

Then we stayed quiet for a stretch, me wanting to bail the apartment suddenly while the bailing was still good. But instead I stupidly stayed, and even invested into the conversation some more.

"Me and you," I couldn't help from saying, while feeling that that dream was getting to me again, "we should take a vacation together. Just the two of us. What do you think?"

Moms looked at me, though, as if that trippy thought that'd been on my shoulder had suddenly fluttered itself up only to land on the tipend of my nose. Then she slowly noed her downtilting head.

"Why not?" I said, suddenly wanting to talk her into it. "Only a one-week vacation. We could take a Greyhound busride, for example, to anywhere in the United States, or maybe even boat it over to Catalina Island! The island's so close we can almost jump on it from the Point Fermin cliffs. Or maybe we can even—"

"Toomer!" moms interrupted me, though. "Quiet up! I could've done that stuff when I was younger, but now I'm not and I'm only used to being right here where I am in the projects." Her stare drifted back to my shoulder. "And anyways, that's a family thing to do. Maybe if the deadbeat hadn't disappeared, things might've been different for us."

"We'll make 'em different!" I told her all determined. "We don't need him to do things together. Don't let some—"

"Toomer enough!" she shouted then. "If I was off on some goddamn bus or island trip with you, how in the world would I be able to make my afternoon date with Goldie!" Then, whatever it was that my face had suddenly done, I knew it wasn't good, because the next thing she said was, "See! I *knew* you were jealous. I knew it!"

I left the apartment a veryhothumiliated.

At Third and Palos Verdes I busted a right and headed towards Pacific Avenue. The morning air was breathable clean and the sky perfect clear, as if some god had given the world an overnight scrubdown. Colors jumped off all around. The occasional tree was a very green green and the upabove sky a very very blue. Even the here-and-there sidewalktrash had a nice sharp color to it. Damn, I thought, glad to be outdoors and away from my moms once again, everything feels so new. Then I noticed some more of those looking-right-at-me pigeons squatting hard on a tireless, up-on-blocks car. They saw that I was feeling better about being out and about and I said, "What's up uglies?" to them all and kept right on walking. Not even the sad gray windowdirty apartment-fronts would get me down anymore. Today, I told myself, would be a very good day indeed. I'll make sure of it.

Then, a few strides before Third and Center Street, a blur of a person came jetting around the corner right at me. In a panic I froze, not knowing which way to juke, and the blur, suddenly grown big with its head turned a one-eighty behind it, slammed into me a very meatyreal. As I airborned against a parked car, landing between it and the streetcurb, the blur never seemed to break its stride and kept highstepping it down the street. Then several L.A.P.D. squadcars came angling around the same corner that the blur had come around. It was a topspeed chase. While I laid there by the carside, I listened to the squadbrakes slam, the doors open up, and the rollerboyshoes scrambling to a very loud yelling sound. I slowly got up just enough to peek through the windows of the car I'd recently flown against.

And what I saw from a distance—him in the middle and the rollerboys in a whaling-away-at-him circlestomp—was like some humungous picture frame that'd suddenly shrunk and sucked towards me, crunching and clanking side-to-side as it did, until it'd maybe lessened to the size of a PeeChee folder and left me an upclose nose-to-nose with none other than Goldie himself. The sight had at first had my mouth mumbling and knees quaking, but since the rollers had already beaten the guy unconscious, he luckily couldn't notice me. And though very knocked out, two or three coplegs continued to work him over anyways: ribs, head, gut—gut, head, ribs. That was how it could work in the Ranch. If you got knocked out, it didn't necessarily mean that your ass-whoopin' came to an all-of-a-sudden end, but that you could possibly be beaten to death and not even know that that was happening to you—something that Goldie'd almost done to that big guy just hours earlier. It was called being stomped. And when the rollerboys finally stopped their stomping session, Goldie was a genuine mashpotatoed mess.

Then, out of the corner of my eye, I saw a line of re-flections coming from the just-across-the-sidewalk yard-grass. In the early-morning sun the line glittered and shimmered like some golden grassresting serpent. I laid down on my belly, mostly rollerboyprotected by the car I was next to, and reached across the sidewalk for it. But when a squadcar suddenly zoomed past I scampered back to my spot. On the second try, though, I gripped it and brought it back across the sidewalk with me.

It was the amazingest thing I'd ever handled. The metal had a very soft heavy to it that was nothing like a rockhard iron, and the suddenly-upclose and bloodcolored jewel im-mediately made me think up something crazy, like the piece had come from some deep, shouldn't-have-been-messed-with hole in the ground; or even that the jewel itself was more a bad thing than a good one—proof enough being that it'd already had the ability to send Goldie on a more-than-usual violencespree the last six to seven hours. I couldn't help but feel that the necklace had some sort of awful evil attached to it that could bring out the deepdown dangerous in a person. It was the kind of sensing that'd instantly had me wanting to toss the thing back onto the yardgrass, which I probably would've done had I not spotted Deadeye, one of those shavenheaded RSP Locos who'd gotten his nickname for this deaddrooping eyelid that he had, deadeyeing me from the nearestby apartmentwindow. As soon as I'd seen him I'd quickly automatically shoved the necklace deep into my backpack, but knew damnwell that he'd probably already seen it. We just stared at each other with maybe that packed-away serpent on the both of our minds. Then he disappeared, only to rightaway show himself again behind his barelycracked frontdoor. Again we just stared at each other. When I checked towards the L.A.P.D. activity, I noticed a suddenly-arrived ambulance with the EMTs already putting a gurneystapped Goldie into the back of it. Then I attentioned myself back to a Deadeye still peeking through his doorcrack.

"That ain't yours, wedo," said an almost-whispering to me Deadeye.

"What ain't mine?" I said, still crouching hard by the car and whispering some myself. Maybe, I thought, he hadn't seen that it was a necklace.

"What you put in your bag, ey," he said.

"What do you mean what I put in my bag?"

"You know what I mean, vato. The rope."

Damn, I thought, he'd definitely seen the thing. "Like hell it ain't," I said to him, though, all know-it-all offended. "That dude the rollers beat down knocked it out of my bag when he ran into me."

"Like hell he did," said Deadeye. "It was his and you know it, ey. He dropped it on the chase, so give it up, homes."

"Why should I give it to you?" I said, again going for offendedsounding.

"Because of possession, brother," he said. "It's ninetenths of the law, no? And you snatched it from my yard, ey. You should also give it up 'cause you know I'll beat your little ass if you don't."

I noed my head, though. I knew he was only trying to stall me with talk till the rollerboys all left, and that he wasn't coming out-of-doors because he was somehow hot himself. "Now you're all about the law, huh? From breaking it to backing it. If you're such a good citizen, why don't you come out and take it from me?"

"It's all in your point of view, homes," he said. "I know I'll get my shot at you when the time is right."

Again I checked towards the ambulance and saw it suddenly gone with only two squadcars left.

"Let's go ask those rollerboys which one of us has possession," I said. "You got ownership papers, don't you?"

"You sure you wanna fuck with me, wedo?" said a way nastiersounding Deadeye. "I know who you are *and* where you live, ey. Use your pinche cabeza, fuckhead, and give up the rope while we're still cool. I'll even cut you in on the fence, ey." Again I noed my head, getting ready to bail. "All right then, motherfucker. Expect the unexpected."

I took off just as the last rollerboy left.

Halfway to the schoolhouse my legs cramped some because of the extra weight in the backpack. Maybe it weighed more than fifteen pounds; more like twentyfive. Get to the safety of the schoolhouse, Toom, I told myself then, any second expecting a whole fleet of lowrider hoopties to come swoopin' up on me to jack me of Goldie's goods. Then I noticed that my eyes were darting around out of control and realized I was expecting not only the Locos, but any other people to be checking me out because of how badly my backpack was sagging. I felt something like an attention magnet. But when I looked around I noticed nobody eyeballing me at all. Didn't they all know, I thought, the people in the cars, on the sidewalks, or even the ones behind the office windows? Everyone's brains had to be on the mountain of gold on my person, no? I mean, it was a queen's necklace! How many of those could there be in the world? Especially like the fatty of a one I had? But at Ninth and Gaffey I passed two old men talking quietly on a busbench and neither paid me an atom of attention. I even looked back at them maybe five times and not once did they miss a beat in their conversation to look my way. Nevertheless, a block before the schoolhouse and the awful feeling hit me of someone's hand about to tap me on the back. I quickly spun around, but noticed nobody there. You're slippin', Toom, I told myself then. You need something like an ice-cold shower to bring yourself your ass back to center right quick. After I'd rounded the final corner for school, though, I ducked out and peeked back around it into the direction I'd just come from. But once again there was nobody there.

Trying to keep any thoughts of attention magnets or being followed out of my head, the worst ideas of them all crossed my mind. For example, had Goldie seen me? I mean, could I be positive he hadn't gotten a glimpse of me when we'd collided? I didn't know. And what'll he think happened to his necklace anyways? That the person he'd bumped into gripped it maybe or that the rollerboys had done so themselves, no? Why not them, I thought; they'd been known to do that type of thing. Hell, it was practically expected of them. Nevertheless, Goldie maybe having glimpsed me started to get to me a bit, so just to be safe I found myself hoping hard that all of his earlier morning memory had been cop-beaten clean out of his system. And anyways, there was always the jailhouse to keep him a good distance away. How long would he get for whatever they'd arrested him on? I wondered. Resisting arrest should alone get him a solid six-to-eight months, no? By that time who knew where I would be? Forget about all of that nonsense, Toom, I suddenly scolded at myself. Just think about getting your day back on track.

By the middle of third period, though, it felt as though a dozen lifetimes had skipped past, with me every time shooting through all the years of my life without a single chance to experience anything at all. Just birth and death, birth and death over and over again until I thought I'd disappear in my chair. It's the type of timetripping I wouldn't recommend to anybody with a heart.

During the entire class my on-the-way-to-school nerves had continued to jump off like fleas from one dog to the next. Between periods one and two I'd actually gone to the restroom just to inspect the necklace—to touch it, curl it, and plain feel its softmetalweight cool in my hands. Then, during the second half of third, all I did was wonder about the necklace's worth—especially that bloodcolored jewel. It had to have serious buying power, I decided; or at least a lot of topnotch trade-in strength. None of the pawnshops in San Pedro, I knew, could handle such an expensive item. And even if they could, what would that get me? An endless supply of rifles and handguns, guitars and watches, and maybe even some ridiculous-ass wouldn't-know-what-to-do-with-it-if-I'd-copped-it-as-an-extra-anyways lawnmower to boot, all of which I'd probably just sit around staring at with not a drop of satisfaction to show for. In my heart I knew the necklace was worth more than all of that silly nonsense ten, twenty, a hundred times over again. Instead of pawning it, I decided, what I'd do was bust down to this store on Sixth Street below Mesa called Union War Surplus. There I'd get what I wanted. Union War's long gray storesign in all big seriousness read: Be It A Hunting Knife Or A Battleship, We Can Get It For You.

When I was younger, maybe seven or eight, I used to pass that knife-and-battleship sign and badly wish I'd had something important like the necklace to trade in. What I'd wanted most back then, believe it or not, was my own train, complete with an engine, sleepercar, and caboose. It was silly how I'd had it all worked out too. Before my first railroad vacation, for example, I'd get the train all painted up orange and blue with brightred stars—fifty of them for each of the states I'd visit. Hawaii, I knew, might've been a problem because I wasn't even sure whether it had any railroad tracks to speak of. But say if it had, I'd used to think, I'd been positive some kind of arrangement would've been figured out between me and the president of the Hawaiian Islands to get my train over there. At the time I was absolutely certain he'd have understood my special situation too—a boy with train visiting all fifty states. But just in case he hadn't been I'd have told him all about how the bad publicity he'd surely get by letting Hawaii be the only state not to've let me, a simple little boy, visit it, would most likely have hurt his chances at being the islands' president the next time around.

Anyways, back then I'd hoped to visit Iowa and Nebraska just to see where the corn grew, Kentucky to watch this horse race I'd heard of once, New Orleans for this crazy music and costume parade called Mardi Gras, New York to go up in the Empire State Building and maybe even to surprise my never-seen-him-before pops. I just wanted to travel around and around doing ordinary American sightseeing like any other tourist would, except by train and with me a very very glad to no longer be in the rough-and-rowdy housing projects without any quiet or quit. Don't get me wrong, I wouldn't've moved out of the neighborhood for good or bailed on moms and the fellas. After my fifty-states trip I simply assumed that the train could've been this occasional out from all the everyday nonsense of that packed the place, that's all. And not just for me either, but for all of us. In fact, moms and the fellas would've had an always-open invite to come along to wherever we wanted to travel or even take the train out themselves as long as they knew how to drive it right. In that way, I used to tell myself, it would've been everybody's train to use. Everybody's, that is, except Goldie's.

What I'd decided to get this time, though, wasn't exactly a too-much-to-ask-for train or battleship, but it wasn't some kind of simple-ass huntingknife either. What I'd settle for, I'd decided, was a nice little boat, complete with engine and windsails. Nothing less. And maybe hopefully filled to the decktop with sandwiches and orange juice for that first ever voyage with moms to the island. The food, went my thinking, couldn't be that much of an extra to a place like Union War Surplus. I mean they were in business with the government and advertising battleships of all things! What would a trip's supply of O.J. and sandwiches be to them? And anyways, they'd be getting that very heavy necklace in exchange. A queen's necklace. My very own boat, I thought. . . . The day had gotten back on track in the best of possible ways, with my mood following a very nicely behind.

But then Deadeye plus a partner showed themselves during that third-period class and my heart damnnear shut it itself down for good. I was just sitting there in class, my brain full of boating dreams, when these two very round faces suddenly showed themselves at the classroom's doorglass. Only one crazy thought crossed through my mind: that thank god it hadn't been Goldie. But still, all I could think was trouble, trouble, and more trouble while all three of those eyes had me dialed to my chair like an old telephone. From that moment on, class felt like another dozen, but-not-very-minded-much-, though lifetimes. Then right before the lunchbell rang, the Locos disappeared. Just to once again play it safe, though, when the bell finally did go off I stuck to my teacher's side until we got right up on the cafeteria hall, where I quickly ducked out.

All through lunch, Deadeye and his partner sat a very quiet on the hood of their car (which was the same exact one I'd gotten airborned against that very morning) just outside the schoolhouse fence. When I grabbed my tray and headed for the basketball courts on the other side of the school, the surveillance of me didn't stop either. They'd simply gotten into their ride and driven around the block until they'd found me again, parked their ride, and got back on its hood to eyeball some more. Needless to say, my lunch stayed mostly untouched right on its tray.

Before sixth-period gym I claimed a terrible chestache (and even showed a starting bruise from the earlier impact with Goldie to prove it) and the instructor let me stay fully-dressed. With the wolves all about I refused to leave the backpack unguarded alone in some easy-to-break-into gym-locker and instead sat at the top of the bleachers watching my classmates do one long lap after another while the just-outside-the-fence-again Locos continued to keep me tabbed. Then the final schoolbell rang.

One block off and everything was fine, sort of. The necklace sat snug in my bag and Deadeye and company hadn't introduced themselves to me either, and hopefully, after the way I'd snuck out of the back of the schoolhouse, they never would. But still, you couldn't help but feel an ambush in the air. Luckily for me, though, it wasn't but a matter of minutes, or twelve cityblocks, before I'd be at Union War Surplus negotiating that trade: queen's necklace for a nice little boat. The more I thought it over, the more I believed it an all the way around fair situation. Union War, I believed, would make at least many times its money back and I would get to sail my boat to Catalina Island the very nextcoming weekend if I wanted to. Which I did.

Then, right before Twelfth and Pacific, the nose of a car shot out of an alley, almost taking out my knees in the process. As soon as I checked the windshield to complain about it, though, the driver's door flew wide open to show Deadeye's coming-to-mess-with-me partner. I rightaway turned to run, but instead crashed smack into a suddenly-standing-tight-in-back-of-me Deadeye, who quickly bearhugged the all of me right off of the ground and carried me into the alley, where he forearmed my throat hard against this trashdumpster while his partner yanked and yanked at my backpack, which, to my very painful credit, I held strong against my body to the point of socketseparation. They'll have to knock me out to get this badboy off of me, I promised myself.

"Guess how many classes we had to search to find your little ass?" sprayed Deadeye at my face. Because of that throatpressed forearm, though, I couldn't give him an answer. "Guess, you fucking pendejo!" he said while his partner continued with that yank yank yank. "We decided you're gonna get as many bolos as classroom searches, ey. How do you like that?"

Then, with two fullstraining hands, I pushed Deadeye's forearm away just enough to blurt out the first number to come to my mind. "Seventeen!" I said, to which Deadeye and company suddenly stopped with all their forearmpressing and backpackyanking to look at each other a very shocked and confused. Then they looked back at me.

"What'd you say, homes?" said a full-of-mean-intention Deadeye.

"Seventeen," I said, trying to sound as donerealwrong as possible.

"How'd you know, ey?" he said, starting to press that forearm again.

"Know what?"

"How many classrooms, bitch, that's what! You got someone following us, homes?"

"No!" I quickly said.

"Yeah he does, Deadeye," said his partner then. "How else would his punk-ass have know?"

"Yeah," said Deadeye. "How else would you have know? Huh!"

"My favorite number?" I said, hoping to ease things up some.

" 'My favorite number?' " mimicked Deadeye back at me, though. "You think something's funny, ey: us having to do a class-to-class search? For a thief?"

"No!" I said ASAP fast. "It was just a lucky guess, Deadeye. I swear."

Then the partner quickly ripped the backpack away from me, dug all through it, and handed the necklace straight to Deadeye, who, with his free hand, put it around his very thick neck.

"Whose got possession now, vato?" he said to me. But seeing the necklace hanging on his chest suddenly robbed me of any and all ability to speak. "Who, bitch!" I looked into Deadeye's good eye and finally said, "A nobody," to which his face turned a full-of-fury red. "Who told you you could call me by my nickname anyways?" he said, and cracked me with a stiff and caught-me-by-complete-surprise jab to the jaw that instantly doubled me over. For a big guy, I later thought, he'd had some serious handspeed because for the next several bolos thrown, my ducks, I knew, were on, and yet I'd gotten cleanhammered by them anyways. And as a rule of the rumble, if you get stung once real good with two guys on you, that was pretty much your ass.

After that first jab the partner had stepped into me with a left knee to the temple, which immediately had me seeing twos of everything. And double vision, I quickly realized, had very little to do with the eyes themselves because mine felt fine, sort of. It was my brain that'd felt this instantly-misfunctioning hurt from having been rocked so hard and unexpected, with my eyes only becoming a kind of droopyfeeling drunk because of it. Which was really too bad, because right about then I could've used a good amount of normal vision to know exactly what was coming at me next, and from what direction. I mean you had to move different to different bolos thrown. To a simple jab, for example, you did a quick and easy off-to-the-side headmovement, to a right or left hook you ducked down under it, which was what you did to a quick cross too, and against an uppercut you arched your body backwards till it passed past the front of your face. Not to mention all the different counterbolos you could throw. Because of the doublevision, though, what I felt and noticed weren't any single kinds of bolos, but this two-headed, eight-limbeded, split-into-a-vicious-two octopus whaling wildly away at me. And since that octopus had already gotten the backpack, I was suddenly in no mood to live up to that knock-me-out-if-you-think-you-can promise I'd made myself either, only to wake up a way later to the very sorry sight of my sure-to've-been-stomped-to-the-ground face and body. So I tried the Ali rope-a-dope for everything it was worth, and even prayed not to get tagged too solid again, but when I later came to had to admit that the rope-a-dope wasn't really meant to be used in alleys versus two bloodthirsty Locos, or especially by an awfulfighting amateur like me, but in the boxing ring and executed by the likes of Mr. Muhammad Ali himself. Again and again the octopus connected with the jaw, the forehead, the ears, the nose, and I suspect most other places they'd wanted. The very last thing I noticed before my sun began to set beneath that sweatyangry fist-and-foot barrage was the bloodcolored jewel twinkling very strong just below Deadeye's jawline, its bloodred color seeming as if to drip right down to the alleyfloor with me.

For the longest time I watched these big heavy clouds floating by way up high, not too sure I really ever wanted to move again. I didn't know where I was at first, only how I'd gotten there, which sent the stupidest of stupid and dumbest of dumb pangs all throughout my system. How could I have walked into an ambush that I knew was coming to happen? I thought at myself hard. Might as well've just silverplattered them the goods way back at the lunchbreak. After maybe a selfpitiful, lying-on-my-backside hour, though, I finally sat up to take a look around. I was in the alleydumpster I'd gotten jacked against. It's a goddamn shame, I thought suddenly; beat a young guy down and out and then simply toss his knockedout-ass into an alleydumpster! I mean, the asswhoopin' I know had come with the territory. But to be treated like so much rundown rubbish *after* they'd gotten the goods from me?—it was dammnear unforgivable. I climbed out into the alley and almost stepped right on top of my backpack, looking as it did as if run over by a 4x4 and afterwards ripped into by a pack of hadn't-had-a-meal-in-months-and-months wolves. I picked the raggedy thing up anyways and put it on.

My face hurt nonstop, and when I made a move for the neighborhood my feet just wouldn't go that way. Of all my aching bodyparts, it was my feet that didn't have it in them to head for that everyday familiar yet. Then my legs and arms and the rest of my body lost that interest too, with my heart finally giving in as well. So I started to wander in the neighborhood-opposite direction for awhile. In fact I wandered so much that I eventually ended up all the way at Cabrillo Beach, where I sat my stilldizzyself down on the late-afternoon beachsand to watch the babywaves breaking a nonstoplong. Not until later, when the tide had started its ebb and the sun had piece by golden piece snuck back behind the horizonline, did I finally manage to get myself up to head for the crib. I walked along the boatbobbing marina, the very fishingboat-quiet Deadman's Slip, and the just-as-quiet railroad tracks. At Sixth Street, though, my feet once again acted up, so I made an uphill left for Tommy's Bar instead, where the bartender, Deek, had always been cool with me dropping in for a glass of cold water every now and then before heading onto the projects on my tougher of days.

"Damn it," said a suddenly-up-on-me Deek as soon as

I'd sat myself down at a dark corner table. "What the hell happened to you?"

"Got jumped," I told him, my whole face hurting from doing so.

"No you didn't," said Deek. "You got mauled. The bastards. Did you know 'em?" I gave him a small, surprised-at-the-question look. "You're right, Toomer, I know. No more questions. It could only make for more trouble. I got it. But just seeing you like that makes me wanna put my hands around one of 'em."

"It coulda been worse," I told him. Then I thought of the necklace and felt as if to sob up for the first time in my life. "In some ways it was."

"Sit tight," said Deek, heading off.

The clock between the bar's liquor bottles read seventhirty. At seventhirtytwo Deek was back with a glass of water and a towelwrapped icebag.

"Here," he said, putting the water on the table and the icebag in my hands. "The ice is for the swelling, so use it. And I put a little extrasomething into your water tonight. It's just for tonight, though, for the hurt, so don't go getting used to it, you hear?" I smiled, but instantly unsmiled from the hurt that Deek'd mentioned. "Go on and drink up. And stay as long as you want, okay?"

I yessed my head and Deek headed for the bar again.

For the next three hours I sat there and sipped on that tampered glass of water, my thoughts coming and going to their own content without them really meaning a damn. I'd lost the boat, I'd every now and then told myself. After you've had something that'd given you a great holy hope for maybe the first time ever, and it's suddenly ruthlessly taken away from you, thoughts had a way of becoming these pretty worthless things, leaving you left with lots of hard-to-figure feelings and emotions that only rode you till they'd become tired of riding you.

"You want a refill on that poison, Toomer?" said a jolting-me-back-to-reality Deek then.

"No thanks, Deek," I said. "I'm nice with this glass."

"Well, you can skip the tip tonight. How's that?"

I halfsmiled with the icebag on my jaw.

Later, when I finally stepped out of Tommy's, I stood still before the entrance as a couple of looking-at-me-strange longshoremen entered it. Once again my feet wouldn't move towards that less-than-three-blocks-away-from-'em neighborhood, though this time they wouldn't make a move for any other place else either; they just stayed there sidewalkstuck in front of Tommy's Bar as if forever cemented down. I looked around the nighted-up street until I came across that completely-forgotten-about, just-one-business-over-from-me storesign: UNION WAR SURPLUS, it read, with the capital-lettered motto just below it. The battleship was painted gray at the center with two blue stars fixed around it, and next to the battleship was the big gray battleshipsized huntingknife. I just stared at that sign as if it'd suddenly come to life and then just as suddenly died again right in front of me. And the longer I stared at it, the deader it seemed to get, until all it was was what it'd always been: a storesign. As soon as I saw it like that my feet woke right up and decided it time to finally head for the neighborhood and my bedroom deep in the heart of it.

Over at Third and Center, though, I noticed some emergency lights hammering hard against the apartmentwalls, disturbing the night with their soundless discofever. As a rule, whenever the rollerboys swooped on the projects and suddenly made a scene, me and the fellas—or any sensible ghetto-ite, for that matter—mostly stayed a goodways away from them. Especially if that scene happened to be Deadeye's very frontyard, with Deadeye himself having just beaten you to a close-to-comatose pulp. An animal like him was the last thing you'd have wanted to see. Plus, snooping-all-about Looky-Loos were an absolute perversion in our book, forever eager to witness the sad misfortune of others just so they could scoop themselves some tragedy to add to the neighborhood grapevine. A Looky-Loo was a creature never mindful enough to leave a person caught in negative circumstances alone. We couldn't stand them. For some hard-to-explain reason, though—maybe because my day had been such a longdrawn mess or because I couldn't help myself from knowing whether Deadeye and company'd gotten busted for possession of the necklace—I felt myself drawn towards those emergency flashes like a nightbug to a glowing streetlight.

At maybe a hundred feet away I noticed what looked like an uncovered body on the yard right next to Deadeye's place. Seeing it at the same time quickened and slowed my steps, which was always how it happened at the sight of someone for whatever reason downed. Several uniformed rollerboys stood around the body and by the time I'd reached the yellow Police Line: Do Not Cross tape I noticed a second one in just about the same spot I'd landed at in earlier that morning. Neither of them had been sheeted yet the way bodies usually got sheeted when slain and Deadeye's had that seen-a-terrible-ghost stare that the freshly-taken-out tended to have, along with a bulletholed forehead that I assumed his partner had too. Putting their bodies together with the madmen who'd slammed me in that alley, though, was suddenly the hardest thing to do. And I thought it strange that I really had no anger for them either, or that seeing the two with not a drop of life left in their bones gave me no satisfaction. If anything, I felt a kind of sad and sorry for them both for having have suddenly died the way they had. (But at that point I could've probably felt the sorries for just about anything I came across. Like myself in any mirror I looked into, for example.) Then an iller-than-ill feeling hit me as I took a closer look at Deadeye. The necklace was missing from around his neck. His partner, I saw, wasn't sporting it either. A come-out-of-nowhere panic instantly swamped my system, giving me this armless-legless feeling. Even though I'd lost a sole possession of the thing, part of me, I suddenly realized, had continued to keep a close connection to it while supposedly Deadeye had it. But now that I knew he didn't, I felt a powerful need to know some immediate facts about what might've happened to it; like had it been robbed from him, and if so, by who, or had he maybe hidden it somewhere before he'd gotten shot, and if so, where were its whereabouts? I quickly eased upclose to the rollerboys to overhear whatever their conversation might be, but after several earstraining minutes all I'd picked up was a "pointblank shots" comment here, a "no willing witnesses" one there, and then that forever-arising gang-and-drug talk they liked to throw around. But nil nada nothing about what mattered to me most: the nowhere-to-be-seen necklace. Then it was *all* a gang-and-drug talk, which rightaway told me that they'd file away the case like they did so many others: as a no-investigation-necessary untruth. It was what the neighborhood violence mostly boiled down to to them: a gang-and-drug problem. Instead of hanging around and listening to anymore L.A.P.D. bullshit, and maybe even getting slapped with a curfew violation my-damnself, I decided to head straight for the homestead.

Finally on my block, I cut behind the apartment buildings and walked between the shared backyards. Our up-ahead kitchen window was fully dark, but I decided it better to sneak into the crib anyways. No sense in disturbing moms at such a late hour, I thought, especially on a day she'd missed out on her much-looked-forward-to date. At the backdoor I quietly turned the knob and stepped into the kitchen. For a good halfminute I just stood there in the cool cool dark, very glad to be back home. Then a faint firecracker smell tickled my nose and I stepped straight to the stove, sniffed at its burners, but smelled nothing wrong with them. Because I hadn't really eaten all day I decided to check for some food to take up to my room with me. I stepped to the refridgerator, opened it, found some leftover burrito, and took it out. When I stepped back to close the door, though, I got the shock of my life when I at the same time sensed and saw someone standing right beside me. In the fastest of fast movements I naturalreflexed the intruder a good ten feet away from me, sprang for the silverware drawer, and grabbed myself a knife just as the refridgerator door closed us both into an unseeable dark.

Suddenly, though, a quiet laughing kicked in; a laughing that belonged to none other than Goldie himself. Hearing it'd damnnear made my hardbeating heart wrap right around my spine a few times. Goldie in the apartment! How could it be! He should've been in jail! I struggled for some answers but couldn't come up with any.

"My bad, Toom," said Goldie in a strong whisper of a laugh. "I shouldn't've come up on you like that. You all right?" I didn't answer. "Havin' yourself a midnight snack, huh? Where've you been all day anyways?"

"Out and about," I finally said. "At the beach. Why?"

" 'Cause I've been worried about you, that's why."

"Worried?" I said. I couldn't believe my ears.

"Yeah, worried. It's all right if Goldie worries about Sunny Toomer a little, ain't it? Shit, in the last few hours you've become like a genuine son to me."

Deciding to let that last comment slide right by me, I said, "Where's my moms?"

"Up in her room, listening to that choir music of hers."

For a click or two we didn't say anything to each other. My eyes had adjusted some to the dark and could barely make out some of Goldie's bodyoutline.

"You see anything unusual today?" he said, making me look another way.

"What do you mean 'unusual'?" I said, gripping into the knifehandle some.

"You know, out-of-the-ordinary unusual. Unexpected unusual. *Unusual* unusual."

"In this neighborhood? Nah."

"C'mon now, Toom. Don't be so humble. And especially don't be embarrassed. I know what you tried to do for me today."

"Oh yeah," I said, taking a sidestep towards the door. "And what's that?"

"You know. Recover and hold onto a certain something valuable of mine."

How'd he know about that? shot through my head. I mean, how'd he ever learn I'd had possession of the thing? He's playing me, I quickly decided, gripping tighter onto the knife and expecting him to any second rush me.

"I don't know what you're talking about," I said.

"Is *that* right?" said Goldie then. "And if I turn on this here kitchen light you won't know how your face got beaten blue today either?" I said nothing. "That's what I thought."

Then that strange firecracker smell tickled my nose again and in a fearful flash I knew exactly what it was. A recently-gone-off gun. It was one of those special kinds of smells that, once you'd experienced just once in your life, you never forgot it. Kind of like that first-ever gobbled-down elementary-school lunch or the first time I'd ever breathed in moms's just-out-of-the-shower skinscent that'd smelled so good and clean it'd made me want to just rub some of it all over myself like the naturalest, most-perfect kind of perfume ever.

"Deadeye told you!" I pointblank said to him.

"Say what?" he said back, though. "Who the fuck is Deadeye?"

"You were up there tonight," I said, with a no-doubt-about-it voiceraise to boot. "At Third and Center!"

"Toom, Toom, Toom," said Goldie all relax-yourself-like and wanting me to lower my voice. "Let's calm down and leave your mother out of this, all right? You know you can't trust a woman with anything. At least not anything this important." I badly wanted to argue with him, but thought of that stillcooling gat somewhere possibly very close to us then. "And put that butterknife away before you hurt yourself." Butterknife! I ran a secret finger along the blade edge and sure enough I'd grabbed a butterknife, which I instantly shamefully laid on the counter.

"Listen up," said Goldie, as though letting me in on an I-already-knew-about-it-anyways secret, "I woke up in the hospital, right, and saw these beautiful gray clouds moving past my window and thought I'd somehow snuck my sorry ass into heaven. As I watched 'em float past I remembered some things. I remembered running from the cops, turning that last corner, and feeling some kind of bump that'd immediately made me drop my valuables. Then I remembered looking back to see what I had run into, but saw nothing but a parked car, some empty yards, and the first of that chaseteam comin' very strong around the bend. And that was it." Goldie then got to speaking as though deeply possessed with the justhappened day and I didn't dare interrupt him. "When I left the hospital I headed straight for that corner, right, and covered every quarter-inch of that mug, only to find nothing anywhere at all. I mean, what the fuck could I have bumped into, I asked myself, that'd just disappeared like that? And then my valuables with it! I didn't know what to do, so I walked across the street, sat on the curb between these two cars, and just thought and waited for a while. And you know, Toom, it's true what they say about waiting, 'cause the goddamndest things happen to those who do the shit. I was on that curb no more than fifteen minutes when these two Locos pull up to the bumpspot, right, the shotgun talking loud and crazy with something very interesting hanging around his neck. I'd have made my move right then and there too if what they were laughing about hadn't thrown me so hard."

Suddenly some footsteps sounded in the upstairs hallway

and Goldie stood a speakless quiet for a stretch, with me the whole time wanting to badly call up to moms to tell her what kind of madman lunatic we had in the apartment with us. Then the footsteps headed back to the room they'd come from. Before Goldie even told me about it, I pretty much knew what it was that the Locos had laughed about when they'd rolled up: the way they'd clobbered some uppity kid to a mashed mess, and maybe at that ridiculous-ass rope-a-dope he'd attempted to avoid it, or maybe even at the way he'd desperately clung to his backpack while the one guy's partner tried to tear it from his shoulder. And of course they laughed about their goldgotten loot.

"How'd you know it was me, though?" I wondered Goldie's way.

" 'Cause the shotgun started talkin' about the kid's mother, right," he said. "Described how she looked to a tee and how he was gonna get with her as soon as he had a chance. It was the filthiest, most tasteless shit I'd ever had to listen to, Toom: all tits, legs, and ass comments, excuse my French; and then some disreputable stuff about how loose she supposedly was, which we know is a goddamn slander. Your mother a loose woman? Why I'd . . . Anyways, I felt I got you into this trouble, right, got you banged-up hurt, and I surely wasn't gonna let two good-for-nothing Locos like that get away with punkin' you so bad. I mean you had my back when I was in the worst of ways, right, and you wouldn't believe how deeply that affected me. Shit, I might as well say it: it downright broke my heart, Toom, you takin' care of Goldie and his valuables the way you did. Fighting off two big motherfuckers like that to keep my goods safe. That's when I realized that you, me, and your moms had finally become like first family, and that what I did to them I did for the all three of us. You see I had to scratch back."

"Scratch back?" I said all disbelieving my ears. "It looked to me like two people got taken out for good. That's hardly what I call a scratch."

"Wait up," said Goldie. "Just hold your motherfuckin' horses. There you go again getting all excited. You need to stop that shit, Toom. Look here: do you know why a judge has never had a problem punishing a motherfucker in the courtroom? 'Cause he believes that once a motherfucker's broken the law he's knowingly put himself at the mercy of the system and that all the judge is doin' is making sure that that system's runnin' as smoothly as it can. Since we couldn't go to the judge or the judge's system for some justice, we had to come up with our own brand of punishment; *and* application."

"What punishment?" I said, still disbelieving my ears. *"Murder?* For two good-for-nothings having whooped my ass?"

"You're damnstraight!" said Goldie with some whispered menace. "That *and* theft. *And* talkin' the wrong kinda trash about the right kinda woman. Them are multiple offenses in case you haven't counted, Toom. Shit, you know it's a different system out here. A basic asswhoopin' back would've done what? Started up another cycle of payback, that's all; the very thing those gangster fucks thrive on. Or did you prefer your moms as the latest target of a drive-by shooting?; or maybe you wanted to simply let them get away with what they'd done to us all? The family. Not a chance *I* could've done that, Jack. The way it stands now, though, we've got no problem and nothing more to worry about. Shit, my conscience is clear and *I* did the deed, so you shouldn't have anything to trip off. And anyways, nobody saw me! And it ain't like California doesn't have the death penalty in effect itsdamnself. Did you know in some countries you can be put to death for simply smokin' on a motherfuckin' joint? Believe me, those two easily deserved what they got." Again the hallway footsteps kicked in and then started slowly coming down the stairs. "Toom," said a quickwhispering Goldie then, "we squashed on all of this or what? Tell me now, yes or no, and then forever keep your word." Suddenly the light went on in the livingroom, which for the first time showed how absolutely ugly we'd become since earlier that morning. "Tell me, Toom, *now.*"

"Like first family, Goldie," I said, holding up my not-even-close-to-trembling hand, which he instantly grabbed for.

"Like first family," he said.

Then he actually hugged me.

For seventeen straight days Goldie didn't leave the apartment, making my life a rightquicking headache all over again. Could I get a packa smokes, right quick?; I'm feelin' like a big-ass steak, Toom. You don't mind coppin' me one, right quick, do you?; How 'bout a six-pack?; A newspaper; A bagga chips; Some Eggos for breakfast! Right quick, right quick, right quick. Half my mornings I was late for school, Goldie had me running around for him so much, while moms, who he'd allowed to wear the necklace ("but *only* around the apartment, baby"), simply assumed the man under the weather.

By day ten I'd gotten so sick of Goldie I started staying away from home again. And just like during those El Niño days I moved back into the public library. Instead of the Bahamas, though, I decided to this time read a murder mystery or two to try and figure up the perfect plan for getting rid of someone who'd become a very unwanted in my life. I wasn't thinking of actual murder or anything, but just for a foolproof notion of fading a person out for good. Of getting and keeping him permanently out of the apartment. More than anything I'd hoped the books would get me thinking about it in the right ways. You know, how to set up and trick a person without them knowing it. But two pages into the second book about a man shot to death at night and *on his very own front yard* and I got Deadeye and company so heavy in the brain that I couldn't read on. Instead a shameful-as-charged feeling crept all over me. Ever since that night, you see, I'd got to taking a different route to the schoolhouse, not wanting to ever in my life have to see Deadeye's apartment again or any family he might've had in it. I mean I still couldn't believe I'd somehow been mixed up in his death. And his partner's to boot. Several times a day I'd get into these tense and terrible arguments with myself about it all, with the one side of me saying, Damn, Toom, you should never've backpacked the necklace that morning, and the other part saying, What you did was a.o.k. normal and all, Toom, it's just that when you've got a violenceprone lunatic on the loose in your very own home only the worst kind of madness can go down; and don't think that that night was the end of it either. One day he'll turn against you and your moms too, and think nothing of it. Just you wait.

More and more then, I wanted (no, *needed*) Goldie out of the apartment and out of my life. Not because of that violent streak, I told myself, but because with him gone, maybe the whole Deadeye business would go away too.

Then, just when I'd gotten my deepdownsickest of the man, he'd suddenly started to feel outdoorsy again, leaving the apartment at night every night, which I would've been a very clamhappy about if it hadn't been for him every one of those nights dragging me along with him as his much-demanded-for company. In Goldie's new familymindedness, you see, I'd become something of a Goldie, Jr., to him, and because he suddenly deeply trusted me for having taken that beating while supposedly trying to protect his prize necklace for him, he'd decided he could trust me with anything at all.

At first we just went to the movies. In six days we saw four action films, a comedy, and a not-worth-our-time-at-all romance, and I'd eaten enough popcorn to empty out an Iowa cornfield. Then one night Goldie said he was taking me somewhere very special to him ("Next to the horseraces," he'd said, "it's probably the most special place that I know. I mean next to the horseraces and your mother's apartment, that is.") and that I couldn't tell my moms anything about it until he'd figured out a way to tell her himself. There was lots, actually, that Goldie didn't want me telling my moms about. Like the kind of sidebusiness (very hot jewelry) that he was running out of her home or that he kept no less than three loaded guns in our apartment at all times. ("The woman's crazy," he once told me. "She's terrified of a simple hand-gun!") And then of course there was that Deadeye business.

It was an old abandonedlooking house on Knoll Hill, which was a high round mound of weeded-over land that overlooked this ugly stretch of innerharbor that used to be Todd's Shipyard, but was now a ghosttown of drydocks and mud. Goldie stepped up to its door and, instead of knocking on it, reached for the knob and turned it open as though he himself had lived in the place. A blast of television commercial was the first thing that hit us and when Goldie shouted a "Hello, hello, is anybody home?" a whole stampede of little scream-ing voices and little sprinting feet came flying our way.

"Papa!" they shouted all together and grabbed onto every possible part of him.

Papa! *Goldie,* a father of one, two, three, *four* little boys? What was going on? Then a woman strolled towards us from the televisionroom with another, butbarelyborn little girl in her arms.

"Yeah, what is it?" she said as if badly bored by our sight.

"Ah don't be like that, Regina," said Goldie covered in his crew. "At least *act* like you know me."

"Don't you 'Regina' me," snapped the woman, though. "If you think you can just walk in here after how many deadbeat months and expect to find yourself a buttercup waiting for you, you got another thing comin'. Now: *what do you want?*"

"I just came by to see my boys, that's all. They're mine too, you know?"

"Is that right? Then what's this one's name?" said the woman about the baby in her arms, to which Goldie got qui-eter than the bottom of an unused swimmingpool, and the woman's face dropped into an expressed-it-many-times-before disappointment. "This is what I've had to deal with," she suddenly said to me, "ever since that one there," meaning maybe the second oldestlooking boy on the left knee, "has been been on the scene." Then she looked Goldie back in the face. "He's an unreliable individual, young man. Unfair too. If you were smart you'd keep a good distance away from him."

"You ain't gotta be so mean, woman," said Goldie then, pulling a moneywad out of his pocket. "I also wanted to bring you something to get by on."

"Then give it up and get on out," she said. "I'm already missing my TV show as it is." Goldie counted her eight one-hundred-dollar bills as carelessly as if they were no more than some crisp toiletpapersquares. "Is that it, eight-hundred dollars? You know what my rent alone is?"

"Shit, that's twice as much as last time!"

"Oh yeah?" said the woman as though ready to squab. "And you've been gone twice as long too, haven't you?"

"All right, all right," said Goldie. "I promise I'll get you some more soon."

"How soon?"

"Soon, damn it, soon," he said, and kneed down. "Give your daddy a kiss all over," said Goldie to the boys, who immediately did as he'd said. Then he stood up and looked at the woman. "Can I get one for the road?"

"Can you tell me this one's name?"

Again Goldie got all poolbottomquiet. "You see," he finally said to me as he reached for the doorknob. "That's what keeps me away from here. Her meanness."

"No, no, no," said the woman, though. "What keeps you away is wickedness. Your *own.*"

The next night Goldie got a very important telephone call. So important that he quickly handcovered the receiver and asked me to leave the apartment "right quick," which I once again did. When an hour later I stepped back inside, it was to the sight of a kitchentableseated Goldie looking as though shocked into the best of moods, with his widegrinning mouthcorners stretching ear to ear. On the table in front of him was a sheet of paper with rows of quickscribbled numbers all over it.

"You all right?" I said to him.

"I don't know," he said back, still grinning hard as he folded the paper into his pocket. "You ever think of takin' a trip, Toom?"

"A trip?" I said. "Where to?"

"Doesn't matter where, so long as it's outta Los Angeles." I slowly noed my head, knowing rightaway what the phonecall had been about. Poorfolk, I thought: they expect a few dollars and instantly think they can join the jet set or something. "You serious? Well I guess you haven't been around long enough to be tired of things. All the fighting and hussling and the always having to look over your shoulder—I'm just sick of it. I've been ready for a break for years, and now I've got it all worked out. You, me, and your mother, Toom, we're going to Hawaii day after tomorrow.

Alls you gotta do is pack your swimshorts." For the longest time I just stared Goldie's way as if at nothing but a greatbig emptiness. Then I realized he'd expected some kind of reaction from me. Something like a joy to the world maybe. But then I remembered moms and her attitude about traveling to places at all.

"Sounds nice, Goldie," I said in an instant, "but I don't think my moms would care for something like a trip. She's—"

"—already packed her bags is what she is! Shit, I'm gonna learn how to surf and swim and do the motherfuckin' hulahoop! And we can stay as long as we want to."

"Wait up," said an in-the-same-spot Goldie the very next morning as I was about to head for the schoolhouse. "You've got no school today."

" 'Got no school' " I said. "How's that?"

" 'Cause I need your services, my man, that's how," he said. "I've already spoken to your principal. Told him you wouldn't be in for a couple of weeks—family emergency—and he said cool."

"You talked to my principal?"

He yessed his head.

"Who'd you tell him you were?"

"Why your father, of course," said Goldie. "Who else?"

———

At Sixth and Pacific Goldie gave me some change and had me stand by this payphone. Then he crossed the street and entered a twostory brick officebuilding.

"If you see anything strange happening in front of the place," he'd said to me before he'd crossed over for it, "call me at this number *top*speed. You hear? It's the number of the room I'll be in."

"Sure thing," I'd said to him, all the while looking at the notesheet he'd handed me. "Anything strange, call you at this number."

"That's right," he'd said, sucking in some air. "After this is done, we're set, Toom. You know that, don't you?" I didn't say anything. "Anyways, just stay on your toes and be ready to call."

I believed moms would feel better about her situation after a while, her typical while being rightaround two-to-three months. To Goldie's credit, though, he'd lasted a good deal longer than any of the others had and might've gone right along lasting if it hadn't been for his absolute carelessness. I mean who in their right mind would trust a bittergotten twelve-year-old with, of all things, their security? Especially when a large part of that bitterness had been caused by that truster himself? No more than five minutes after he'd entered the officebuilding, what had to be half the L.A.P.D. suddenly swarmed onto that Sixth-and-Pacific intersection and rightaway stormed the building entrance. By the time Goldie had picked up the telephone we knew it was too late for him to bolt.

"Damn it, Toom," he whispered hard into the telephone, while somewhere behind him a door was being banged off its hinges, "why didn't you call me in time?"

" 'Cause I was thinking, Goldie," I told him as calm as possible.

"Thinking! About *what,* motherfucker? When you shoulda been calling me instead!" Again the door in the background took a bad banging.

"About how absolutely unrelated we are, Goldie. I mean, if we were related, I'd have felt something terrible for you as soon as that first siren kicked in, no? Something like a panic. But I didn't."

"Motherfucker, you *let* me get caught! When I was doing this for us! The first family!" Then the door on the other end cracked wide open and all the usual rollerboy warnings were shouted all about.

"Goldie," I said, "we ain't even last family." And it was the last time I ever spoke to the man. And like I've said: Looky-Loos were a flatout perversion in our book, so I wasn't about to stick around and watch the poor pathetic bastard get stuffed into the back of some squadcar. I mean making that first call to the L.A.P.D. had been low enough of me for a year or two, and making the next day's one maybe low enough for a lifetime.

———

But I really had no choice, you see, because the last thing that Goldie'd yelled at me during that police-raid call was how, when he eventually got out of prison, he'd beat me to a bloody death. At the time the comment hadn't registered really for the simple beautiful fact that there were so many L.A.P.D.s in the neighborhood to keep him away from me. Later that day, though, while I was lounging around in our new-and-improved, Goldie-free livingroom, that "when I get out of prison" of his cut at my brain and ease like a bad pair of scissors. How much time did a guy get anyways, I wondered, for grandtheft necklace? One, two, maybe three years at max? Out in less on good behavior. Or maybe a fivespot to a dime with an already badlybuiltup rapsheet? Even then, though, there was that time off for good-behavior possibility. And then what would happen? I'd be one day strolling home from high school or something and, instead of getting alleypunked by two crazy Locos, I'd be beaten to death by my moms's very own ex-boyfriend. No thank you to that, I thought.

In my opinion, Spiro's Burgers on Third and Pacific had always made the best cheeseburgers on the planet. What I believe made them so tastydelicious was the way that the cheese had smacked like the government's own that we used to gobble down like purestcane sugar. Richard, though, thought it was the grilled onions that did it, Will Man the secret sauce, while the Grizz (in his Spiro's-going days, that is) had always loved them for the simple fact that they were cheeseburgers from Spiro's. Anyways, I was halfway into one of those beauties when a lone undercover ride finally slowed to a stop just across the street, a suited rollerboy-woman getting out of it, who quickly stepped around her car to the curbside smutrack (because of the low morning demand I thought it the perfect stashspot), put in some change, and pulled a big brown paperbag out of it, which she quickly grabbed and drove away with.

A single day later a cussing-and-screaming Goldie was refused his bail and shipped straight to the L.A. County Jail on double-murder charges. Since I hadn't known which of his guns had been the take-out weapon, I'd simply carefully plasticbagged all three of them into a paperbag, dropped them all into the smutrack at daybreak, and a few hours later made that second call from the same exact Sixth-and-Pacific payphone that'd hopefully keep Goldie out of commission forever. It was like A, B, C, it all went down so easy.

Then, rightaround the time Goldie'd gotten sent upstate for good, one of those expected unexpected things happened to us: a prisoner got released who, instead of being a wannabe pops like Goldie had himself been, happened to be one of our very flesh-and-blood own. In fact, he was Will Man's pops to be exact and his name was Hector Hermosillo, a kind of a living legend around the Rancho San Pedro housing projects. Unlike Goldie's very predictable jailhouse sendoff, though, Hector's beeline visit for Will Man's place was mostly an all-of-a-sudden, unexpected shock.

ᖴathers. Whenever a real one came around things felt rightaway strained. Like the man had to force himself to show and the kid to pretend that the visit was something special to him. And then there was all that awful and black-as-bad-motor-oil blood between the parents themselves. The brokendown communication, the quick impatience, and finally those evil looks and was-it-at-all-worth-it good-byes. No wonder they'd long ago parted their ways, you'd sometimes catch yourself thinking. Mondo's pops came up once a year from Mexico, Richard's a few times more from who knows where, and Talea's once in lifetime from Samoa. And except for two already-mentioned telephone calls, I'd never even met mine, with moms just telling me damnnear every day of my life that he'd been nothing more than a spermdonor anyways. But like I said, whenever someone's pops did eventually manage to show, it threw us all for a good loop. Especially the shower's son.

209

It'd been the typical May morning: clear sunnywarm skies and enough time for me to round the fellas together for the haven't-had-one-in-awhile baseball session. Will Man sat on a low cinderblock wall separating the manypotholed parkinglot from the long stretch of shared backyards, while I stood next to him wondering exactly what to say. Across the lot stood the rundown nursery with the beige-yellow suncracked paintjob. It was the place we usually played all our summer baseball games and all our year-round blackjack hands. But Will Man, in his constant white T-shirt, and even though his attention was down at the ground by the gloves, bat, and baseballs between us, had his back to the nursery and wasn't even close to thinking about sports. On his neck were several fat, deep-purple hickies that in the past month or so had gotten as constant as that T-shirt was. Just a week back, in fact, he'd had nearly *twenty* of them suckerfished all over his throat—front, sides, and napeback to boot. From what girl he'd gotten them he still wouldn't say. But those had mostly faded already.

"When'd you find out?" I finally said to him.

"Barely five minutes ago," said Will Man, looking at me with these worryful, definitely-not-baseball-interested eyes. "Moms says he made parole yesterday; that they let him out early this morning." He checked towards the street. "He should be here any minute."

"Why'd she say you have to take a drive with him?"

"I don't know," he said even more troublefaced. "She says he's got something important to tell me."

"Important?" I said. *"Hector?* Like what? How to rob a bank and get caught in the process?"

But Will Man just shouldershrugged as he looked back to the ground. Then he said, "All I know is he promised moms to take me for a drive the day he got out. Why, though, she wouldn't say. Seemed almost embarrassed when I asked her."

I once heard Will Man's parents go at it over his future.

"He's either gonna stay in school or become a cholo like yourself, *I know, I know,*" said a frustratedangry Lydia, "but that's *his* decision, Hector, not yours. You can't decide it for him."

"But I can guide him, though," said Hector. "School's just gonna make him into a square, babygirl. Sitting at a stupid desk, taking stupid tests, just to live the nine-to-five. It's ridiculous, ey. If he becomes a vato like me, though, he'll properly learn the streets. I'll teach him everything he needs to know, ey, so he can become a man who's sure of himself. And proud."

"Proud of ending up in prison," said Lydia.

"That's right, Liddie," said Hector all excited. "That is something to be proud of, a trip to prison. So long as it's not too permanent, though. At every jail I ever went to I made friends. *Good* friends. Real communidad. People I respected and who respected me back. I have no shame of having that in my life. And if he ends up inside a few times, neither should he."

"Well you should be ashamed," said Lydia all offended-sounding. "And anyways, you talk like a crazy person."

"Crazy hell," said Hector. "I'll disown his little ass if he gets like one of those nerdy school dudes, one day wearing a tie and carrying a briefcase around; with no ganas or style and only a bad personality to show for it. Just to imagine him that way, ey, my very own flesh and blood, makes me sick to my stomach. No lie."

"Yeah, yeah, yeah, Mr. Lowrider Man," said a tired-of-the-arguing Lydia. "You're not saying nothing new. And anyways, if you ask me you've already disowned him 'cause you're never ever around."

"That's not true!" said Hector, suddenly all offended himself. "I'd do anything for my boy; you know that. He's already like a prince of the projects 'cause of me. I got the little cabron instant respect and reputation around here because of the organization I created—out of nada, Liddie! Believe me when I say that. In return, though, I get no respect myself. *Especially* from you."

"Well, don't start holding your breath," said Lydia. "Not now."

"Don't worry," said Hector. "I won't."

The organization Hector created was Chuy Lopez's old set, the Locos, when he was only fifteen years old. That's why he was known around the Ranch as "El Primo," the first. At eighteen, though, he stabbed an L.A.P.D. and got fifteen strong for attempted murder. The day he got out was when he'd met a mad-about-him Lydia who was only sixteen years old at the time, but by that very night had managed to get Will Man all started up in her bellymiddle.

How many times Hector'd gotten arrested, I don't know. What I do know though's he stayed in prison a lot. Ever since that copstabbing business, a judge would take one look at Hector's rapsheet and everytime hit him with the maximummost sentence available. Sometimes even made up a maximum, Hector was hated so much. Since prison was one of the best things a person from the Ranch could do to build up some respect for himself, though, we didn't think Hector so terribly off. I mean his respectlevel was already so high, prison must've come very easy to him. And around the Ranch, for example, people actually bragged that they knew him (even when they didn't), had given him a smoke (even when they hadn't), passed a few words with him on the sly, or plain got arrested by the same exact rollerboys he'd gotten arrested by. Just to mention a relationship with the man, no matter the kind, had you an instant status. Hector's was a reputation that could completely nerve a guy under. Especially a young and very-related one like Will Man was.

Since Hector'd just been paroled for a stretch, though, my attitude was suddenly a lot like Lydia's: no matter how prisonhard he might've become, Will Man had to see him. I mean, like she said: who knew the next time he'd be out-and-about around, especially with the way those judges *(and rollerboys)* had had it in for him so bad? Plus, he couldn't be a moving-into-your-crib-to-never-give-you-a-day-of-peace-again Goldie-type anyways since Lydia, unlike another moms we won't mention by name, wouldn't allow it. Will Man, I thought, was lucky to have a pops come around at all; a real-live, wanting-to-see-him-for-a-minute father; even if that father happened to be an intimidating and too-much-to-handle Hector Hermosillo. And maybe the man did have something important to say, because even when he'd the last few times been an out-and-about free man he'd rarely come around our part of the Ranch much, except for maybe that guaranteed-to-happen argument with Lydia. Hector, you see, had years ago hooked up with other women. And supposedly, he was even illegally married to one or two of them.

"Where you guys headed?"

"Point Fermin," said Will Man, his forehead stresslining over his begging-my-way eyes. "Moms says it's a good place for us to be together." He stopped to think about something, his hands all the while wringing themselves dry against his pantlegs. " 'Be together.' Can you believe that, Toom?"

I noed. "You need some aspirin or something, Will Man?" I said then. "You don't seem so well."

"How 'bout if I ask for you to come along!" he damn-near shouted at me. "Would that be cool with you, Toom?"

"Will Man," I said all nonchalanteven. "I'm not so sure pops would want me along for anything this important-sounding. Do you?"

"I'll talk him into it!; tell him I won't go just by myself. Me and him, you know, we're not even that close. You along'll make us both feel better. Trust me, Toom."

"All right," I said, suddenly hopeful in my heart to first-hand hear what Hector Hermosillo, *El Primo* himself, had to say to his hardtrippin' son day one out of lockup, "if you really want me to tag along with you I will."

Will Man got up, eyed me as though I'd become an L.A. Dodger allstar or maybe dropped a laundrybag full of money at his feet and put up his fist. "I owe you one, Toom," he said, and connected his fist with my suddenly-raised own. "I owe you a *big* one."

"No you don't, Will Man," I told him rightoff, damnnear feeling that I'd cheated the guy, my very own good friend, when I'd done so. "Just put the baseball stuff in the crib and when we get back we'll hit some drives over the fence. Cool?"

"Cool," said Will Man. And a splitsecond later this lime-green VW Bug tailpiped it into the parkinglot.

The first few blocks neither of us said anything; just sat back and tried to get used to being in the very tight space of a rumbling sputtering car driven by a man just hours ago come back to society. "So you vatos got nothing to say, huh?" Hector had said to both his son next to him and me in the rearview mirror maybe a minute into the ride, while all the while squeezing hard on his steeringwheel. Of all things for him to be, I thought, edgynervous as Will Man wasn't the one I'd expected.

Hector, wearing a wifebeater tanktop, was fullytattooed at his arms, neck, and upperback. A badlyfaded-all-over *Lydia Girl* was on his right neckside while some less-old tattoos like *Juanita* and *Teresa* were just under that, and then on his right backside was three times the gangtag *RSP.* On his right forearm I saw the big blue cross with the *Jesus Christ* just below it in old-English letters. When I secretly scooted to my far left I saw a brandnewlooking, jailhouse-style *Little Hector* just under an as-badlyfaded-as-the-*Lydia-Girl Will Man. Little Hector,* I thought; he must be a new babybrother of Will Man's I'd never heard about because the tattoo hadn't been there the last time Hector'd been around. Then I wondered if Will Man even knew that he had a most-likely-living-somewhere-right-in-San-Pedro-with-him stepbrother named Little Hector. And maybe even in his very own neighborhood at that. I decided to mention it later. If then.

"Damn! I'm driving with a couple-a lame-Os," said Hector suddenly, again flashing us each that edgynervous look of his. Back at the pickup spot, Will Man hadn't even asked if I could come along, he was so scared of pops. And I surely wasn't going to invite myself. So instead, Hector'd looked at us standing together all dumb and speechless and said, "What? You wanna come along too, little hombre?" to me. "It'll do you some good, ey, if you heard what I'm gonna tell my own little wedo." So I instantly jumped into the back of the Bug, giving Will Man shotgunseat based on circumstance alone.

"Whose car?" said Will Man finally as we leftturned it onto Pacific Avenue.

"That's a good question, hijo," said Hector all impressed with him, " 'cause earlier I was wondering it myself. I don't really know. It's one of those friend of a friend of a friend things, ey. Know what I mean, vatos? All confusing as hell." He laughed hard and shot a side-eyed look at his boy, hoping he'd understood him properly. Then he took a closer look at him. "What the fuck happened to your neck, man!" he said all loud. "You hanging out with a vampire or something, ey?" to which Will Man instantly got this crooked helpless grin on his face and, without having moved an inch, seemed to be shrinking right into his seatcrease. "Don't tell me you've already slid it into homeplate, hijo? Have you or not?"

"Naw, pops!" said Will Man all gollygee-like, but sounding not too sure he'd told him the right thing either.

"Better not've, vato," said Hector, quickly checking me in the rearview. "And you, Toomer? Have you been hanging in the boneyard with any muchachas? Don't lie to me either, ese." I instantly no no noed my head, *Which is the honest-to-goodness truth, Primo!*, I rightaway thought at the man.

Which it was too. Except for a sneaking-off-on-those-hickysessions Will Man, none of us had ever had time enough for girls. I mean if they hadn't been down with the fish or the football, or the pranking and the baseball, or most other things we were into, then they hadn't interested us. "Good," he said all relaxrelieved and once again looking to his son. "That's exactly what I wanted to hear, wedo. I was worried that your urges had gotten the best of you already." Suddenly, though, I wasn't so sure I should've ever come along.

At Point Fermin, Hector parked the VW along the white wooden fence that protected touristy pedestrians and their children from edging themselves off of clifftops a hundred or so feet above the greenblue spread of Pacific Ocean water. From the car you could see the long and slow up and down of that water which, the more it reached away from you to the right of Catalina Island, the more it flattened out to a hazygray horizonline. From the high car, though, you could still hear the rocky roaring, way-way-under-us wave-crash. Slowly, my eyes wandered across that everywhere spread of sea until maybe half a mile out they spotted a small speck of a person on a nearing-in-on-an-oceanbuoy kayak. The paddler was all smoothchurning arms as he upped and downed to the steady swells around him.

"Man," said an also-oceanviewing Hector. "I've kinda missed being out." Then he turned his head to his son.

"That's the one bad thing about prison, hijo. You don't get outside enough."

Until just a year ago, me and the fellas sometimes headed over to Point Fermin to watch the hanggliders take off from that five-feet-away-from-us cliffedge, only to drop nosefirst down towards those waterwashed rocks below and then quickly curve heavenward so fast to even into this smooth, way-above-the-ocean glide. Up in that windpocketed sky the hanggliders had looked to us like the biggest stringless kites of all time as they made their long lazy looping turns on the air. That was last year, though, when the hanggliding was still allowed. What'd made it illegal was when two of the just-taken-off hanggliders ended up down against those cliffbottom rocks. Their downswoops had supposedly been welldonesmooth enough, but neither'd been able to pull up and out of them in time and . . . Anyways, that's what I was staring at, their takeoffspot, when a suddenly cigarettesmoking Hector cleared his throat to speak.

"Tell me, hijo," he said to his son. "You know what the birds and the bees are?" Will Man, though, didn't say a word as he tried his best not to look at pops. "How about you, Toomer? You know what they are, símon?"

"Yeah," I said, feeling my face go rightaway red. "When a man and woman get busy."

"That's right, Toomer," said Hector at the rearview and taking another cigarette hit. "But get busy for what?"

"Babies," I said. "To make babies. Will Man knows this stuff."

"He does?" said Hector, turning to his suddenly-glaring-at-me boy. "Do you, hijo?" Will Man slowly yessed his head. "Tell me then when I ask you something, *carnal,* instead of wasting my precious time." Hector stopped to think. "So what gets the woman pregnant then, ey?" he finally said.

"Sperm," said me and Will Man at the same time together, with me kind of getting used to the questioning.

"That's right again," said Hector all it's-about-time-like. "You vatos are gonna get A-plusses if you keep this up. Now: when should or shouldn't you be with your girls, little vatos?"

I, for my part, thought very very hard about the question. Never in my life, you see, had I considered it the way Hector was suddenly asking it. Especially since none of us but Will Man had gotten any experience in the girl department. I waited for Will Man to say something, but when he glanced at me all I-can't-handle-this-shit-goofyfaced like, I knew he wouldn't talk.

"At night," I quickly said, which had made a perfect sense to me since I couldn't understand why anybody'd be in a babymakingmood too early into a day.

"Say what, homes?" said a deeply-disappointedsounding Hector, though, with a deeper dumber red running instantly up my neck and all over my face. Without really wanting to I looked back to the oceantop for that possibly-buoy-rounded kayaker, but couldn't find a trace of him anywhere. "You vatos think that all you gotta do is say hey, what's up? to a weda for a baby to pop out of her, ey?" I could feel him looking back and forth at me and Will Man, with neither of us in much of an eyecontact-returning mood right about then. Damn, I said to myself. What could've happened to the guy in that kayak? "Tell me this, eses," said Hector. "You know what a monthly is, don't you?" We both slowly noed our heads, still not able to look his way. "Man, what do they teach you in school, typing? On the last two questions, ey, you vatos just slipped to a B-minus. Shoot, maybe even a C-plus, I haven't decided. Listen up, though. The monthly's when the weda—if she's old enough—can't have any babies because she passes all this stuff out of her, símon?"

"What stuff, pops?" said Will Man all I-don't-get-it-like fascinated suddenly.

"You know, ey," said Hector all fidgety again. "Stuff." But still Will Man had that I-don't-get-it face going on. "All right then," said Hector finally. "Blood, okay? And it happens once a month twelve times a year, and the weda can't do nothing about it, ey. It's just mother nature getting her way, eses. Sabes?" We yessed, but in a deep disbelieving wonder. "Now as far as you're concerned, vatos, there's one good thing about the monthly that you should never forget, and that's this, ey: that while the weda's having it, you can get with her as many times as you want 'cause she's got no babyegg inside of her. Since it's come out with the blood, ey, it's the perfect time to get yourselves some lovin'. But you still gotta be careful: 'cause one mistake and you bought yourself the hotdog stand, brother. And that's no joke either, eses, if you know what I mean?" This time we both yessed like crazy, and with the seriousest expressions I'd ever seen on the either of us. Will Man, though, I was sure, had had the same exact thought flash his brain that'd flashed mine: But what about all the blood? And Hector being Hector rightaway saw that brain-flash all over our worried-up faces. "What now, eses?" he said. "You little shits aren't scared of a little blood, are you? I can't believe this! You vatos would give up all that pleasure 'cause of that? *Chalé*. I'm suddenly ashamed for you, ey." Then he looked his son's way. "I'm almost ashamed for my-self." Me and Will Man lowered our heads. "If that's the case, we've got ourselves a serious problem, ey, 'cause I don't know about you, Toomer, but Will Man here's been baptized Catholic like me and Liddie, and even though we've been separated many years now and I've been locked up in the pinta a lot, we're still very religious people, ey, which means, until Will Man's an adult on his own, he's very religious too; which basically means no condoms while bonin' down, ey— the church doesn't allow it; which all of it together has to mean what, eses?" Hector waited.

Again my mind started to grind around for the right an-swer while for some crazy reason not wanting that B- or C-minus to drop to a D or maybe even an F. But I couldn't find it. Then I looked at a Will Man who suddenly had it like he'd never in his life had anything before, making all of Hector's coming-out-of-nowhere talk fall into place like the best, most sensiblest kind of thinking ever. "Always staying out of the babyhole," he said all absolutely sure of himself.

Hector eyed his boy as if a prize student and said,

"Símon, hijo, símon," which instantly had Will Man off of that cliffedge on a swooping soaring hanggliderride of his very own. "It's simple when you think about it, isn't it, *carnal?*" he said kind of affectionate-like, then damnnear even smiling. Will Man yessed his widegrinning head. Then, instead of the rearview, Hector actually turned to me in his seat and said, "Do you get it too, Toomer?" I yessed as well. "All right then, vatos," said Hector. "That means we're down to our final problem, ey: what should we do about it?"

" 'Do about it?' " said a–suddenly-back-to-the-ground Will Man.

"Tell me something, ese," said an again disappointed-sounding Hector. "How long do you think, ey, that your weda's hickygiving's gonna get your little peanuts off? Huh?" And just like that Will Man crept right back into the shell he'd for a very brief second come out of. "Just 'cause it's all thought out and understood, doesn't mean it's going to happen that way, wedo. You ever hear of the instincts and urges, ey?" We quickly yessed. "Then you know that they mostly don't give a damn about what the brain is thinking, símon? Especially when it's you and some hot-to-trot Lola up a tree somewhere and both of you absolutely have to have a piece of each other as soon as possible. Sabes? At times like that, ey, you'd be surprised how quick the brain forgets what'd made the best of sense to it just a minute before. The instincts and urges, though, vatos, they never forget what makes sense to 'em, ey. That's why you have to make some compromises with 'em. And of course with that weda up in the tree. Shit, even me and Liddie had to make a few after you were born, hijo. Out of respect to her father."

When Will Man rolled his window down, I immediately heard the way-way-below-us waves washing strong and heavy against those cliffbottom rocks. Half my attention stayed with their foamrumbling sound while the other half listened to Will Man ask his pops a not-so-sure-I-thought-he-should've-asked-him-the-question question.

"What compromises?" he'd said.

"Certain things, ey," said Hector, "that you and your wedas can do that wouldn't get her knocked up."

Certain things? I thought. Certain things like what? Again I looked at Will Man to once again see if he'd made any sense of it at all. Maybe not the correct answer, but enough of one to shock his eyes up some.

"I'll give you eses a hint," said Hector all calmed and collected. "The pinta's full of guys doing exactly what I'm talking about. You cholos, though, are lucky. You have your wedas to hang out with."

And with that, everything about the compromises fell into place as fast as a two-piece jigsawpuzzle.

"Never underestimate, vatos, the pleasure the rest of a weda's body can give you. *And* the other way around, ey. You can never forget to please both ways, because to leave your weda hanging dry in the pleasure department is wrong."

Will Man, I noticed, had gone a very numb-amazed. Like he'd finally made some close connection to pops; a connection that'd instantly quieted his whole body down.

For the longest stretch we just stared at Hector as if he were the wizard of every kind of know-how. Hector'd said him and Lydia, though, and trying not to imagine them doing the compromises together was suddenly a very difficult thing for me. In fact, trying not to imagine a good friend's moms in the very bucknaked, let alone on her front or backside in the very bucknaked, felt like some impossible-to-avoid bad behavior. I couldn't keep the woman out of my head. No matter how hard I resisted, images of a compromising-away Lydia came and went like so many incredibly nasty brainshorts, leaving me in a shameful excited mess.

"What if the girl's not down with the compromises, though, pops?" said Will Man suddenly. "What then?"

"That's easy, ese," said Hector. "You dump her. A weda like that, ey, will only keep you frustrated and miserable. Who wants to be with a babymaker at your age anyways, vatos? Or a churchgirl. There are plenty of wedas in the sea, ey, who wouldn't get weirded out by this stuff. Not only wedas either, 'cause like I said: the pinta's full of guys doing the same exact thing. Not that I'm condoning that behavior or nothing. But those instincts and urges, eses, they don't just go away behind bars. If anything they get worse, and then they can really mess with your head. If you only knew how it happens in the pinta, ey." Hector's mind drifted back to incarceration for a few seconds. "But anyways, homes," he finally said, "out here there are lots of women for you. Take Mona, for example. You can bet your bottom dollar, eses, she'd be cool about the compromises."

"Mona?" said an ASAP Will Man all surprisedsounding. Mona was Will Man's nextdoor neighbor and Lydia's best friend, neither of which had surprised him, though. What'd done that was the fact that Mona weighed a good two billsplus.

"Yeah, Mona," said a you-heard-me-right-the-first-time Hector. "She's a woman who can offer young vatos like yourselves good times, ey, with none of that girly weda attitude thrown in either."

"Man, there's no way I'd get with Mona, pops," said Will Man, letting out this helpless chuckle of a laugh. "She's not close to my style."

"Style?" said Hector, suddenly surprised some himself. "You're hanging out with a vampire, wedo, and preaching about *style?* Just look at your neck, ey: like you've got some purple skin disease that also leaves your wevos swollen blue. Chalé, homes. Now I can see why Liddie asked me to have this talk with you, 'cause your little ass has no imagination. And getting down has a lot to do with that, ey." Hector took another cigarette drag. "Because I'm doing this for your best interest, though," he said, blowing out the smoke, "I'll try and be patient, ey. You see, eses, it's not so much looks you should be after—though looks can be pretty damn nice—as it is pleasure."

A strain hit Will Man's face; a trying-hard-to-get-at-Hector's-meaning strain that was sure that his pops was sharing another something important with him. But Will Man just couldn't figure what the man had meant by pleasure being more important than looks. In the small backseat, though, I'd already imagined an on-all-fours Mona naked as the day she was born, and then her and Hector working hard on the one then the other compromise, and just like that I'd gone right off of that cliffedge myself, soaring the sky in the longestlasting windpocket that'd definitely ever happened at the Point Fermin cliffs. Up there I wondered whether Juanita and Teresa had been fat women too, and what they must've looked like in their compromising-away bucknakeds. When I finally looked in Will Man's way, I saw that he'd made it off of his carseat too, and into that high blue sky with me. Up there together we smiled at each other and damnnear giggled.

"You see, vatos," said a down-inside-the-car Hector to us, "the best thing about Mona is that she's a very lonely and very misunderstood woman." He looked at us closer, smiled, took a final drag of his cigarette, and tossed it out of the window. "I'd bet big money she's even fantasized about you vatos before." Me and Will Man looked at each other, shocked. "I know how that woman's mind works, ey, and trust me, she's even been hoping you wedos would make a move on her."

Mona? Have fantasies about us? Was that possible? All those years of being around her and we'd been a possible bootybucknaked in her mind the whole time? The steady waveroar suddenly filled my floating ears up to the brim while Will Man once or twice let out a nervous, pops-has-gotta-be-pulling-our-legs-sounding chuckle. Then, back inside the VW, things began to shrink while the world outside seemed to stretch forever and ever out of my reach. Mona bothered me. In fact she now bothered me as much as Hector had terribly interested me. Though she'd always had a nice-enough personality, I'd mostly tried to avoid the woman. I mean Mona was a person with no kids, no man, and, except for Lydia, no friends at all, yet she somehow managed to live in our neighborhood anyways. Only her younger brother Johnny, who we sometimes played blackjack with while he got looped on these vodkaheavy screwdrivers, once in a while dropped in on her. And whenever he did, so did we, because Johnny, being a bank teller, always had these ten-dollar quarterrolls and the best of attitudes as their quarters came out of their paper-packets, chinged into the pot, and dropped straight into our pockets. With a steadily-liquored-up Johnny, the winning was a guaranteed automatic. Until, that is, he'd gotten to that point of telling us, "Okay, you guys, two more drinks and I'm warning you, I won't be in fullcontrol of myself." And because he most likely meant what he'd said, we'd bail the apartment way before that second drink was poured, the real signal to hit it usually being Johnny's touchyfeely phase. For example, he'd lay a sloppy hand on your shoulder and say something like, "My goodness, in a couple-a years you'll be such a strapping young man," or, "Won't you come upstairs and model some of my socks for me?" We'd laugh of course, but quickly finish whatever hand we'd held and hit the road like some gotaway-with-it-all bank robbers, our pockets packed to the full with coin.

But that'd been about as much man as we'd ever seen around Mona—and ourselves as much kids. Suddenly, though, right in the back of that VW Bug, something new about Mona dawned on me. She at times during those black-jack sessions had behaved a bit inclose with us. I mean sure she was a big woman in a very small apartment who often enough had to squeeze tight by a young guy to get from point A to point B. But even back then I had once or twice wondered whether or not her big breastbrushes hadn't been a bit on the overlyfriendly-intentional side, if you know what I mean. For example, I'd be looking over my blackjack hand, right, when *blam!,* there'd be one of those big Mona breasts all up against my back and shoulder and sometimes even headside to boot. And then there were those times she'd asked me to grab a too-difficult-for-her-to-get-at-herself plate or bowl from a cup-boardtop while she gripped my legs to supposedly steady me on the chair. And then there'd even been that moment I could've sworn she was dreaming my way with a little too much mist in her eyes, until she'd suddenly come to, that is, and quickly turned her head away. Maybe Hector hadn't been all that off, I started to think; about the woman, her fantasies, *and* her loneliness. Especially since everything else he'd already told us about had had so much of a solid sense to it.

"Any questions, vatos?" said Hector all matter-of-factly then. "If so ask now, ey, 'cause you know me: here one day, gone the rest." He started laughing again. Me and Will Man, though, looked at each other and rightaway went back to our own, but very-separate headtrips apiece. "I guess now you'll be showing your vampire friend a thing or two. Right, hijo?" Will Man smiled at Hector, who again laughed until he started coughing like a sick person. "Thanks for the talk, pops," said Will Man then—and like a suddenly-grown man at that. Hector put a hand on top of his boy's head and rubbed it around some. "I wish we could have 'em more often, hijo," said Hector back. "I know how much you need 'em, ey, so we'll see just what we can do about it in the future. Símon, little ese?" "Símon," said Will Man no different than his pops would've done. Then the engine got fired up and the VW was eased away from the cliffedge.

"By the way, vatos," said Hector as a last word, "the first chance you get, find yourselves a car with a decent back seat. You won't regret it, ey."

Over-the-line was how we played. I was in the outfield while Will Man was waiting his turn at bat next to a bunch of sunworn and groundpainted seals and dolphins. Besides me and Will Man, Richard was pitching from a tugboat deck, David playing shortstop by a giant seahorse, and Mondo waiting on a whaletail to swing or not swing at Richard's next delivery. Suddenly a high flyball sailed off of Mondo's bat, over my head, and over the outfield fence. I immediately went after it.

Even though the nursery's fence had always been high enough to keep the nurseryschoolers in, it'd been easy enough for us to climb right over it. Those nurseryschoolers, though, they'd stopped playing in the nursery a year or two back. That was when the school'd been open and they played and played alldaylong while me and the fellas had to wait for the last of them to go home before jumping into the schoolyard ourselves. But the nursery had been a different place then. All kept up and clean and run like the perfect little garden. Usually while we'd waited, the parents of the nurseryschoolers stood outside the fence right beside us, staring our way no different than the L.A.P.D. would do: like they were trying to memorize our faces while at the same time warning us with their eyes. "We know who you are," they'd eyeballed at us, "so you better stay a goodways away from our little ones." But even way back then we knew their looks to be full of shit. As if any one or all of them could've stopped those waves from washing against those cliffbottom rocks. As I headed back to my position I was suddenly as glad as Will Man had been that Hector'd let me tag along with them. How else would I have learned about the birds and the bees? Not from some scared-to-death-over-a-bunch-of-hoping-to-play-a-little-baseball-like-us-knuckleheads parents, right?

Under the stillwarm afternoon sun, Mondo was yelling for Will Man to step to his turn at bat. Will Man, though, was looking across the infield, past that thirdbase seagull, and over to his porch at a just-come-out-of-her-apartment Mona who'd rightaway gotten into one of those several-times-a-day chats with his moms, Lydia. "Will Man!" yelled Mondo, then Richard, then all of them put together. But never once did he hear them. A far away universe, you see, was a long long way for a name to have to travel just to make it to a young guy's ears.

Almost immediately after the Hector talk, me, Will Man, and all of the fellas went on this monthslong crimespree that'd started up so fast and furious even we'd been caught off guard by it. While it'd happened we pretty much lost our control to the point of forgetting all about our summer fishingtrips along the waterfront, our football and baseball sessions at the Big Park and nursery, and anything else that had to do with a basic common sense. We drove into the highs (the rich neighborhoods like Palos Verdes and Rolling Hills that sat way up above the Ranch, known that as the lows) almost every night in these ritzy rental cars we'd GTA'd from the just-across-the-street-from-us cruiseterminal, robbed uncountable houses, fenced all of our crimegotten goods, and habitgambled most of our money away.

During that whole crimespree too, I couldn't help but think that that Hector talk had somehow derailed me and

Will Man from being the simplesimons we were before we'd heard it. Suddenly, though, we'd get frustrated and angry at the smallest little thing said or done to us, be prone to start up squabs with the fellas themselves, and have terrible dreams apiece about a wanting-to-lie-right-on-top-of-you Mona, for example, or, only in my case, a suddenly-naked-and-knocking-at-your-door Lydia ready to tell your moms about all of your very recent bathroom behavior. And maybe as a result of all that new agitation in our systems, we'd somehow managed to derail all the fellas too—especially since me and Will Man had more and more become something like the group decisionmakers; and then me much more than him.

Then one night at the very end of July, the two of us, instead of being interested in the usual craps session with some of the just-as-usual older heads, convinced the fellas to hit up the Hotel La Salle with us over on Seventh Street. It was finally time, me and Will Man'd decided, to bring to life as much of Hector's wisdom as possible. And between the lot of us we figured we had just enough in the way of bankroll to pull the experience off.

The Hotel La Salle wasn't the seediest hotel in San Pedro (that was the just-about-cattycorner-from-it Cabrillo), or the most drugrelated (that was the up-on-Twelfth-and-Pacific California), or even the violentest (that was the Barton

Hill). In fact, for a place located just a couple of blocks from the Ranch the La Salle had a downright classiness to it. It had a clean and quiet lobby, a deskman in a threepiece suit and handlebar mustache, and a buildingfront that claimed the concretechiseled date of 1923 right above its doorway. And the La Salle had had some history to it too. For example, it'd been a main part of this formerly worldfamous stretch of bars and buildings known as Old Beacon Street; a place that every sailor on the planet had known as "the toughest few blocks in the world" and which some of the oldtimers still called it. Old Beacon Street had had bars with the names of Shanghai Red's, the Dollar, and Goodfellows that'd been packed all night every night with sailors, drunks, tourists, and prostitutes who'd kept the local jail as packed as the bars had been themselves. But all that was before the place'd been bulldozed under for a supposed rat problem. It's a hard thing to believe: knocking down a whole worldfamous community just because of some rats? Only in Los Angeles, right? Anyways, that's where me and the fellas were headed, to one of the only buildings to've sidestepped that historyhammering wreckingball.

In front of the La Salle we saw a curbstanding woman who had Hector's top two requirements absolutely down, for she was much more on the plump than unplump side and in her hairnet and rollers was a mile-and-a-half from having good looks. On top of that, she had some badlystretchmarked breasts and a bubblebootied backside to boot. "She's perfect, isn't she, Toom?" said Will Man as soon as he'd seen her, and as if in a perfect dream. "Only if she's down with the compromises," I said to him. Then me and him headed up to her to hopefully negotiate somekind of group discount, seeing how we were so many to her single one.

"How you doin' tonight?" I said all I've-done-this-a-thousand-times-before-like.

"Beat it, junior," said the woman, though, no more than glancing our way.

"What do you mean 'beat it'?" I told her, trying hard to sound insulted. "We're here to talk some business and you get rightaway disrespectful."

"Yeah," said Will Man. "Business *and* pleasure."

"You guys wanna talk business with me?" she said, suddenly impressed as she looked us up and down. "All right then, talk." We did. "Two for the price of one!" she said.

"Or the regular price," I told her. "But for the full treatment."

"You want *everything?*" she said. We yes yes yessed our heads, with Will Man's damnnear coming off his neck. "You sure you guys can handle everything?" Again we yessed like lapdogs. "And then some," said Will Man. "And them too?" said the woman about the rest of the fellas standing across the street. And yet again we did like lapdogs. "All right," she said, "but only this once. Follow me."

She walked into the La Salle's frontdoor, through its

checkerfloored lobby, and up a wide flight of stairs with our whole train in tow, making me feel like some duck in a pond. Whenever I looked at Will Man or another of the fellas, I saw nothing but two widebulging eyes glued to that steadilyrising backside in front of us. At the third floor the woman went into the hallway, opened the first available roomdoor, asked us in, and shut the door behind us.

"Money first," she said all business-like. I pulled a rubberbanded wad out of my pocket and gave it to her. "I'll count it in the bathroom—while I freshen up. Why don't you all get comfortable. If you know what I mean?" Then she stepped into the bathroom, shut its door too, and started the water running hard.

"We're finally gonna get some!" whispered a terribly-happy Richard to us. "First one naked's first to go." We all undressed as if getting out of some fireflaming clothes and, to my surprise, Will Man, having tripped and stumbled out of each and every one of his redhot garments (socks included), was deadlast to the raw. "Looks like you got the caboose," said Richard to him.

"Fuck that, ey," said Will Man all Hector-like. "You wouldn't even be here if it wasn't for me and Toomer. I'm going at least third," to which nobody disagreed a word.

For the next minute or two we bounced around listening to that water run, our skins getting cooler and cooler as we waited.

"You're not drowning or anything, are you, lady?" said Richard finally through the bathroom door.

"Of course not," yelled the woman over the hardrunning water. "Just gimme another second to finish freshening up."

When I looked around I noticed the all of us an already very-wellrisen for the occasion. On the floor our clothes looked like some kind of lumpy, soon-to-be-sewn-together quilt.

Suddenly there was a *boom boom boom* at the roomdoor, though, which had us instantly spinning in its direction.

"Oh shit!" said Will Man all around. "It's her pimp, ey."

"Time to get ready to rumble then, fellas," said a quickly-grabbing-for-his-trousers Richard.

Then a voice behind us that sounded nothing like the person's we'd been waiting for said, "Come on in!" and we once again one-eightied around to the sight of our supposed-to-be-as-naked-as-we-were woman with a police badge hanging around her neck. A splitsecond later and the room was filled with so many L.A.P.D.s that our you-know-whats started dropping like so many bad habits. For some strange reason all I could do was think of old Goldie in a not-too-different-than-ours situation no more than a block and a couple of months off.

One by one and all through the night each of our moms came to claim her boy from the police tank with there everytime being a terrible amount of slaps and shouts echoing throughout the station, and after each pickup at least one gleeful rollerboy always showing his mug at our bars to let us know that we'd be the next in line until there was nobody left but me alone waiting, my own moms having stranded me until way into the next morning.

Things had gotten worse than expected too. While in police custody one of the fellas had slipped up and actually mentioned the cruiseterminal, and the next thing we knew, on top of that original solicitation charge, we'd been hit with damnnear a dozen counts of GTA apiece. Everybody's moms had gotten so angry by the news, they'd altogether made each of their boys promise them *and* the police that neither'd any longer hang out with the supposed ringleader of their set—*me,* Sunny Toomer—or if they did they'd rightaway be given a year apiece in juvenile hall. Not only that, but some of the fellas each got these crazy punishments anyways. Lydia, for example, had Will Man donate all of his sports and fishing equipment back to the where-he'd-bought-'em-all-from-in-the-first-place Salvation Army, Richard's moms, Dee Dee, arranged for him to do three months in juvy anyways, just to give him a taste of what he was headed for hanging around a person like me (but luckily for him the Grizz had stepped in to get the juvy judge to give him only a month, and then at some juvy ranch with cows and horses on it at that), and Mondo's moms sent him to deepdown Mexico to stay with his knew-him-barely-at-all pops for the rest of the year. Needless to say, I thought it very evil and extreme of them all. That is until my own moms had gotten the punishment fever herself which, when I later thought about it, had seemed like one of those way-out mysteries to me.

On top of losing all the fellas for who knew how long, moms, the third morning after my arrest, sat me down in a kitchen chair, had this brandnew boyfriend of hers named Caesar hold my arms behind the chairback, and proceeded to scissorsnip my hair until I was left with these very ugly, mangylooking scalpclumps. Who knew she'd cared so much about her boy's good or bad behavior, I said to myself as I watched the scalpclumps fall, never having shown the slightest interest in it before. But suddenly she was on this correctioning crusade.

"For many many months to come, Toom," said moms to me with the haircaked scissors inhand, "that's gonna be the style. And if I ever see or hear of you wearing a hat or a bandana or anything at all, I'll make sure you end up rightalongside your buddy Richard. Do you hear me? But for much more than three months."

"Why're you punishing me like this!" I said to her finally, all the while trying to get out of Caesar's hands. "It's cruel and unusual punishment, and maybe even against the law. Like child abuse."

Moms took a step back. "Caesar," she said, regripping the scissors daggerstyle. "Give us a second alone together, will you?"

"Sure, sugar," said Caesar with a suddenly tighter-than-before armsqueeze. "You're gonna be nice to your mother, right, coño? I mean, she is your mother, after all."

"Yeah," I said. "Of course I will." Then he let me go, gave her a kiss, and stepped outside.

She squatted herself low right in front of me, her bare legs showing when her dress slid to the sides some. I could see my snipped-to-pieces and differentlengthed headhair all over her knees. It just clung to them as if a longtime part of them.

"Now you listen to me, Toomer," said an armchairgrabbing moms all upclose in my face, some dirtyblonde strings wedged between her pink and never-so-angry-at-me lips, "if you think this is cruel and unusual, you've got another thing coming. What you did to Goldie—*that* was cruel and unusual. Don't think I don't know about that story either. You have no idea what I've been through because of you." I could tell she felt like screaming at me. "We were planning to get married, you sonofabitch. Did you know that? On our trip to Hawaii. And you fucked it all up." She just squatted there and glared at me with those dirtyblonde strings in her lips that'd beaded all over with sweat. "You're lucky you're a minor, Toom, 'cause I couldn't think of anything sweeter than you having ended up in the same place as him. I'm not kidding. And that wouldn't've been cruel and unusual either. Just poetic justice, you lucky bastard."

Again I looked at my headhair on her also-sweated-up knees. I wanted to reach out and brush it off of each one of them and even apologize into her ear that it'd landed on them in the first place. Then I looked at her you-are-the-enemy eyes. "Goldie did some bad things," I said as casual as possible, knowing damnwell it'd angry her up real good and, more importantly, keep her right there close in front of me.

"To bad people!" she whisperscreamed, staring at me as if wanting to drive those daggergripped scissors deep into my chest.

"Why don't you just send me to my father then?" I said to her. "Like Mondo's mother."

She immediately stood up, which made my heart sink to the floor, and started pacing around the kitchen with those scissors still gripped daggerstyle. "If I could I would," she finally said. "But it's not that easy. For one, he's no longer reachable; nobody knows where he is. And for two," she stopped, looked straight at me, and pointed those scissors my way, "you owe me. With Goldie I might've been able to start something new. But now all I have is this place—and you."

"And Caesar."

She checked at the door. "He's temporary and you know it," she whispered all insulted.

"What, I've gotta stay just so you don't lose your welfare checks?"

She inspected at me as if I'd guessed her weight, then flashed away. "Toomer," she said. "We don't really hate each other okay, so let's not get ugly about any of this. You've taken something major from me. I don't care if he'd done bad, we were gonna get married, Toom. To surprise you." I saw the wet building up in her eyes and couldn't stand to look at them anymore. In a way, I knew she was right: in order to make my own life better off I'd taken something very big from her. Maybe even something bigger than the both of us put together. Suddenly I felt myself getting weak and a very scalpclumpdeserving.

"So what do I owe you then?" I said.

"Just what you said," she told me, wiping at her face. "You'll stay here till you're eighteen-years-old and deal with my every foul mood."

"And if I don't?"

She stepped up to the chair and squatted down in front of me again, this time those scissors pointed right at my nose. "You will, Toomer. And you know why you will?"

"Why?" I said, staring at nothing but her angry-at-me mouth.

"Because you need me more than anything else in the world," her mouth said to me. "That's why. You've got nothing else but me. And viceversa."

Coming as they did from my moms they were maybe the bestsounding words that I'd ever heard. Then she added that I wasn't allowed any further than the front or back porch and got given only fifteen minutes to make it the two-plus miles all the way home from school.

"Yes, maam," I told her as if giving her a kiss.

And that's how things went all the way around for, as moms herself had promised, many *many* months to come, until one day in mid-November when she told me that it was finally time to get myself out of the apartment for a stretch, and that a short trip she'd arranged with some of our local family would be just what the doctor ordered. And damn was she right, because right about then I'd happened to feel myself on the verge of a possiblypermanent kookoo, I'd been cribrestricted and apart-from-it-all so long. A drive through the Mojave Desert, I thought, did sound like a perfect doctor's note. But there was one little problem: the family I'd supposedly be going with.

"They're crazy!" I told her. "Always trying to hurt somebody. I don't wanna be stuck in a car with the two of them."

"What do you mean 'crazy'?" said moms back at me, though. "You're getting all your friends arrested for grandtheft auto and soliciting prostitutes and then calling my brothers crazy? What've they ever done to you personally?" I thought about it some. "Well what?"

"Nothing," I said. "Yet."

"That's right nothing. And they never will. But instead you, a known criminal, sit around badmouthing a couple of guys who've been nice enough to offer you on a trip with them."

"All right, all right," I said to her. "I'll go."

"Damnright you'll go," she said. "And you'll be nice to them too. No lip or attitude, do you hear me?" I yessed. "Anyways, they've lived like model citizens lately. Yancey's even had a job for three or four months now."

Fantastic.

And at least *going* to Las Vegas it was a perfect doctor's note. Never could I have imagined a bunch of sunbaked and foreverspreading sand to look as beautiful as what I saw, and with so many different cactus shapes to boot. And the trip to Vegas had been beautiful for another reason too. My uncles, Angel and Yancey, had planned this get-rich-quick scheme while they were there and talked on and on about all the wonderful things that they'd do and buy after we'd made it home with their new pile of loot. They'd supposedly quit their jobs, buy a house, a motorhome, new cars—even said they'd move my moms out of the projects. They told me they'd read up on all the different kinds of gambling Las Vegas had to offer (which sounded like just about all of them) and had finally decided something called roulette to be the best way to "beat the system," as they kept calling it. Anyways, that what-all-they'd-buy-with-their-winnings talk had been some of the bestsounding I'd ever heard, at times getting as interesting as Hector's own had been. And the fact that it'd lasted for hundreds of those goldendesertmiles didn't seem to hurt it either. Unfortunately, though, things that first night in Vegas didn't turn out as perfectly as the uncles had hoped they would, and, to be terribly honest, had turned out rather the opposite of that. And then, a goodways into our quicker-than-expected U-turn back to Los Angeles, they got even worse.

Then it was hanging from the rearview mirror swaying side to side at the end of a shoestring and, what bothered me terribly, bent and pointing sometimes at Angel and then at me, at Angel and then at me, at. . . . A shameful nauseous feeling came and went in my throat and stomach. Both of my uncles, though, had these happy, crazed, and quivery expressions on their faces. Like cartoon gargoyles. It was too much to think that I was in any way related to either of them.

We'd already been rolling though the desert for a good hour when we noticed the figure of the hitchhiker on the shoulder of the nightroad, his arm held out and thumb cocked high. Though we hadn't quite gotten to him yet I saw him as clearly as if he'd been sitting in the car next to me. Black leather jacket, Hector-like neck tattoos, greasyratty hair tied in a bloodred bandana with a beaten-down backpack at his blackbooted feet, the hitchhiker's face was meancreased and weatherworn—from maybe a lifetime of being in the exact same middle-of-the-desert situation he was in when we'd come upon him. A night animal in need of a lift, I thought, and one I wasn't sure I wanted anywhere in the car with us. When the headlights finally lit the hitchhiker up dayglo, he squinted this beamy pair of razor-red eyes that reached right into our car; eyes that showed he had an ageold bite. Then, for a splitsecond, everything about the man softened some. He became simple, almost friendlyfaced, standing there with that needy thumb of his sticking straight up to the sky. But behind the wheel Angel stiffened and tried his hardest not to look at the guy.

My uncles had arrived in Vegas with the hopes and excitement of scheming warriors, and a mere few hours later'd retreated defeated, with Angel's yearyounger brother Yancey sprawled out long in the back seat from having hammered too many on-the-housers at the big hotels while losing his paycheck piece by speedy piece to one dealer after another. And because Angel hadn't done any better he'd started to motor us back to Los Angeles and the anybody lives that they led, flat broke and on the meanest of tilts. But then, an angry hour into the desert, there was that hitchhiker with his thumb sticking up and a very highwayhopeful to latch onto the mobile misery coming his way—though he didn't actually know how much of a misery my driving and passed out uncles really were. And to be honest, neither did I at the time. I mean I had a clue from past rumors and events that Angel and Yancey could be far from goodygoody when their heads were high and their spirits beneath the curb. But later, after Angel had done that U-turn to go back for the hitchhiker, I was shocked at the way they'd treated the man. And I'd never dare say that he'd gotten what he'd deserved either. But anyone standing in the middle of a dark desert night at three or four in the morning and needful of the good mercy of strangers should know better than to underestimate a single soul rolling past them. Especially if that soul was headed towards Los Angeles, a city filled to the brim with the violent and unstable. Streetgangs, rollerboys and freewayshooters, earthquakes, riots and poisonous smog—not to mention all the heatwaves, droughts, and canyonfires it got, or even that occasional, believe-it-or-not flashflood, Los Angeles was the city of all three of our lives. Not that I'm sure that explained anything that my uncles had done before or after our U-turn back. But on the highway that night it seemed to boil down to something like a Los Angeles frame of mind. It's funny, but that was all I could come up with at the time: a Los Angeles frame of mind. Las Vegas, which we'd only been in for a quick couple of hours, had seemed another city altogether. A desert wonderland of a city, really. The whole time Angel and Yancey were rouletting away their hardearned bankrolls, I was off riding rollercoasters and bumpercars and grubbing down on ten-plus hotdogs done up with the works in the very middle of the town. Everything about the place had had this makebelieve feel about it: the cars and the stopsigns, the streets and the buildings. It was like a some blown-up toystore. Even the people and their money'd felt fake. In fact, Las Vegas was a place where you heard and imagined more money than you saw. Every hoteldoor you passed it was a *ching ching ching,* but whenever you snuck a peek inside to get a glimpse of all the riches, the only things you saw you saw were these buckets of coins and these differentcolored plastic chips posing as big money. Like I said, make believe.

But at least *I* quickly got hip to that and realized that Las Vegas was mostly a moneytaking machine; that a person had to be intentionally ill to think that he'd had a chance to "beat the system," so to speak. Humongous hotels, neonlighted boulevards, *rollercoasters*—they had to come out of *somebody's* pockets, no? None of that godawful glitziness had grown up out of the bonedry ground on its own, right? Right. It took lots and lots of money to build it. Other peoples' money. But the uncles hadn't accepted—no, didn't want to accept—that that got-over-on-'em glitz was strictly a suckermagnet that hypnotized grown fools such as themselves. And damn did the didn't-know-what'd-happened-to-'em frustration later show in their eyes like steel spikes. During departure alone I knew not to say a word to either of them, they were so absolutely mad. So if the hitchhiker would've just asked me, maybe with some kind of eye communication or hand signal of some kind, if he should've done what he did by flipping off the man sitting next to me, I'd quickly secretly have told him a no doubt about it NoFuckingWayInThe*World*DoYouDo-SomeStupidShitLike*That,* Fool! Are you out of your fucking mind! But instead of playing it respectful and safe, the guy just had to uncurl that middledigit, stiffen it at the end of his alreadyoutstretched arm, and blast it right at my uncle's face. And that was pretty much that. During the U-turn, I almost asked Angel to be an angel and let me out of the car, but knew that he'd only disregard whatever I'd said anyways. So instead I watched him as his hand reached behind our seat and double-and-triple shook Yancey from his latenight slumber. When Yancey'd finally made it to a sit you could tell by his first face that he instantly knew both by the shake he'd been given and by his brother's very hard hardquiet that something awfully real was on the verge of going down. Yancey then stretched his hand forward, patted me on my shoulder, and said absolutely nothing to the fact that we'd just passed a sign that read Las Vegas, 75 miles. For all he knew Angel had U-turned it around in order to rob a hotel casino in order to reclaim all the money that he'd lost. I mean Yancey just completely trusted his brother's moves and motives and was simply very game, which thoroughly intimidated me. And though I was in no mood to witness a two on one on the desertfloor, especially since my uncles were to be the so-called instigators, I had no other choice but to try and imagine my suddenly-jumping midsection to be made of something that could hopefully take the soon-to-be-happening squab. Make it like a strong metal of some kind, I told myself, like iron or steel. Hell, make it into an aluminum even. My heart, though, was a different matter. As soon as the U-turn had been made it'd gone to a shook, shaken, and reshaken Jell-O. That sonofabitch off the road, I kept telling myself, he should've just asked me if flexing his ignorance the way he had when we'd come up on him was the intelligent thing to do. Suddenly I wished I could've had a serious adult conversation with the guy about the way he'd decided on his actions. Who owes you anything anyways, I caught myself thinking at him. Just assuming people have to let you into their cars, their lives, their motherfucking misery. But I knew that thinking this way was only a sorry-ass attempt to forgive my uncles in advance for any of the sure-to-happen damage that was soon to come. To Angel I did say a weak something like, "He isn't worth it," but in his state of mind he wasn't really reachable. His brain, you see, had gone into some automatic-delirious mode while his face had gone that cartoon gargoyle. Life, said his face, was being hard on him again and now he was set on a good amount of payback. So when Angel said the word *knife* and Yancey popped out this big ugly six-inch blade of a one, I quickly crossed my fingers tighter than ever and hoped that that goddamn hitchhiker had come to his disrespecting senses and at least hidden himself behind a thick cactus or big round rock of some kind. Just don't be there like the fool idiot you've proven yourself to be, I thought at him again, or tonight could be your last one alive. You don't want to die alone in a no-man's-land, do you? But then I saw the sonofabitch looking over his shoulder at us like he'd been expecting us for company for quite a while now. He even sported this *please,* I've-been-through-this-type-of-shit-a-thousand-and-one-times-already expression on his mug. And maybe you have, I thought at him again, been in some similar situations before, but not with these particular out-of-luck-*and*-bankroll sticks of dynamite coming your way. Angel then veered across the broken yellow highwayline and drove straight at the hitchhiker who, to my total surprise, didn't even budge. The guy is either stupid and loony, suddenly crossed my mind, or he's got a very dependable weapon on him. But after slamming the brakes and skidding to a dustyclouded stop, the hitchhiker busted out no weapon at all, not that Angel and Yancey would've cared about it much. They just jumped out of the car after him and the scrap began. There was a first wild exchange of fists, kicks, and grabbing, and, what'd caught me completely off-guard, none of the three said or shouted a single word to the others. Just silently got down to the business of the scrap like it was an old job of somekind. Then the hitchhiker, who'd been swinging as if with four frantic arms, ran onto the highway, back onto the dirt, and so fast around the car once, twice, three times that it looked like he'd grown himself a tail. I almost started to laugh, it seemed so ridiculous. He'd gotten on the swiftfoot, though, because he'd suddenly realized that he didn't have the firepower to beat the uncles back. Then Angel caught him with an overhead right that knocked him straight to the ground, where Yancey commenced to stomping him into a very-difficult-to-witness unconsciousness. Finally, the uncles stepped back, dusted themselves off, and looked at the raggedy mess they'd made of the hitchhiker.

Then they talked with each other in a cool calm wondering way about the brightness of the moon and the stars and the night air all around, which they thought altogether beautiful when experienced from a desertfloor. As I listened to them I felt the coolness of that air myself as it moved in through the leftwideopen cardoors. On the ground the man's arms and legs were spread so wide apart you'd have thought him trying to moontan himself. His nose and left leg appeared broken and both his lips were split in two, while all the while his stomach upped and downed to these quick, short, hyperventilating-like breathings. To top off the sadness that he'd become, he was thoroughly sandcoated. As I checked for any headlights on the highway, I pulled some of the cool desert air full into my lungs so as to keep myself all right. How it was that my uncles just stood there chatting with a man close to dead on the ground and our car pointing down the wrong direction of highway, I don't know. A trooper, I thought, could creep along any minute and tic-tac-toe arrest the fool three of us. Then, when I looked at them again, I suddenly finally realized what it was they were doing: savoring the situation. Right there in the night desert and over the busted-up-misbreathing hitchhiker they'd come upon this strange-to-see-it-happening-to-'em peace of mind that you could tell they hadn't experienced in quite some time. It chilled me just to see it. The beatdown of the hitchhiker had actually been a kind of religiousness to them. Again I looked both ways up and down the highway but saw no headlights coming.

Then, pointing out the stars that he knew by name,

Yancey cracked a just-grabbed-from-the-back-of-the-car can of beer, took a good guzzle, and handed it to Angel. Without paying the hitchhiker any attention they started to laugh about a neighborhood woman Yancey'd brought up, but agreed she was a special lady as far as women went and talked about another star. Then Angel bent down and took the hitchhiker's hand in his own and the desert'd never heard a more sorrow-and-painpacked scream as the one the hitchhiker let out that night; a scream mixed with enough deep and high howl so as to make my entire hotdog collection jump right out onto the desertfloor.

Sometimes I think it would've been best if at that very moment I'd have just turned my eyes away. But to look at what? The nothingness of the night? My own hands and middledigits right where they should be? No. Without Angel's act to connect to the scream that'd happened, my imagination might've haunted me for the rest of my days and maybe even forced me to never again go on a drivingtrip, no matter how simple or short. Instead, I let the hitchhiker's pain suck me in in the same way its sound had been sucked away by that cool desert air, only to leave me stranded in that lost and gone middle for a long long time to come.

But who'd have thought that such an unafraid and meaneyed man would've let out such a loud unproud cry and then pass out again to take him some more of that moontan?

Before we drove off and left him there the strangest thing happened. Yancey knelt down by the hitchhiker's boots, undid one of his shoestrings, and put it into his pocket. Somehow, that theft had seemed to me more hateful than all of the other stuff put together and, without any thought or control, I said, "Yancey! *Put that man's shoestring back on his shoe,*" with a small part of my brain instantly hearing how ridiculous the demand had sounded. Yancey, though, stopped in his tracks and without looking at me much said in a rough but uncold voice, "We deserve it, Toomer. On this night we deserve all of it." It was a voice, I realized, that'd cared deeply and honestly for me. "But by the way," he then said. "You need yourself a little mantraining. Be expecting me a visit from me."

And many many miles down the road and ever closer to home it swayed and pointed from the rearview mirror the way it did: over at Angel and then at me, at Angel and then at me, at Angel. . . . It's the way it went for hundreds of miles and for many years to come. And then their faces had that mad uneraseable happiness to them that seemed to've crawled up out of some deep dark hole in the ground. While I stared at the pendulumlike motion, I decided that the nail itself was the eerist thing that I'd ever seen; like a halfmoon or undergrown seashell of some kind. Then I looked out of the window and wondered how cold the desertfloor must get in the deepestmost middle of a coolcold night. It would always be hard to believe really that the same kind of blood flowed through all of our veins.

It was New Year's Eve and I was sitting on the backyard porch working over some beans and tortillas on a paperplate when Yancey strolled up to me out of the night with this darkeyed musclebound stranger in tow.

"What's haps, Toomer?" he said in his gravelgritty voice.

"Just having a little bite," I said, showing him the plate to prove it. "If you're looking for moms, she's upstairs in her room." I always assumed when he or Angel came around, which was rarely to never, that they wanted something with my moms who I'd several times that evening tried to talk into heading down to the fireworks celebration on the waterfront with me, but who wasn't at all interested in the turn of the clock, which was exactly the mood she'd been in ever since that Caesar dude had harshly unexpectedly broken up with her about a month back. Moms not leaving her room much even had me once or twice wishing that Goldie was still around just to lift up her spirits some, or that a night like tonight had at least been a trashtossing one. Hell, I'd have even been down with another triplet of mannequins to get her out and about for a stretch. Anyways, at least she'd had it in her to finally remove me from that not-allowed-past-the-backyard-porch cribrestriction I'd been on for so long.

"I'm not here for that, Toom," said Yancey. "Just wanna talk with you for a second."

"With me? About what?"

"About the fact that you're gonna tag along with us tonight," he said, staring steadily into my eyes.

"I am?"

"Yeah. It's time you had that mantraining I told you about. You remember; back in the desert that night. That hitchhiker." I looked at him as if I'd never in all of my days heard of a thing called a desert, a night, or a hitchhiker before. "Don't worry," he said with a laugh. "You'll be all right with us. Plus you're gonna make yourself a little money."

I put my fork down and porched my plate. "Doing what?"

"Don't worry about that, Toom," he said. "You'll find out soon enough."

I looked at Yancey and his rockround partner, knowing damnwell I should simply be getting up, saying a no, no thank you, fellas, but I'm feeling a little bushed tonight; beans, you know, can have that effect on a young guy; and then stepped right into the crib. Somehow, though—and maybe because of how hard the big darkeyed one that Yancey'd brought along with him was staring at me, or maybe because of that aggravating-me-terribly mantraining stuff he'd once again mentioned, or even because of how terribly terribly lonely I'd gotten having sat night after night on that porch by myself, but I couldn't do any of it. I couldn't get up, couldn't say no, and couldn't even complain about the beans. I simply felt stuck.

"Meet us at the Big Park about ten," said Yancey then in this I'm-not-taking-no-no-for-an-answer voice. "All right?"

"All right," I said with a slow headyes, not liking the idea of the Big Park ever since Monet had gotten paralyzed at it from an out-of-town walk-up, which was basically an onfoot drive-by and a tactic that some of the gangs had lately considered more honorable than just a slowing-by-in-the-deathride drive-by. "At least have the ganas to look your enemy in the face before you squeeze it off," we'd heard one of the Locos say. But Monet getting shot had maybe been the saddest day of many sad days to happen to the Ranch—especially since he'd been so well on his headed-for-the-pros way, doublesportstaring it for a toplevel college program he'd signed with his last year in high school. The neighborhood, which'd been so happy and proud of him, had suddenly gotten so deeply depressed about the tragedy that the very mention of his name was enough to have age-old mothers screaming revenge—which might as well've become Papa Pierre's middle name.

Then Yancey and his friend took off into the same dark

night they'd suddenly come out of. Before they got too far, though, I yelled what was a had-to-be-asked question in our neighborhood: "How much?"

"Don't worry about it, Toom," said Yancey, though, starting to laugh and talk aloud with his quietstrange sidekick. "Just show!"

Whatever, I said to myself, and walked into the kitchen to check the time. Ninefifteen. I sat back down on the porch and heard a cat fight jumping off just around the way and for some crazy reason hearing it'd made me want to kick something hard. Then some crickets started up and I picked up my plate, lifted a forkful of beans to my mouth, and chewed them as slowly as I could. I had almost an hour to kill.

At just after eleven the corner of First and Pacific got very hot with black-and-whites. They seemed to've doubled and tripled at that hour, so we were watching for the rollerboys too. We were sitting in Yancey's car maybe fifty feet off Pacific Avenue and checking out the entrances to three different bars, each of us watching one of them. The bar I had was called the Kan Kan, whose doors opened almost straight out at our car. Whenever someone entered or bailed from the bar those doors'd flapped in and out like a clothesline in a twoway-wind. Like most of the buildings on First and Pacific, the Kan Kan had a shabbybeige paintjob to boot. At the moment nobody was coming out of it.

If I wouldn't've hooked up with these heads, I told my-self after the first jack, I probably would've given a guy a helping hand. Kept him from nosediving or drunkdriving after he'd stepped himself onto the street. But as it was I was locked into the jack and somehow even in the upfront shot-gun seat, my hands steadily rubbing against my knees. Though I mostly wasn't aware that my hands were rubbing my knees.

The first two had come from their bars looking lit and tilted and stumbled along Pacific Avenue and the streets cut-ting across it, never moving too quickly, and maybe not too sure they were moving at all. Hell, maybe they'd thought that they were still at their barstools draining that nerve magic of theirs. The first one Yancey'd taken out and the second his sidekick, named a T-Dubs. Me, I'd been night-eyes for them—Sunny "Nighteyes" Toomer—while they'd gone off and had their tagteam turns.

With all the extra rollerboy buildup on Pacific Avenue, though, I suddenly said, "What if one of those guys shows back up? Or maybe calls the rollers on us?"

"Won't happen," said a positive-voiced Yancey, not let-ting up an inch on his barwatch. "They're still out for the count. Drunk out, dead tired out, and KO-knocked-out. You'd be more likely to see one of 'em over your morning eggs, Toom. If then."

"Why, you nervous, little man?" said T-Dubs suddenly, his voice sounding made of as much solid sandpaper muscle as the rest of him.

"Nervous?" I said, hoping to sound a deeply offended. "Hell no; just careful. With all the rollerboys on the street I just didn't want us to be caught sitting at the scene of the beginning of the crimes that's all."

"Uh-huh," said T-Dubs then, giving me this I-more-than-a-little-bit-doubt-you look.

"Just relax, you guys," said Yancey finally. "We've got a nice snug spot well off the corner, and I guarantee you, Tooms, that those two never saw what hit 'em. Right, Dubs?"

"Right," said Dubs. "And anyways, all these rollers'll be heading back to the station in a few minutes." They started laughing hard, knocked fists, and sat back as if bigmealfull.

True, I suddenly remembered. Not a rollerboy in the city'd be foolish enough to be out and about when the hands on the clock struck a midnighttwelve. That was the hour damnnear anyone with a gun stepped out-of-doors to unload at anything L.A.P.D.—especially if that anything was the police station itself, where all the rollers'd be basement-huddled and waiting calmly for the hell upabove to let finally up. I turned my head back in the direction of the Kan Kan. For maybe the next fifteen minutes, though, guys only entered the place.

"Damn!" said a suddenly-frustrated Yancey when a threegroup suddenly exited his bar. "Look at these fucks, Toomer. Take a note. You should *never* leave a bar without a female or alone. None of that buddybuddy barhopping bullshit. You hear me?" I told him a yeah. "Bad-for-business motherfuckers."

"Correctamundo," said T-Dubs then. "One less and I'd have been down for the doubleteam, Yance. Three, though, that's one too many for me."

Wait up! I suddenly said to myself, my body damnnear tensing to a cramp. He's talking as if I weren't even in the car with him; as if I'd been counting for no help at all. Or even as if a young guy had to have a bunch of overbuilt burly muscles to get over on a stumbling-all-over-himself drunk. Hell, not even Yancey, my very own uncle, thought of defending my presence in the car. Again they started to laugh about something and the longer they did the more I believed it to be a secret pleasure against me. Before the red pushes all the way through my skin, I decided, I've gotta step up and defend myself.

"I'll take number three down," I said suddenly, the words racing down my brain and out of my mouth so fast I thought I hadn't done so. But I had, and finally giving in to that trying-to-wrack-me-terribly bodytension. Having said it, though, had me suddenly feeling bigger than usual in my seat; as if as importantly involved in the wronggoings as my carmates were.

Yancey and T-Dubs, though, just looked at each other and then casually rolled their eyes my way.

"Don't be too hasty, Toom," said Yancey then. "You'll get your shot. We had it all planned that way anyways."

You did? I thought, the tension rightaway coming back a little.

"That's right," said T-Dubs as if reading my mind. "As

it stands, though, we'd have much too much to think about; there'd be too much happening at once. But like Yance said: you'll get your turn."

"Besides," said Yancey, "you know one of those three doesn't have a dime on him. A threegroup's always got a leech tagging along."

"Right again," said T-Dubs.

We again got silent while a small relief and tension mixed itself in my system. The relief from having shown them I was downer than they'd thought I was, and the tension from knowing I was the very next in line.

"Like I said, Toomer," said Yancey then. "You'll get your turn. And as a matter of fact I've decided that the next one is yours. We'll cover you, driver and lookout, and you'll be all on your own: the jackhammer."

"And collector," said T-Dubs. "You can never forget to collect on the jack. It's why we do it in the first place, isn't it, Yance?" He laughed to himself.

"Think you can handle it?" said Yancey to me.

"Of course," I rightaway told him, and as strong and solid as I could.

"I hope so," he said. " 'Cause you shut down on us in the desert that night. I swear, if I ever see that father of yours again I'll kick his deadbeat ass for not having stuck around long enough to at least make a man out of you. You know what we're doing tonight is called, Toomer?"

"Jacking people," I said.

"Yeah, it's called that," said Yancey. "But it's also called a rite of passage. You know what that is?" I noed. "That's when an older man such as myself puts a younger guy like you into a situation that'll make a man out of him—which at the moment you're nothing like."

I felt a warm blood running up to my face as he and T-Dubs looked me over for a long terrible minute. Then I quickly forced my eyes back to the Kan Kan. One of its bardoors that'd been opened had stayed that way, letting me see all the way into the place. The barcounter was lined elbow to elbow, which only moved to take drinks to mouths and then go elbow to elbow again. A heavy barsmoke floated along the top of the open door and up into the latenight air. From a goodways away I could even hear the loud-and-lively music inside of it. But still I sensed Yancey and T-Dubs holding their eyes on me.

"I'll be all right," I said to them finally, going for that strongsolid voice again. "Just keep the lookout like I did for you."

"Sure enough," said Yancey back to me. "That's the spirit of the thing. But just remember: this isn't a punishment against you or anything for having had no stomach. It's more like a tough kind of love."

"You're damnstraight," said T-Dubs. "And the tougher the better."

We dropped into the silence again—on the outside, that is. Inside, my heart, lungs, and stomach felt as if in a terrible civil war with each other. I quickly fullbottomed my window for air and, just as I did so, the number three jack came stumbling through that stuckopen door.

We never owned a television in my family. Anytime others in the neighborhood or at school had rapped about a show they'd seen the night before or coming on that day or the next I'd simply felt them to be talking in some kind of strange foreign language. One time, though, maybe at Richard or Will Man's place, I did see this crazy old show about an old whitehaired man who chased animals just to staple some sort of plastic tag to their ears. Loony, right? But anyways, way before that old man had busted out his staple-gun, he'd be hard after the animal, say a rhino or a deer, in a jeep or helicopter moving topspeed, and would always be a superconfidentrelaxed about the hunt and with very little excitement to his voice. It was just him, his chasingmachine, and that wild what-the-hell-is-happening-with-me animal doing about one-o-five in a fiftyfive zone, though some-times the old man did have this assistant along, a big buffed guy named Jim or John or something, who'd always do all the rough and dangerous stuff like tackle an alligator, catch a just-gotten-into-its-flight eagle, or slam a waterbuffalo and hogtie its legs. And always with this big-ass smile on his face to boot. The ones Jim or John couldn't really beat down, though, the old whitehaired man would simply shoot. And for an old guy he was tough. From that helicopter at a serious clip, *pow!*, and he'd dropped a lion or a zebra in full desperate zigzagdodging sprint, as if having fullwellknown that a highpowered rifle had been dialed right onto its running-as-hard-as-it-could backside. Even from the faraway of the television set it'd been a crazy sight to see. But check this out: the gun, it had no bullets and was called a tranquilizer gun. Just aim and fire like normal, right, but with no injury, killing, or death. Only this nice and unexpected sleep. And of course that *clip clip clip* earstapling business. But that tranquilizer was the kind of gun I didn't mind. You could shoot something with it, even if you'd only wanted to staple some ridiculous-ass tag to its ear, and what you shot would later wake up, feeling maybe a little drowsy and offbalance and tripping that this piece of plastic was stuck to its head, sure. But a very very glad to be a healthy and alive.

As he stumbled past us we all three ducked down, not wanting to be recognized by even a very-out-of-it drunk. He headed uphill along First Street towards Grand and Yancey turned the car around to follow him. At Grand, he stumbled right towards Santa Cruz. The other two we'd followed in the opposite direction, to Fourth and Mesa and Seventh and Grand. Yancey'd made sure that they stumbled a good distance from the bars and into the quieter neighborhoods before he and T-Dubs got out of the car to do their business, which, not unlike that desert situation, had seemed as much about delivering a more-than-ruthless asswhoopin' as it did about robbing a person of pocket money. Number three, though, besides being as big as a moving van, had a quickness to his step that moved him along much faster than those other two combined. It was as if, like those wild wild television animals, he'd known we were at his back. At Santa Cruz Street he crossed and continued towards Sepulveda, where he quickly reeled a left for Gaffey, a cementdividered, freewaybusy street that couldn't be crossed by car at that point.

"All right then, Toom," said Yancey suddenly as he pulled aside the car. He was holding out his hand to me. "Take this." It was a knife; the same exact knife that he'd handed Angel back in the desert before he'd eventually claimed his souvenir. It had that same six-inch blade and, from where I was sitting at least, had nothing tranquilizing about it. Yancey, though, stretched it out to me as if simply offering me a frenchfry.

"Take it, Toom!" he said. "It's only in case he's too much for you. The sonofabitch didn't look too little. But you've gotta hurry! He didn't look too slow either."

"But I thought you guys would have my back?" I said.

"We will in terms of police," he said as though I were a very dumbstupid. "When they kick back in again. Like you did us. Shit, Toom, you know how this works. Stop eating cheese! You said you could handle this."

"That's exactly what he's doing, Yance," said T-Dubs all

disappointed agreeing. "Eating cheese. What happened in that desert anyways?"

Before Yancey could answer him, though, I snatched the knife from his hand and opened the door.

"Atta boy!" said Yancey. "We'll catch up to you on the other side of the street, all right? A block up; no more than two."

Feeling somewhat dazed, I stepped out of the car and headed after him. But then Yancey's car was next to me again.

"Put the shank away, fool!" a suddenly-shotgunriding T-Dubs said to me in this punched whisper. Then they drove off up the street and into an alley.

I looked down at Yancey's knife dangling loose in my hand. It felt a very out of place in it. When I lifted it higher, the clean silver of the blade reflected some nearby streetlightglow blue and white against my eyes. The flat and wide bladeside had a deep and rough groove down its center. As I stood there staring at it, I wondered what it would say to me if it could speak, and a "no mercy" and "no forgiveness" were the first things to jump to mind with a just as quick "injury, killing, and death" following right after them. I put the knife into my waistline, handle first between belt and stomach, and started to jog after the guy before Yancey and company showed themselves again. At the corner of Gaffey, though, I saw him already crossed to the other side. Somehow, in his very drunken condition, he'd gotten himself through the traffic, over the centerdivider, and through the traffic again without getting hit. Then I crossed over between the traffic, jumped over the divider, and continued to follow after him.

To those of us living in the Ranch, the streets above Gaffey were dead streets—meaning a lot less rollerboys on the lurk and practically no witnesses to witness a crime carried out. Damnnear total deadness. Especially more so tonight since it was New Year's Eve and all and most of the residents were down along the waterfront waiting for the fireworks while the rollerboys were waiting in their basement stations for the last of the hadn't-even-started-to-land-on-'em-yet lead to fall from the sky. Whenever I got close enough to the guy to make my move, I'd be free to do so with more or less a peace of mind. Slowly, I closed the gap between us. By block two above Gaffey Street we were only five or six carlengths apart. The knife I rearranged some after it'd cut against my midsection a bit. I quickly wondered where Yancey and T-Dubs were and just as quickly imagined them hanging down below Gaffey still, laughing and talking loud about their jacks and then tripping hard to a churchlike silence.

From where I was, I suddenly thought, I could easily've dropped the guy if I'd've had that old whitehaired man's tranquilizer gun. At the moment that he'd crossed under this large bushy tree that grew right over the sidewalk to the top of this big streetparked motorhome, for example, *blam!,* he'd have gotten dropped like a runaway circus elephant. No blood, no messiness, and no questions asked. Just a little sidewalkburn from the fall and that very sweet sleep he'd most likely been headed for anyways.

Without that old man's piece, though, I suddenly had a lot of things to think about: like what, if anything, do I say to the guy to get his bankroll from him? Yancey and T-Dubs'd forgotten to tell me that; just kicked me the knife and moseyed on their way. Should I say nothing at all and straightaway bust out the blade? Nah, I thought; the blade's gotta be a last resort thing. But what then? First blindside him, then knock him on his ass with a terrible flurry of punches the way Yancey and T-Dubs had done, and if he doesn't go down quietly simply stab him in his leg a few times. Maybe even a buttcheek. A person couldn't stay still-standing with a knife stuck into his buttcheek, could he? Or maybe I'd just talk to him first; see if he's not so drunk he understands me. If after that he shows any stubbornness then I'll just have to bust out the blade. That'll let him know the time. He wouldn't try any dumb shit then, would he? I mean not with that long and sharp chunk of steel pointed at his gut. But what if that all fails? What if none of my tactics convince him any and he starts to get the better of me? Then what? I could always outrun his wino ass, right? Even if he could highstep himself after me some, it wouldn't be in a very straight line, would it? He'd probably have a wild wobbly stagger to his footchase. Knowing that one thing suddenly made me feel much better about my chances in dealing with the guy. Then Yancey flashed my mind again. Not really Yancey, though, but what he'd said about that rite of passage stuff. About pops not having made a man of me. I lifted my shirt to check on the knife against my midsection. Ready or not I've gotta pick my spot, I rhymed to myself to ease myself. Then, at the corner of Sepulveda and Walker, the guy stumbled right.

When I turned the corner myself to finally make my move, though, I was shocked to see him gone. On both sides of the street I couldn't find a trace of him anywhere. He'd just disappeared.

As I eased into the middle of the street I drew Yancey's blade from my waistline and held it tight to my leg. To my surprise the drawing had been the naturalest of moves for me. Then I noticed my head was doing these just-as-natural side-to-side movements, as my eyes, those badly wanted nighteyes, darted around spotting every strange angle and shape that Walker Street had to offer. The street and the neighborhood, though, were completely dead, with no lights showing in the houses. They were fully unlit. Then the streetlight yellow from the far corner away died midway. Around me somewhere I could feel him like some hiding-out-for-you fever. Where was he, that man who'd been in front of me? In one of the perfect little houses that lined both of the streetsides maybe? Does he live around here with some already-in-bed wife?

I stayed in the streetmiddle, stepping slowly over the broken yellow centerline. As my eyes continued to shoot around I felt the blade pressing hard against my pantleg and legleg, my tensiontight arm ready to lunge it out at an angry fastforward. Then, halfway to the Summerland intersection, the streetlight died all the way. I was in a dark and swallowed up darkness, not able to see the trees or the gates, the parked cars or sleeping yards that were everywhere around me. For maybe a five full minutes I stood and waited and heard not a sound. Maybe he was good and gone, I finally thought; maybe off in that yellowless bedroom jammed tight up close behind his deep-asleep wife, smelling strong as he did of barsmoke and alcohol. In the dead of the night, with the sun halfwaygone and halfway on the way, I listened just one more time around me northsoutheastandwest and finally put the blade away against my midsection between belt and stomach.

My eyes hurt bad from straining most of the night down by the bars and then on the jack and finally needed some rest. I feel like a full-on fool, I thought, having offered myself the way I had down on First and Pacific. "I'll take number three down," I said low and hard at myself. Trying to step up as a superhero or something. I'll show you older heads I got the man in me too; that I'm good for more than just nighteyes; that I'm as capable as . . . but wait. What kind of men could they be claiming to be anyways, jacking guys as they did who were a foolishly holidaydrunk? Chickenshit cowards was what that was. No; cheese-eating, chickenshit cowards. Which was what I had become too. Hell, there had to be more to becoming a man than drunkjumping, no?

Two, three, four against one—and then with a knife as backup? It was all chickenshit, I told myself. And would I really have shanked the guy if it'd come to that? For no more than some possible chumpchange maybe? I'm sure that Yancey and T-Dubs had done theirs—but me? *Damn,* I suddenly realized, I might be carrying a murder weapon. I mean it was already a piece that'd cut into the flesh and bone of another human being. That much I was sure about. Then I felt the blade against my midsection and wondered how that would feel, a straight-up stranger stabbing some sharp solid steel deep into a place that'd had no chance against it. Then all that bleedinghurt and fear that nothing could be done about any of the happened-inside-of-you damage. I listened around the dark again, but this time not for him but for the hoped-they'd-still-be-basemented-away rollerboys or maybe a return resident creeping around the block. No way I'm getting caught with a possible murder weapon, I told myself. I've gotta find a place to hide it until I see Yancey again. Then I thought about the drunk guy and was glad he might've been all pressed up against his in-bed woman. Locked-in-doors protected from a psychothree like me, Yancey, and T-Dubs. Full of relief, I decided to head back down to First and Beacon and stash the knife along the way. There on the street without angles and shadows because the yellow had died away I started to turn in the dark invisible quiet when suddenly that far corner streetlight started its slow fade back to on. All around me the invisible black lightened to a low yellow glow until finally the street was everywhere seeable again. Then a closeby and heavy-footed sound suddenly made me jerk myself around and at the same time cut myself hard against my midsection, sending a sharp sharp pain from my belly all throughout my body. I quickly looked around but saw nothing, and when I felt around my bodymiddle and the suddenly big openbellied blood that was there, my head began to run in these tight and tighter circles. Why the hell had I done that? I asked myself hard, not able to take a look under my shirt; too afraid of the cut's deepuglyopenness. Yancey, I thought; now I'll have to hide the knife *and* myself from him. He'd laugh at me for the rest of my days if he knew how this'd happened. When a heat built itself up in my body, the bellypain started to get less and less sharp. Then the heat surrounded me like some sort of thick and heavy bodycoat and my head spun around in these evertighter circles. Shit, Toom, what've you done to yourself? For a splitsecond I felt my knees buckle in and my neck limp up, and then I felt as if I'd hit the ground and rolled right against a car tire. Start walking, I told myself, feeling as if to give in to sleep; get up if you're down and start walking yourself to First Street. Wave down a car, any car, even a roller if have to. Just don't fall asleep on the ground. With my head feeling heliumlight, I finally felt as if I'd made it up when in front of me and in full high silhouette he stood over twice my life. He seemed to've sprouted right up out of the concrete, I thought, and have not a start or a finish to him, but only this everywherespreading size. How could he have hidden anywhere?

I asked myself, suddenly wondering if he'd even hidden at all and not been at my back the whole dark time.

Then he made a not-so-humansounding grunt that had me instantly automatically lifting the blade still in my hand. Not a word came from my lips as the knife rose up and headed its stabbing way. Before I knew it, though, his giant arm was coming at me too. It moved quicker than it did slower and grew bigger as it got closer. As hard as I tried I couldn't make my stabbing motion go any faster than it did. Then the giant arm slammed into me hard and I instantly heard the knife clanking right near the place that I'd landed. Instead of working me over Rancho-style, though, he just hurdled me and rumbled down Walker towards Summerland Street.

That wasn't a man, flashed my mind as he'd gone over me, but something like a man. I mean you've got men and you've got women, I said to myself, and then of course that animal world, but he hadn't been any of the three. The cigarette and alcohol smells had been missing from him too, replaced instead by this terrible terrible odor of soggyskin and badlyburnt breath.

I got up and turned in the direction that he'd run, listening to his heavymoving steps maybe half a block away. Then I felt something hard underneath my shoe. It was the knife, but without any of the blood it should've had on it. I just stared and stared at it the same way I'd done when Yancey'd reached it out to me. Where was all of my blood? I wondered. I lifted my shirt and saw not a drop of it there either. What happened to my stomach? When a light suddenly came on in the nearestby house to me I snatched up the knife and headed in his direction, feeling a never-beforefelt confidence surging through my system. I was healed and closed and hadn't been cut at all, I said to myself, my legs running after him as if strictly born to do so. And where there had been a heat all around me, there was now only a very cool cold. After maybe a running-along minute I'd already gained on him. Then at Summerland he bolted left and was headed for Peck Park. The knife I felt a weightysolid in my hand and I knew I wouldn't drop it again.

Up ahead, I heard his heavy footsteps and even heavier breathing. In fact he was really sucking hard for air. From a nearby house a dog suddenly exploded and charged, barely held back by a sidewalk gate. His loud barking set off another dog in the not-so-faraway distance. Then I noticed how the guy moved: like a crooked broken bear of a man limping badly into his every contact with the ground. When he suddenly looked back at me his face was too terrible to look at; terribler and crookeder than his movement even; worse even than that not-human grunt or that stronger-than-ever soggyskin smell. The face'd almost froze me in midstride, it was so ugly. The eyes, mouth, ears, and nose all looked a very twisted out of place. Why was I running after him? I wondered now. After something so sad and ugly and twice my size? Was it still the chumpchange I was after? It didn't make any sense to me. Or maybe because I had the knife? Yancey's words haven't finally brainwashed me to a senseless recklessness, have they? To prove myself a man of men? Turn around, Toomer, I told myself; go back to your porchfood and leave the night alone. But my legs wouldn't let me. Just like after that Deadeye beatdown, they'd suddenly copped a life of their own and kept me right on stepping after the man until they'd closed our previous distance to a much muchshorter half again.

He ran and rumbled. For limping so bad I couldn't believe he was moving so well. As he neared under a streetlight in midblock his groundshadow jumped towards me like a black flickering flame of a man, caught him like a high noonnightedness, and then ran out in front of him until it'd disappeared back into the shadoweating dark. Then my own front was lit and I got chased by my longrunning groundshadow, which also got snatched by another noonnightedness that had the shadow hiding an up and down underneath my fastmoving feet, before finally stretching ahead of my running. Then, when he crossed the last street and went into the park, the night and the dark took my selfsurge away.

I stopped at the corner and watched him slow to a walk. He was getting tired and weak. With the knife strong in my hand I crossed that final street and entered the park myself. When I stepped onto its grass, he once again looked back at me. His face, I finally saw, was covered with these deformedlooking lumps and crusty patches of skin, while his eyes were full of a wild wild death. A fear flooded my veinways and blood, but still I couldn't keep from closing on him. Then he turned his head away and grunted more powerful than before.

For a while I followed along with the same exact space between us. Then, just before the parkcenter, he started into this insane and funnylooking sprint that looked as if both of his hips were busted, and suddenly he shrieked as-if-gunshot loud, which scared a bunch of these never-knew-they-existed-before squareheaded blackbirds from a big green mushroom tree. The birds fluttered and complained as he rumbled and rolled towards the parkcenter. When he finally reached it, he tripped a facefirst to the broad and lawny parkgrass. With the knife gripped everhard at my legside I steadily neared him. He was stomach down on the grass and when he saw me coming close behind him, tried to crawl away. Seeing him do so angried me up bad, and the closer I got to him the angrier got my gripping hand until finally it'd felt too tight and mighty to ever drop the knife again. My legs stepped across the grass with more power than ever too. The knife, I knew, was moving to the great powerful rhythm of my body. A rhythm and power that could kill almost anything at all. Even a lame-and-limping, crawling-about-like-some-sick-to-have-to-look-at rainworm of a man. When I was finally up on him, he slobbered and whimpered as if badly hurt; even squirmed some to that same old grunting sound of his.

The parkcenter, I noticed, was lit up by a shouldn't've-been-there-at-all piece of the moon floating milky and round in a whitespotted sky, while the very green smell of nightgrass and trees had gotten a deep and full into my nose and lungs. Somewhere, I thought, had to be those shapes without angles and that seeing without yellowness, no? Why not here? Then a sound like a low and calm hum trembled up the quiet and everything around me. When I raised the angry knife high over my head, the moon's reflection hit it hard on the hardstrong silver of the blade. His hurting needs hurting, said the blade to me, my hate moving strong inside my system. Then I heard the new sound, though: a light crying into the dark and lawny parkgrass. He knows about the knife held high above his life, I thought. The new crying made my knifegrip even tighter, though, until my ears and my mind got agonied up with too much pressure to hold. When all of my control finally left me I lunged to the ground, releasing a hateful hurtful force from every place in my body, sticking and sticking as if I were killing the whole entire world. And only after dozens of those stabbings and strikings did finally I come to a stop; not to a quiet one, though, but to the sound of a heart pounding hard throughout the park; it pounded against the grass and the trees and the whitespotted night above. When he finally turned to me he smiled me a twisted smile that quickly disappeared when he saw the knife stuck deep inside that ripped-up and manyholed earth. He started scrambling backwards on his hands and backside until I grabbed for the knife, held it up high, and showed it to him. He froze. Then I threw it far off into a row of mushroom trees. Again he twisted his smile at me, stood up, and was once again twice my life. From way up above, his eyes looked me over.

"Go home," I said into the air at him, and finally turned to do so myself. At the edge of the dark park I turned around and saw him completely disappeared.

On the street where I'd fallen, Yancey and T-Dubs drove up to find me sitting on the curb. My body hurt terribly.

"Where've you been?" said Yancey all upset. "It's four in the morning! We've been looking everywhere for you."

"Where've *you* been?" I said right back at him, my belly feeling like some hotscalded water.

"What's up with the Raggedy-Ann look?" said T-Dubs then. "You get into a squab with that guy?"

I yessed my head. "He jackflighted on me, though, and got away from me at the park."

"What happened to your stomach!" said Yancey suddenly. I looked down and saw the sticky red. It was all over my hands and pants and shoes too. "You look like you've already bled to death, man." He got out of the car and stepped right over to me. "What happened?"

I looked up at his worriedlooking eyes and knew I couldn't tell him about it. "It happened during the squab," I said. "I'm all right, though."

They both stood staring at me in this very-impressed-with-me silence.

"And where's my knife?" said Yancey then. "You did hold onto my knife, didn't you?"

I noed my head. "I lost it during the scuffle."

"In that case, Toom, I gotta keep your cut," he said. I shouldershrugged. "You're not gonna tell your mother about this, are you?" I noed my head. "That's what I thought!" he said, slapping me on my back. "So you want us to drop you off at the hospital or what?"

Again I noed my head. "Just give me a ride to the crib."

"Atta boy!" said Yancey all proud and happy. "I knew you'd come around. Didn't I tell you, Dubs, that my nephew'd come around? Jump into the back, little man."

I did, and thought about that man part the whole way home.

I don't know how word got around the neighborhood that I'd been badly stabbed, but it had, and like a recordbreaking supersprint at that, which even had the Grizz stopping by to pat me on the head and tell me all seriousvoiced how he was looking into the matter. Then one by one each of the fellas snuck by the crib to see if the rumor was true, how it'd happened, who'd done the shanking, if they could see the cut, if I was all right, and, best of all, when I'd be able to hang with them again. And everytime I'd answered them a yeah, yeah, it's true, I was just sitting on the backyard porch eating my rice and beans when, *wham!,* some never-seen-him-before dude jumped me for no reason at all and we fought and fought like a couple of pitbulls until he cut me where he'd cut me and finally ran away while I'd cussed him terribly as he did so; but I'm doing okay now and I'll show you all the wound later, and of course I want to get together again, as soon as I'm up and at it and have enough energy to get us all in some degree of trouble again. And we'd laughed after each of them had sat there and listened a very slackjawed, damnnear wishing it in their eyes that they'd been lucky enough to've been jumped like me and lived to tell and joke about it all the same way I did.

Supposedly the news of Toomer's stabbing had finally softened up the moms's hearts my way for the first time in over five months too, though one of them (who I've decided not to mention out of respect to her very-close-to-me son) did say that what'd happened to me had actually served me right, since I'd in her and a lot of other peoples' eyes always been "an exceptionally evil young man." Those were her very words: exceptionally evil. It wasn't a big thing, though, and not as if I'd never thought about myself that way either.

But the nicest thing to happen in a long long time was that moms had personally made me some meals to eat in bed, took my temperature maybe four times a day, and dressed and redressed my bellybandages whenever it was necessary. And never once seeming to mind either. For all I cared (which was more than only a lot) my rest and recovery could've gone on lasting forever. But I, of all people, knew better than that.

We were all three looking at the man. He was a beatendown fiftyfive to sixty, shirtless, had a bloated stomach, man titties hanging from a caved-in hairless chest, and skin that showed a shineless ashybrown under the very hot midday sun. His toes stuck through his shredded shoes and his drawers out of a sad sagging, caked-and-crusted pair of shorts that were covered in some brown and yellow stains to boot. His hair was a dustyweedy clump and, to top off the general sadness he'd become, his out-of-orderlooking body had not a dime of definition to it, but only this shapeless size. Slumped down against the fence like he was, he looked a very lost and defeated in the world.

"Who the hell is he?" I said to Richard and Will Man, who were sitting on the nurserysteps with me. "He's been there now what, three days? Maybe four?"

"I don't know," said Richard as he looked from his cards to the man, "so long as he doesn't get stupid, he can lounge and laze as long as he wants." Richard went back to his cards. "Stay."

"True," said Will Man then, also checking his cards. "We don't *own* the nursery, ey." Then he took his own long look at the man as if for the first time. "But why's he gotta kick it *in*side the fence and not outside somewhere else? And for all these days."

"Maybe we should say something to him," I said. "See if he's okay." But neither Richard or Will Man said a word, instantly getting back to the cards. My eyes, though, wandered to some crushed and scattered glass on the ground by us that glinted strong from the overhead sun and cut very sharp into my eyes, for a moment even hypnotizing me into forgetting the cards in my hand and that Richard and Will Man were sitting no more than a foot away. For all the past months, I started to think, I'd at times wanted so bad to be back on these steps flicking cards to these same exact heads that I thought I'd go loony if I didn't, and suddenly I couldn't feel them anywhere near me anymore. Not only that, but ever since we'd started hanging out again it'd been a greatbig struggle just to understand their simplest joking or care about their silliest cares. For example, as soon as they'd mentioned a blackjack session, my first thought'd been for the library again. For its books and mysteries and quiet for myself. Somehow, in the time we'd spent apart, the fellas had become a harder to take kind of company.

"Toomer!" said Will Man then. "Wake up and deal me a card, ey. What's gotten into you?"

I came back to earth but didn't answer him. "You need a hit?"

"Nah, I'm cool," said Will Man. "What do you have?"

I flipped my cards in front of me. "Twenty."

Will Man flipped his three. "Push."

We looked at Richard, who slowly flipped over his down card. "Twentyone!" he yelled, gripping the pot of its money.

Suddenly the fence rattled. After three-to-four slumped days the man started to move. One hand then next of his grabbed at the diamondshaped fenceholes as he slowly strainfully pulled himself up, never not eyeing us as he did so. Once on his feet and he tried to balance himself still. Then he started moving towards us, his large stunned legs taking these short shuffly full-of-drag steps as his shoebottoms scraped a rough and hard against the ground. His closing-in-on-us legs looked like jointed, leatherwooded treetrunks, tough and scarred at the shins and baggy and wrinkled at the knees, where a yellow fluid was slowly oozing out of them. By the time he'd reached us, it seemed another four years and not days had gone away. The man smelled terribly.

Trying to stand in front of us he wobbled, caught himself, then gave up the weakest of sheepish smiles. His behavior, I told myself, said drunk as a bendered skunk, but there was no way that he could be. The four days he'd been fenceslumped he never once handled a bottle or can. No, I thought, his wobble was more serious than drink; more like his nervous system had gotten miswired or rusted from so many days of sitting on the ground. I wanted to speak to him, ask if he needed a doctor or something—you know, healthrelated stuff—but was still too shocked at him having gotten up and actually walked his way over to us. When he again smiled that same weakish smile, I suddenly noticed the tiniest bit of tearwater built up in his eyes.

"How wonderful you've become," he suddenly said in this deepsounding voice. "Like angels." Then he slowly climbed the steps we were on and entered through the door of the boarded-up abandoned nurserybuilding.

Me, Richard, and Will Man sat numbheaded and mostly looking back to the part of fence the man had been stuck to. Four days he'd been sitting there, only to suddenly wobble up to and past us like some big heavy ghost. And then there were those strange words. When Richard finally got up to head after the man, I quickly fulldecked the cards and went to stop him. I could tell he was mad that a wigged-out-and-wobbling stranger had entered the nursery without permission.

"Check it out," I said to him. "The guy looked pretty bad off. Let's just leave him alone for a while and make him get out later."

"Bad off or not, he doesn't belong in the nursery," said Richard all upset. "It's our hangout, not his." He paused for a click, then, with a challenging-us, no-joke-about-it eye-contact said, "I'm going in and he's coming out. Simple as that. You guys down with me or not?"

Inside the nursery, which smelled like it always did of cool and musty sidewalk rain, there was no immediate sign of the man. So we grabbed the three churchcandles that we used for light, lit them one by one, and held them out in front of us to a dusty candlelight cloud that rose itself all around us. On our way to the first door, Richard and Will Man picked up a two-by-four apiece that the boarding men had left when they'd shut the nursery down. But he wasn't in the first or the second room, which left us only the final backcorner one to check out, where we stopped before its usually-open door. Richard gave us both that same are-you-down-with-me-or-aren't-you look and, full of negative nerves, me and Will Man yessed him our heads. Richard turned the doorknob, cocked his two-by-four back, and shoetipped the door open, which rose up more floordust in swirly suctiony puffs all around us. Then our candlelight reach showed the man. He was reslumped in the door-opposite corner, his hands limp at his sides and these sweatlines easing heavy down his forehead and temples. Again he was staring dead at us.

"You can't be in here, mister," said Richard, uncocking his two-by-four.

But the man only twitched up that same weak smile, which suddenly turned into a painful kind of grimace.

"If he sat on the outside for all those days," whispered Will Man to us, "he might try and make this his permanent home."

"Mister," said Richard again, "you gotta get up and out. *Now.*"

The man, though, just blinked his eyes our way without the slightest bodybudge.

"Beautiful young angels," he then said, and again that painful grimace hit his face, but this time wracking it bad. Then his head suddenly slacked forward to a very loose hang.

"Hey, *mister*," said Richard. "Wake up! You can't go to sleep in here."

With the candle out in front of me I stepped forward and kneed down next to the man, struggling hard against his smell, which was like a cheesyhot tar. I put my hand to his shoulder and gave him a good shake. "You gotta wake up," I said. But he didn't answer. "Hey; you okay?" My voice, I noticed, had gone a slightly highpitched with worry.

"Toomer," said Will Man then in his own troubled-sounding voice. "I don't think he's breathing."

I put my hand in front of his nose and mouth and waited for a sign of some in-or-out-moving air. When none came, I turned to look towards the door.

"He's dead," said Will Man to me, the words featherfloating through the candlelight quiet and moving right through the cool dark dustiness of the rest of the nursery. I stood up and backed away from the man, trying in secret to pantswipe the death from the hand that'd touched him. In the candlelightgold, uncountable dustspecks had gathered around him and looked like some strange grayblue mist. Then I looked at his legs. They'd become like two great fallen trees and his toes like so many sidewalkbreaking roots. Just outside the nursery a police siren suddenly highed and lowed through the projects on yet another business call. Richard, I noticed, had gone into this raw and angry silence, while Will Man seemed to've doubletroubled up with worry.

"What's in his pockets, Toom?" said Richard.

I dug through them and in a back one came across an old wallet, opened it, and found not a single beat-up dollar. What I did discover, though, was a maybe ten-year-old photograph of two young and posing children in something like their Easter outfits sitting in front of a proudfaced man and woman. It was all that was in the wallet. I showed the photograph to the others, who checked it out to the candlelight.

"Let's head out," said Richard, which we rightaway did.

Outside my window that night, the sky showed a clear and high darkness that was poked full with a million shining stars and had a big beautiful moonhole in it. Whenever I woke up or couldn't sleep, I just stared at those stars and moonhole while they reminded me of other things. Like that cool cool night on the desertfloor, for example, or the young Alonzo's walks to the Green Turtle Market-Bar, or even the time on the wharf after Tom-Su had gone. Then I thought of the men like the Grizz and Mr. Kim, Hector and the uncles, or even Goldie and the set leaders. I couldn't figure why they'd been the men we'd all had to know, instead of some normal everyday ones that most people in the world seemed to get to grow up around. Late into the night I noticed a wide, Pacific-born cloudbank gobbling up one star-cluster after another until that big and beautiful moonhole itself was almost all that was left. And after it'd been gobbled too, I finally decided what had to be done and fell into a couple of hours of sleep.

The next day we were back on the steps, trying hard to focus on our blackjack hands. Richard and Will Man looked as drained as I felt, which was like a stayed-up-a-solid-week-straight drugaddict. Will Man had the deck and me a six in hand with a four down and a queen showing. "Stay," I said.

Richard showed a five and called for a hit, which he got. A five and two showed. Again Richard called hit and again he got a two. "Stay," he said, scooping up his fourpile.

At various times each of us had glanced to where the man'd been slumped for all of those days. A strange leftover fence-impression was still there. During half-a-dozen black-jack games we hadn't mentioned him once; just pretended the most interesting important thing was the blackjack hand. When Will Man suddenly fulldecked and handed me the cards, though, it didn't surprise any of us. We sat in the usu-ally-not-so-quiet nursery saying nothing for many many minutes on end.

"Why'd he have to go off and die?" Will Man finally said. *"Here?* Not only die but watch us for all those days straight?"

"It was like he'd planned to die on us," said Richard. "As if he'd said to himself: 'These would be some good heads to die on today.' "

"Maybe it's why he said what he said yesterday," I said.

"Said what?" said Will Man.

"You know, that you've-become-angels stuff."

"That was some strange shit to say, no?" said Will Man.

"Yeah it was strange," I said. "Like he knew us or something. And to top it off, they were his dying words."

"But where would he know us from?" said Richard. "Had you guys ever seen him before?" We thought about it and noed. "Wait up, he did kinda remind me of my. . . !"

"Who!" said me and Will Man together.

Richard held his breath for a second, then let it out in an I-must-be-crazy headno. "Damn!" he said, playing something off. "It was on the tip of my tongue and now it's gone. You know how that sometimes happens."

I looked over at the fence again and then at a Richard and Will Man who were suddenly staring at that same crushed glass from the day before. It sparkled strong against their also-seemed-to've-hypnotized-'em faces. Then those strange-sounding words came back to me: "How wonderful you've become; like angels." As if he'd understood a thing about us that we didn't even know ourselves; as if his whole last purpose in life had been to tell us just those words. But why? I wondered. As I watched them I did suddenly notice something. An angelness. Not a wings and halos kind of angelness, but something that'd still had a special kind of goodness to it.

A goodness coming from them simply being two young guys on a step who hadn't already become all hard and grown and tripping out the minds and lives of those ten, twenty, or thirty years younger than them. That kind of goodness. It's the way they'd been the first time I'd ever met either of them, and I wondered if I still had any of it, too. Or even if I'd ever had anything like a goodness in me to begin with.

"I think you're right, Richard," I said as a bait throw. "He did pick us to die on."

"Say what?" said Richard all notunderstanding.

"Why?" said Will Man in hot pursuit.

"Maybe because we're being tested," I said.

"Tested?" said Richard. "By who?"

"You by me and me by you," I said to him.

The calmquiet suddenly made me think of how byhimself the man must've felt as he sat day-in, day-out against that fence, knowing maybe the whole time that he was going to die. And besides me, Richard, and Will Man, no one in the neighborhood seemed to've seen him at all. And now that he was dead and in that secret backcornerroom not too far from us, no one ever would. Thinking it made me feel somehow important. The kind of important that a person might feel knowing he had a very hidden possession of something very very rare—like another human being's dead body, for example. The more I felt that importance, though, the more I needed to feel it properly out of my system.

"What do you guys think we should do with it?" I said to them.

"You mean the body?" said Will Man.

"No, he means the birthday suit," said Richard, making a you–sound–ridiculous face at him. "Yeah the body."

"Call the dude with that Cadillac stationwagon," he said. "He always does the pickup when somebody's killed."

"Ain't *no one* been killed," said a disbelieving–his–ears Richard. "Anyways, that's no good. You call the bodyman and then you gotta deal with the rollerboys swarming all over the place. And anytime they roll on a dead body, you know somebody's getting charged with murder."

"Nobody murdered him!" said Will Man. "At least none of us. You just said so yourself."

"Yeah but they'll tag us with it, anyways," said Richard. "Say we poisoned or suffocated him; or maybe that we didn't call him a doctor in time. You know how the roller-boys work. They'll trump anything up on you. No matter what, though, they'd shut down the hangout."

"Then maybe *we* could jack the Cadillac stationwagon?" said Will Man all excited. "Move him ourselves."

Richard looked at him like he was a stone fool. "You need to be slapped," he said with a me–versus–you laugh. "Could you see your midget–ass swoopin' around in that big sonofabitch? Shit, you probably can't even drive."

"Fuck you, punk!" said a getting–up–as–if–to–squab Will Man. "You got a better idea?"

"You're damn right I do," said a staying–cool–in–his–seat Richard with a headpeck on the "right." "We'll break open the nurseryfloor, dig a deep–ass hole in the ground, bury him in it, and put the floor back together the way it was. Nobody'll know a thing."

"But just yesterday you said you didn't want him *in* the nursery," said Will Man. "Now you're getting all hypocritical with your no-carpentry-knowing ass."

"He wasn't *d-e-a-d* then, fool!" said Richard, getting up to finally go toes.

"Ho-ho-hold on a minute," I said, jumping between them. "No offense, Rich, but I gotta go more with Will Man on this one. We definitely have to move him ourselves, but without bodyman's stationwagon." I waited for Richard to argue with me, but when he didn't I went on. "If we move him, we do it right; no inbetween, Mickey-Mouse nonsense. We do it as if he was someone we knew."

"But we didn't know him, though, or anything about him, Toom," said Richard.

"Maybe five days ago we didn't," I said, "but today he's the dead man in our hangout and we're the only ones anywhere who know about it." Neither of them said anything. "He's ours," I finally whispersaid to them. "He *belongs* to us." I watched as their faces slowly tried to understand what I'd said. "He's yours, mine, all of ours," I told them, to which first Richard's, and then Will Man's eyes brightened up big.

"How do we move him then?" said Richard.

At those words I broke down a plan that I thought was tops, though a little risky in a different way than stealing bodyman's stationwagon would've been risky. It was a plan I'd thought about the night before when all those stars and that moonhole were on their way out. After a stretch of co-ordinating things we split up so that each of us could do whatever was needed to make the plan go smooth. At right around sundrop we'd hook up again.

Having elbowed the last of the daylight over the hill and to-wards the coastline and ocean and everywhere else that day-light had to go to come back as morning, the night spread itself long and low over the whole entire neighborhood. Back on our steps we listened as a mother's voice called loud around the darkened-up streets for her child, who we could hear laughing and running its way up to her before their voices disappeared to the shut of an apartment door. Out-side the nurserygate the occasional walker came and went while we watched and waited for the world to go a com-pletely quietdead.

After a quick *clip clip clip,* Richard returned from the fence with wirecutters in hand. At the same spot the man had been slumped against, he'd made two up-and-down, five-foot-wide wirecuts so the fence could be peeled bot-tomup, one of us holding it open from above, the other two moving him through. Next to us stood the freshlyborrowed shopping basket full of the sheets, towels, and shortrope. We tilted the basketedge against the nurserysteps and got to ar-ranging the sheets and towels around inside it. At one point we moved as if three sneaky spirits, our hands lifting towels, folding sheets, and lighting up churchcandles to head into the nursery again.

The thick smell of bad meat hit us as soon as we'd opened the door, getting stronger the closer we got back to him. When we finally saw the body I was surprised to see it in a new position. The upper part of it had bent head-to-knees forward as if, because the man'd forgotten to pray before he died, his body'd decided it for him after we'd left him in peace. His badly sunken-in skin had turned a deep-dark purple and a thick mucousy string dangled from his nose to his kneecaps, gobbing up some on the ground. For a long terrible minute we just stood and stared at it all. None of us, I was sure, wanted very much to touch what'd become of the man, who was an awfulsmelling sight to take in.

We quickly spread the sheets, though, on the floor next to the body. With Richard at the feet and me and Will Man at the back, we rolled it head down onto the sheets, a stronger second dose of funk hitting us when we did so. Then we wrapped it up, tied the sheetends into these big gnarly knots, and me and Will Man pulled away at the head end while Richard pushlifted hard from the legs end. And even though we had a six-armed straining in full effect, we could mostly only drag the body along the nurseryfloor. Once outside, though, and we slid the body upsidedown into the basket, which took every bit of strength that we had. Then we wedged a churchcandle between it and the basket, checked again for any cars or nightstragglers, and, comfortable that the coast was clear, headed for that freshly-cut section of fence. After we'd angled the basket through the held-open fencepeel we were finally on the street.

Then my mind was on many things at once, like the questions I'd forgotten to wonder about. Like would the longrope be strong enough to lower a guy so heavy? Or what would we do if we ran into any of the portpolice? Or even suddenly: was this really the right thing to be doing? I mean, was there something after all wrong with the latenight moving of a body in a shopping basket? As I skateboarded the noisywheeled basket down the street, Will Man rode along on the side of it. Then my feet were off the ground and we sped like a cageysounding streetsled towards Harbor Boulevard, where Richard had run ahead to check for any passing traffic. His wave, though, meant that me and Will Man, who was footbraking the basket to my steering, should continue for the Harbor corner and the tugboat docks two blocks to its right.

"You get the cinderblocks?" I suddenly asked Will Man over the basket's loud rattle.

"Yeah," he said, his voice all a-vibrate. "I put 'em where we decided."

Between us the body bounced around from the cracks and lumps in the passing-fastly-under-us street.

"And the longrope; did Richard get the longrope?"

"Yeah," he said. "I saw it at the tugboats when I dropped off the cinderblocks." Then Will Man looked at the bouncing body. "Toomer, you sure we're not gonna sink, ey? I mean us three and him and all those cinderblocks? That's a serious load, no?"

"Don't worry," I said all whatever. "We'll be all right. This kind of rowboat can carry a ton or more."

"What's that in pounds?"

"Two-thousand."

Will Man did the math in his head. "We should be way all right then," he said with a full-of-relief smile.

"That's what I said, wasn't it?" I said, hoping to calm him off the subject.

Of course I didn't really *know* if we'd have too much weight or not; only that we couldn't start changing up our plans while in midplan. I quickly snuck a peek at a staring-straight-ahead Will Man, whose face had gone a very very troublefree. I'll keep any doubts to myself, I decided.

At the tugboat docks we leaned the basket sideways for the wooden docktop but it slipped from our hands and landed hard with a bang. Then we pulled the body out and strained it to the dockedge. Richard climbed down to the rowboat under the dock and threw us the hidden-inside-of-it lon-grope, which me and Will Man had tied around the body before Richard'd made it back to the docktop.

Though my head was a very cool clear, my stomach felt knotknotknotted from all of our fast secret action. At a one and a two and a three we eased the body off the dockedge and held hard to the rope as we lowered it to the rowboat below. The ropeburn damnnear made us want to scream. When the body was in the boat, though, we let the rope fall right on top of it. Then we all climbed down, me with the candle inhand, and got into the rowboat. We're moving a dead body, crossed my mind again; a person not too long ago watching and breathing and more or less moving around like we were doing. It all felt so normal abnormal.

Along each side of the body we put four of Will Man's cinderblocks and freed up the longrope and, on one side of the rowboat looped it through a cinderblock, banded it tourniquet-tight around the body, and did the same with a cinderblock on the other side of the rowboat until all eight cinderblocks had been fastened like so many bigblock barnacles. Behind us every one of our oarstrokes turned the harbor flatness to an upset waterswirl. The rowboat, Will Man mentioned, was a good six inches above sinklevel, which made him grin anew. For the first few minutes we kept close against the right waterwall, barely able to even see the boxcartops in the railway yard just a hundred feet away. Then up on the harbor walkway we saw two bums digging deep into a dumpster, only their baggy leglows sticking out. A small spotted dog was at their side. In a deepasleep city, I thought, we've got some nightowls for company. Though the bums couldn't notice or hear us hushing by them, their dog did. But instead of barking, he just stared our way like some kind of slackjawedwonder with a sidetilted head. Then I realized

I'd stopped my rowing and that one of my hands was resting flat on the body's back. It just laid there holding it steady as if always meant to do so. The man, I thought, once again seemed like some person from our past. Someone we'd known and who knew us back strong. Why else would he've said that "you've become" and not a "you are" to us? I quickly checked if Richard and Will Man had noticed me, but saw that they were still eyeing that staring-at-us dumpsterdog and I slowly pulled my hand away.

Ports O'Call village passed steadily by, all its shops and restaurants a lightsoff shut, its walkways without the usual tourists. Across the harbor the old naval drydocks were busy with nightshifters working at the hullside of a large water-worn vessel. We watched as the sparks from their fixing machinery sprayed all around them to the water below. Then to our tight right a whole noise and action kicked in along Deadman's Slip, where we saw maybe two-dozen people putting up booths and banners for the soon-to-be-jumping Fisherman's Fiesta. Suddenly I felt the rowboat moving as though from a more surefocused rowing.

We closed on the end-of-the-breakwater lighthouse while its neongreen beacon lit us up several times a minute during its steady circletrips. Closer to the lighthouse the bigger swells started to pop and splash against our boatside, too. Will Man, checking out the swellsplash, went right-away back to his troubleface. A few minutes later we bobbed against one of the breakwater's huge graniteblocks, the white, tubelooking lighthouse standing tall and quiet over us, its beacon too high up to catch us in its path anymore.

Then we sat in a triangle with the body between us and I took a pack of matches from my pocket, placed the candle on the granite blockedge, and lit it. In the land distance, the few scattered lights showed a San Pedro in a deep and dark sleep while the candlelight glow showed the stiffwrapped body still and quiet between us. Then we closed our eyes and, like we'd earlier agreed, thought a good thought apiece for the body and the man who used to be a part of it. It wasn't really praying, we'd told each other back at the nursery, but a simple solid way of giving up a respectful enough send-off to a person recently died, the candle being for just in case he'd had a religion he might've followed. After we'd finished with our thoughts, we knocked fists and blew out the candleflame. Then we shoved off the granite and headed for the breakwater gap.

As we rounded the lighthouse the swellcurrent instantly picked up and we all three rowed with an extra effort against the rougher seawater. After many hard minutes we were on the wide-open Pacific where, from maybe a hundred feet back, the beacon once again caught us in its neongreen circlesweep. Then we stopped our rowing, grabbed onto the body, and tugged and pulled it to the rowboatedge with all of our leftover strength. Though we bobbed hard to the heavier swells, and though Will Man had a fearing-deeply-for-his-life look on his face, me and him still managed to lift the body's leg end onto the rowboat stern, while Richard leaned himself over the bow so as to keep us in a good bobbing balance. Then me and Will Man tilted the feet into the sea, released our grip and watched the body ease heavy towards the water. And though cinderblocked, wrapped, and roped, it just floated there on the oceantop like some suddenly-happening miracle. I looked at an already-looking-my-way Richard and Will Man, who then looked at each other before turning back to the body. We couldn't believe our eyes! The cinderblocks hung concreteheavy from both sides of it, trying their damnedest to go for the oceanbottom, but the body wouldn't let them. It was as if it couldn't accept it'd died and didn't want to be buried because of it. I didn't know what to say, do, or think, except that to try and manage the body back into the rowboat would've been just about impossible for us. Then a very shocking thing began to happen: the sheets began to suddenly tear long and loud straight right up their middle. Even though the ocean swelled and splashed all around us we still heard that sheet-tear as if it were our very own eardrums. Then, just as the green beacon swept past again, what looked like a steam started to rise from the tear and turn into a gaslike gather that just hung there in front of us. Then the gather did the beautifulest thing ever: it changed into something like a billion brittle goldflakes that started a slow and steady rise right up into the night sky, at the top of which they seemed to fix themselves into a cluster of stars that'd never ever been known of before. When the beaconlight again swept past, the body finally started its sink. Then it was gone and, for the first time all night, we could smell the seasalt and ocean-brine all around us.

Richard and Will Man had their backs to the lighthouse as we slowly rowed for the tugboat docks. For a while the beacon caught us again and again in its lightpath. As it did I'd everytime witnessed these wonderful green halos that'd come and gone around Richard and Will Man's heads. Then they were there and then they were gone, there and then gone, there. . . . That was how it went until eventually the beaconlight could no longer reach us from our rowboat moving so swift and light into the harbor channel. The body, I thought, would be somewhere on the oceanbottom by now, maybe hopefully resting in a wild seaweed garden of some kind. And hopefully peacefully, too. I dropped one of my hands heavy into the water and for the rest of the night and the next day after that we said not a word to each other.

(Ne and Will Man didn't hear the cars until their accident happened just a few feet away. They must've flooded out each other's fullspeed engines. But then it was *kablam,* with the big beige fourdoor with the pregnant woman in it veering right for me and Will Man at this very quick motordead clip, making us sidesprint hard like a pair of longlegged landcrabs onto the nearestby yard from where we watched the fourdoor plow into, over, and past the corner firehydrant. Next thing an anger of water shot high up over us, the car, and the intersection, and none of it could've happened on a stranger weirder Sunday afternoon in the history of the housing projects.

Sunday was the last and biggest day of the Fisherman's Fiesta down at Deadman's Slip and, as long as I can remember, fiesta weekend had been our neighborhood's number one go-to event. Rickety rides, carney games, junkfood, and a chance to hang loose with the nonprojects-living part of the population for a change, the fiesta was the only once-a-year party everyone got invited to and no one ever missed, me and Will Man included.

But come Sunday morning and the idea of doing up Deadman's for a third straight day had hit us with this old stale done-it-to-death feeling. The same as it had Richard, who nevertheless had to attend it again because of Dee Dee and the Grizz wanting to make it a family outing for them. So instead, me and Will Man decided to stay behind in the neighborhood for the day—a day we discovered just how popular the fiesta really was. And we'd never seen anything like it. The projects had become a right-out-of-a-western ghosttown to the point of us expecting a tumbleweed or two to come bouncing down the street. Never before had so much still and quiet happened to our neighborhood blocks. The normally people-active sidewalks were suddenly a goodfoot-free, the usually football-busy Big Park was a pass-and-catch empty, and the forever children-noisy backyards were a very sleepysleepycalm. Me and Will Man had strolled around the place for hours as though taking in some strange abandoned planet. And until the accident'd shaken us from our daydream senses, not a single car drove past either. Not even the always-present rollerboy kind, all of them having followed the poorfolk down to Deadman's so as to keep a close tabs on them during their only loose weekend of fun.

What'd collided with the pregnant woman's fourdoor was a big blue brandnew truck that'd managed to roll onto its roof and slide along the street for a stretch before coming to a screechmetal stop. That was when the fastestmoving man we'd ever seen scrambled out of the truck's upsidedown window, ran through the firehydrant's downdrop to look into the fourdoor's busted-up windshield, showed a worriedwild expression spread across his face, and hurried out of sight like a long-gone wind, never once noticing me and Will Man standing just on the other side of the car from him. When I myself finally looked through the downdrop and into the fourdoor's windshield, I saw a lone and grown man in the driver's seat who'd rumpled faceforward with his head on the steeringwheel. It was then, at that staring-through-the-downdrop moment, that our afternoon suddenly went from strange to superstrange.

I can't really explain it, but it sometimes happens that I know I'm being watched. Call it some freakybrained ability, nerves, or whatever you want, but much of the time I'll turn around and catch a real-live person actually eyeballing me—or sometimes even a bird, cat, or a dog. On fiesta Sunday, though, my I'm-being-watched feeling was so strong I actually almost spoke to the most-likely-right-there-next-to-me watcher before I even turned around, I was so sure of the presence. Maybe ask him why he hadn't said anything about the accident or the need to call an ambulance yet; or why he hadn't at least oh-my-godded once or twice, if only to let us know he was there. Instead of speaking to him, though, I one-eightied myself around to check up and down the block for that set of I-can-see-you eyes dialed my way, but found none. Immediately, that is. What I did finally notice was this open front-door at the top of the corner apartment's threestep rise. Again I flashed a peek around the block for any staring-right-at-us people and, seeing none, looked back to the open apartment door. A goodways into it and all I saw was a cool-looking darkness. But then, maybe five feet into that pitchblack middle, I started to make something out. It was a face staring out at me; a face that seemed to float a perfect unmoving foot right above my very own. I took a step forward and suddenly saw it as clear as if it were my very own in the center of a dark square mirror. It had scabbed, mold-old skin, unseeable eyes, and a badlycombed mess of very toothwhite hair. Next to the hair, the skin was as gray as a raincloud. I took another step forward.

"Excuse me," I said to the face. "But did you call an ambulance?"

But there was no answer.

"Could we use your telephone to—"

"No phone," said a deep and tiredsounding voice, as if it'd expected that very question some time ago. As if it'd expected everything that was happening some time ago. When I turned to Will Man, I saw that old familiar look of his: nervousness.

Being of the projects, I rightaway knew what he wanted to do: get a move on. If we did, not only would we hopefully not get involved in a sure enough hit-and-run situation, but we'd also hopefully miss being the only witnesses to've seen a more-than-likely grandtheft auto suspect. None of that, said Will Man's nervous look, could come to any amount of good for us. Especially after that Hotel La Salle business. I mean, what would we say to the rollerboys, for example, at being the only ghetto-ites to've missed the very last day of the everybody-and-their-grandmother-attending Fisherman's Fiesta? I could hear them in our faces already. "Looks kind of suspicious, don't you think?"; "What no good were you punks up to?"; "Huh?"; "Maybe it was you two who were driving that truck"; "Can you prove that you weren't?"; "Can you?"; "Huh?" And then that nonstop rampage of whens and wheres and hows and whys all the time leading to a *guilty, guilty, guilty.* Uncountable rollerboy questions that always had a way of twisting the casual or accidental into the no-doubt-about-it criminal. They ask a young guy enough of them and eventually they'll figure out *something* to charge him with because, in their evil opinion, *somebody's* got to be taken down for a crime, any crime, or the whole trip or patrol had been nothing but a greatbig waste of time. Hell, they were probably down at Deadman's that very minute arresting some of us for simply having jumped on one too many a ride, or for having joyed it up for a third day straight. It's too bad how a thing not really connected to you like an out-of-nowhere auto accident could suddenly be about nothing but you and your life. Which, in a way, wasn't really that much of a mad leap to be making, since to continue on our stroll, for example, might suddenly be a much riskier thing to do. Not only had that old man already seen us and not only had our clothes sogged up strong from the firehydrant gush, but only a fool rookie of a rollerboy wouldn't know not to connect us to the scene of the accident. Even on our strange, neighborhood-empty Sunday, we still had to expect at least one of those cruising-around-the-corner, everjacked-for-some-action squadcars, no?

Anyways, that's pretty much how my head raced along to Will Man's nerves when several long and loud moans suddenly drifted our way from the inside of the wrecked-up fourdoor. Sounds, I was sure, not belonging to the steeringwheelrumpled man, but to a much-in-pain, maybe-sliddento-the-floorboard-below woman. When I checked Will Man again, all he had for me was this weak, what-the-HELL-do-we-do-now, Toomer? eyebrowraise.

Though I'd seen my share of pregnant women, I'd never seen a single one to match the big belly roundness of the woman we found flat on her back on the backseat of the car.

She had a belly that seemed to rise right up against the four-door's headliner and look an at-the-point-of-explosion tight. Not only that, but the woman herself was all thrown together. She had on an oversized orange bathrobe, a pair of fuzzy pink slippers, sported an all-over-the-place jungle of jetblack curly hair, had a steady heavy sweat on her face, and she huffed and puffed as though oxygenstarved. When I smiled her way I knew immediately that all her hurt brown eyes wanted to know was how the man behind the wheel was doing, who I quickly glanced at before coming back to her.

"Please tell me he's all right," said the woman in a higher-than-I-expected voice, putting both of her hands on her belly and starting to cry. "Please. He hasn't said a word to me."

Again I turned to the man, this time forcing myself to check him out some. His head was openeyed my way and he had a thick goopy blood hanging dark and strandy from where his cracked-wideopen forehead had connected with the steeringwheel. His bare legs, I saw, were covered in the same red goop that'd covered his head and steeringwheel.

"How is he?" said the pregnant woman. "Tell me he's all right!"

"I'm sorry," I told her, "but he's not all right. He wasn't wearing his seatbelt."

"Yes he is!" she shouted, and started punching and shaking the back of his seat. "Wake up, goddamn you!" Then she wildeyed me. "You're just a kid, not a doctor! What do you know? He has to be all right! Do something!" Then she screamed his name so loud that it hurt my ears. I slammed the cardoor closed.

"She's crazy, Toom," said Will Man as I automatically looked to the corner apartment's open door with that same gray face steadily staring out at us. Again the woman screamed the driver's name. "Let's get outta here before the rollerboys show. Forget her and that old man; he's probably blind and can't see us anyways."

"Yes he can," I said, and headed straight to the bottom of his steps. "I need a towel," I told the gray old face point-blank, its eyes a suddenly-seeable yellow color.

"No towel," said the same tiredsounding voice to me.

"What do you mean 'no towel'? Everyone's got a towel in their apartment."

Instead of saying anything, though, he just looked past me to the back of the fourdoor, where the woman had once again screamed a big blue murder. Hearing it'd made those barely-yellow eyes large up and his mouthsides twist as if to smile.

"What's that expression you're making?" I instantly said, which just as instantly made the expression change to a glare my way. I stepped onto his first step. "If you can't walk, I can—"

"No!" he said, freezing me with a suddenly-gripped cane that he *slam slam slammed* against his floor.

Will Man said something.

"What's that?" I said, still looking hard at the old man's face.

"I'm gonna go call an ambulance," he said. "From the rec center payphone. All right, Toom?"

I looked his way, quickly guessing the other reason he wanted to bail. "Yeah," I said, trying not to sound too disappointed. "I'll be right here waiting."

Will Man left and I took my foot off the step. For the next minute I paced around near the rear of the car. When the woman again screamed for help, I stepped back through the downdrop, snatched open the cardoor, and told her some was on the way. Holding onto her big belly, though, she moaned this new moan—like some wild, injured, about-to-be-split-into-two animal-moan.

"It's happening!" she yelled. "Please don't leave me again, okay!"

What was happening, of course, was that soon there would be more of us. That bellytight condition could only've meant the woman was going to drop a helluva bomb at any minute; a bomb I'd minutes before hoped not to be around when it went off.

Even before I'd slammed the cardoor closed, I knew they'd been in the accident because of a hospital rush. I knew it when I'd asked for the towel that I'd told myself would've been for wrapping up a newborn baby, and I knew it while I'd been pacing back and forth to buy some valuable time away from the situation while stupidly hoping hard for her to've delivered her baby on her own somehow. Instead, though, it was still inside her but now on the very verge of going for that end-of-the-tunnel daylight. Suddenly, all that went through my mind was a Will Man on the payphone, breaking down to whatever operator he'd connected with every necessary detail to get the woman her SOS ambulance ASAP. Say the right streetcorners, Will Man, shot through my head; and that she's about-to-bust-it-bigtime pregnant and full of pain and screaming at me for speaking the asked-me-to-say-it-to-her truth. What in the world do I know about delivering a baby anyways? I thought at the woman. Tell the operator that, too, Will Man. Tell her that the young guy waiting at the car with her knows just about jackshit about bringing a newborn into this world with him.

Then she was eyeing me in this lonely, helpless, more-afraid-than-I-could-ever've-been way, which actually loosened me up some.

"I didn't mean that kid stuff earlier," she panted. "But he's my husband." She started crying again.

"Don't worry," I said, "I'm not going anywhere."

"Thanks."

"What's your name?"

"Helen," she said, wiping at her eyes. "What's yours?"

"Toomer—Sunny Toomer," I told her, instantly wishing I'd left out the last name. Again I checked her extralarge belly. "You know, Helen, I'm not sure I can do anything for you."

"You'll be fine," she said with a quick smile. Then she moaned that same wild animal moan, her fingertips gripping hard at her belly. "As long as you don't leave me, Toomer, we'll be fine together. Okay?"

When I yessed my head I again thought about Will Man on that payphone call. Tell 'em the right corner, I thought at him again. Santa Cruz and Beacon Streets, one block off of Harbor Boulevard. Get the streetnames right. But then an important something flashed into my brain. "Don't I need to wash my hands!" I said to the woman.

"It wouldn't hurt," she said right back with a wince. "And try and find a sharp object while you're at it. But please hurry!"

I broke for the firehydrant and held my hands against its strongshooting upgush, which popped and stung them to a clean-as-possible powerwash. Then I searched around the yards and sidewalks for that sharplooking object, but when I couldn't find one headed straight back to the old man's steps.

"You better give me a knife, mister," I said to the gray old, still-staring-out-as-if-hung-into-midair face. "I *know* you've got a knife I can borrow."

"No knife," said the gray old face, though, without a care in the world.

"You're full of shit!" I shouted at it. "You know what's happening in that car? A woman's gonna have a baby!"

But he just shouldershrugged. *Shouldershrugged* at an out-of-nowhere, no-doubt-about-it emergency happening just a few feet from his door. Not if my brain had been some simple bucket of tapwater and that old man's shouldershrug the biggest chunk of steel would his response have sunk in.

"If something goes wrong with her," I warned him hard, "or her baby, I'll—"

But suddenly the woman *super*screamed and I ran right down the steps, searched up and down the still-people-empty street, and actually spotted a bottle half a block away. In one smooth motion I sprinted over to it, snatched it up, cracked it on the curbedge, ran the sharpestlooking piece to the firehydrant, rinsed it like I'd rinsed off my hands, and finally hurried back to the car where the woman had closed her eyes to a very fast in-and-out breathing while all the while mumbling some sort of praying to herself. Then she opened her eyes.

"Tell me," she said. "Are the people in the other car okay?"

"It was only this one guy," I told her, my breathing suddenly fast as well. "But he jetted off a while ago."

She tried to hold in another moany scream, but couldn't. "I'm sorry, but I have to start pushing! Are you ready?" I yessed.

Then she bit down on her robecollar, lifted her knees, and spread her legs wide, making the robe fall off to both sides. "Oh my god," she yelled through her teeth as if on ferocious fire. "Can you see anything!"

When I finally looked to the birthing place, I saw a silverdollarsized piece of skin bulging out of her.

"Yeah!" I said, suddenly feeling as though I'd done something great. "I see it! Keep pushing!"

Aaaahhgggrr! she screamed into the bitten-into robe, then huffed and puffed some more. "What now?" she shouted.

"I can see half its head!" I said. "Again!"

Aaaahhgggrr!

"Its shoulders!"

Aaaahhgggrr!

"Its back and elbows!"

"Pull it some!" she said. "Gently, though? Really gently!"

I did, and just like that the whole naked little bloody thing slid right out into my hands as hairyslick as a mango pit. "I've got it!" I said, hoping that I really did. "I've got all of it!"

The baby was ragdoll limp, had a goopy, peachfuzz face, and, what surprised me most, was totally blueskinned—its toes and fingers included.

"Cut the cord!" shouted the woman then. "Quick, cut it by the navel! But be careful!"

I took the bottlepiece and sliced at the cord, which broke right into two.

"Now tie it off!"

I did, and very much like an old pro.

"It's not breathing though!" I said as soon as I'd realized it.

"Clean out its mouth!" she shouted. "Hurry, Toomer!"

I fingerscraped some brownblue mush from the baby's mouth and just like that it started to cough and cough. "It's coughing!" I said, for the first time seeing the weenie. *"He's coughing! It's a boy!"*

"Now hold him upsidedown!"

"Upsidedown?"

"Yes! Just do it!"

I flipped him as told and lots of fluid instantly drained from his nose and mouth onto the woman's legs and carseat. Then, as his coughing kicked into an out-of-control crying, a very unbelievable thing started to happen. The blueskinned little baby quickly lost its deep blue color and turned a kind of very dark pink instead. It was as though a very soft light had gone on inside of him. When I held him rightsideup again he hollered around as if extra hungry and started twisting in my hands like fiesta taffee. Everywhere the baby was smeared in a thick dripping purple blood that'd gotten all over my hands and arms to boot. The purple, suddenly crossed my mind, though, wasn't like any blood I'd ever been around. There seemed a lot of something good about it. Not in a longdrawn ghetto year could I have imagined human bodyblood to be a good thing *outside* of the body. In all my life if it hadn't been held-in-protected *inside* the body by all that skin and vein, then a very bad thing had happened. That's just how it was; if ever I saw the stuff, somebody'd gotten a very messed up by somebody else. Like that suddenly-undershoe, street-and-sidewalk-globbed-from-you-name-the-violence morningblood we'd sometimes accidently come across during our walks to the schoolhouse, it'd been bad because it always had us wondering who in the neighborhood had gotten stomped or stuck or capped into this time during the middle of the night, and next thing the whos and hows and whys would get so strong into our heads we'd often had no choice but to follow the dripaway to whatever alley, door, or abandoned car it led to just to ease our worried minds that the bleeder hadn't been someone somehow close to us. Needless to say, in that sudden headspace the schoolhouse had a very quick way of becoming a very meaningless memory to us. The babyblood all over my hands, though, reminded me of none of that awfulness, and the longer I stared at it while the newbie wailed and wailed, the more I could feel my face wanting to crack into a thousand pieces from how hard my smile was smiling at it.

"Here," I said, reaching the baby over to his mother, who quickly took him and wrapped the hollering little thing right into her bathrobe with her in the naturalest of natural movements. For the next halfminute or so all I did was watch the new mother as she made one small adjustment after another so as to give her little boy the most perfect of possible resting nooks.

From many many blocks away the police siren sounded like a hardbarking dog, ten million capped-at-me rollerboy questions, and a permanent migraine headache all wrapped into one. "I've gotta go," I told the woman then, ready to step back through the downdrop. "You'll be okay now. I can hear 'em coming."

"Can't you stay just a little while longer?" she said in a dis-believing kind of beg. "At least until they've made it here?"

I quickly noed my head, which instantly sent a small and rotten feeling through my system. I knew she didn't want to be alone with the man on the wheel; the man who'd known her and been with her and most likely'd very deeply cared for her; the same one who was the other half of the robed-up little bundle he couldn't any longer hear. But it was an aloneness that, once it'd kicked in, I knew I couldn't do any-thing about no matter how long I stuck around to keep her company.

"What are you gonna name him?" I quickly said.

"We were thinking of Benny or Jacob," she told me, starting to cry again. Then an aftercramp hit her and faded right away. "Which one do you like?"

"Jacob," I said. "Jacob sounds perfect to me."

"Jacob," she whispered to her baby with another small adjustment. "Okay then. Jacob it is."

"You won't tell 'em my name when they get here, will you?" I said, keeping steady tabs on the closing-in-on-us sirensound.

"No," she said. "Not if you don't want me to."

"Thanks."

As I broke for the corner I was stopped dead in my tracks from a very nearby telephone ringing off the hook. It came from the old man's apartment, the old man himself quickly closing up his already-barely-open door as soon as I'd spotted him.

All of a sudden, with only the few seconds I had left, I wanted nothing more than to charge up his sorry-ass steps and smear something stupid like a big purple IT'S A BOY, MOTHERFUCKER! all over his frontdoor. Not that I would've wasted a drop of the babyblood that way even if the siren hadn't existed, or if the downdrop hadn't already washed my arms and hands clean of it as soon as I'd stepped back under it. I just thought it might've been a way to draw some neighborhood attention to a person who had tried his uglyutmost to be harmful by doing nothing, and that, whenever the fiestagoers filed back home, maybe a very lively question-and-answer session could've happened that might've forced him to apologize to everyone around who maybe just once in their lives assumed the slightest bit of good in him. I mean all of those days that he'd supposedly been among us and he'd most likely never had the consideration to just a single time help a person out when needed. Really, you had to feel sorry for a nobody like that.

So instead of any smearing I sprinted for the corner, all the while feeling sorry for a person given the opportunity to be the first one ever to help a hollering, blueskinned mangopit of a baby into the world and not take advantage of it. I promised myself, though, that soon enough I'd make a very special trip back to the old man's apartment just to tell him what it'd felt like.

But I never saw him after that. I even returned the very next morning and knocked knocked knocked on his door, but he didn't answer it then or the several visits after that. The last time I went by a family was moving into the apartment, which had me heading straight to the housing office.

"What old man?" said the deskwoman.

I explained to her everything about his face and the towel, the knife and the telephone ringing—even chanced it and mentioned the auto accident.

"But that apartment's been empty for the last month," she said. "For renovations."

"You saw him, right?" I said to Will Man a few days later.

"Yeah, I saw him," he told me. "Too damn ugly to forget in just a week."

"Then the two of us together can't be crazy."

After the ambulance had showed that day, me and Will Man actually returned for the rest of the fiesta. We didn't know what else to do with our day, and I, for one, needed the strong distraction it had to offer. The neighborhood quiet, you see, didn't feel the same as it had before the accident, with both of us all the time expecting another one of those out-of-nowhere carcrashes with every step that we took. Not only that, but fiesta stragglers had already started to work their way back to the empty streets and blocks and shared backyards. The neighborhood normal was already well on its way back.

At first the screaming laughing people and the mixedtogether smell of junkfood and harborbrine had me right where I wanted to be: drunk with a dizzy distraction. But then another kind of distraction started to slowly catch my attention: the distraction of small, medium, and large-bellied women popping up all over the place. It was strange, but I couldn't help but to zoom in on each and every one of them as they passed and notice how, in the middle of such a loud-crowded ongoing, each of them moved about as if in her own perfectly peaceful patience, and as if they each had this special kind of forcefield that made the crowd around them always automatically part as they passed. Have they always been this way? I wondered about them.

Then I saw this one with that riper-than-ripe, ready-to-go belly that I'd seen earlier that day. She even had the same black curly hair. As she split the crowd, I followed her past one noisy carney game after another and watched how she placed a single careful hand on her belly to feel maybe a kick or just to let the little blueskinned rider know that in all that outside noisiness she was all the time right there with him. Then a man showed up with a pretzel in his hand that the woman took and bit right into. The soon-to-be father, I thought.

"She looks like the woman from that car today, no?" said a suddenly-next-to-me Will Man.

"Kind of," I said, not able to not keep staring at her oversized belly.

"You think she's gonna have it today?" he said.

"Who?"

"The woman from that car."

Will Man said something else to me but I couldn't really hear him anymore. Everything around me, you see, had gone a stone stone quiet; everything, that is, except that bigbellied woman eating on her pretzel. And as she did so she parted the crowd around her like the queen of the fiesta.

"Today, yeah," I said. "And everyday for the rest of her life."

Acknowledgments

A major thanks to Sue and Mike Painter for their truly unconditional love and support; to my positively untoppable agent Leigh Feldman; to Bill Thomas for his keen editorial sense and vision; to Debbie Cowell for her couldn't-do-without-'em smarts; to Anni Bergman for her friendship and the sharing of her very special home; to Stephen Dixon for his early and ongoing support; and to Alice McDermott for her warm invaluable insight. A special thanks to Elzbieta Matinyia and Judith Grossman; to Noel King for being a wise old friend and to Nubra Floyd and David Anthony for their faith and compassion; to coach Mark Henry for pushing my brain beyond the roundball and to Johnny St. Igneault for saving my life and still not knowing about it. Also a fat thanks to a few of my no-doubt-about-it, listed-you-in-alphabetical-order friends Richard Caughlin, William Cliff, Obadiah Tarzan

Greenberg, Alessandro Isolani, Peter Kim, Po Kutchins, Kathleen Murphy, Toby Poser, Andrea Soeiro, Eric Yetter, and Tucker Zinke; and to my listed-you-mostly-by-your-ages sisters Shanaz Ardehali Kordich, Noucha Jasanis, Geraldine, Anya and Zayha Hecker, and Ninette Lewis; and to my brothers Mario "Bear" Meallet (who lived a lot of this book and knows it), and Patrick Meallet; and also to Robert Hecker and the Kordich family. And a final family thank you to my only-made-one-of-'em-like-this-one moms, Sigrun Hecker. Joshua Painter, Kristin Lang, Alexis Kaufer, Howie Sanders, Sarah Malarkey, David and Cally Graham, Storm Large, Michael Cavaseno, Alissa White, Eric Rathhaus, Jamal Rayyis, Samuel Rosenberg, Matt Kass, Raindog, Liesbeth Van Robison, Rachel Warden, Zachary Matz, Tom Garvin, Rachel Cantor, Betsy Murphy, and Scott Benjamin have been awesome in their own ways; Sarah Challinor Smith, James Smith, and Julia Challinor very excellent in friendship and . . . places to live. Sacred Grounds, San Pedro and Cucina Viansa, Sonoma for places to write. Readers' Books Sonoma for existing and Kathleen Caldwell for her very sage counsel. And last but definitely not least, I want to give it up BIG to the hometown heads from the Rancho San Pedro days: Glenn Allen, Armando Correa, Richard Allen, Carlton Mayfield, Gerardo Castillo, David and Ricky Owens, Dip Owens, TT Fala Kuaea, Sam and Malae Pele, Willie Jaramillo, Bobby Cook, Heather Olsen, Coop, Bear once again, Cheetah, Mitchell Waters, Rollie, and a spine-full-of-pointblank-buckshotblast Salunga. You were flatout beautiful.